Highcliffe House

OTHER PROPER ROMANCES
BY MEGAN WALKER

Lakeshire Park
Miss Newbury's List

Highcliffe House

PROPER ROMANCE

MEGAN WALKER

SHADOW
MOUNTAIN
PUBLISHING

For Owen—

When your moment comes, I hope you'll take the risk.

All rights reserved. No part of this book may be reproduced in any form or by any means without permission in writing from the publisher, Shadow Mountain Publishing®, at permissions@shadowmountain.com. The views expressed herein are the responsibility of the author and do not necessarily represent the position of Shadow Mountain Publishing.

This is a work of fiction. Characters and events in this book are products of the author's imagination or are represented fictitiously.

Visit us at shadowmountain.com

PROPER ROMANCE is a registered trademark.

Library of Congress Cataloging-in-Publication Data
Names: Walker, Megan, 1990– author.
Title: Highcliffe house / Megan Walker.
Other titles: Proper romance.
Description: [Salt Lake City] : Shadow Mountain Publishing, [2024] | Series: Proper romance | Summary: "The last thing Anna Lane wants to do is spend a week in Brighton with Graham Everett, who is hoping to make a financial investment with her father, but then she discovers a hidden warmth in her one-time rival in this enemies-to-lovers romance"—Provided by publisher.
Identifiers: LCCN 2023046550 (print) | LCCN 2023046551 (ebook) | ISBN 9781639932443 (trade paperback) | ISBN 9781649332547 (ebook)
Subjects: LCSH: Man-woman relationships—Fiction. | Great Britain—History—Regency, 1811–1820—Fiction. | Brighton (England)—Fiction. | BISAC: FICTION / Romance / Historical / Regency | FICTION / Romance / Clean & Wholesome | LCGFT: Romance fiction. | Historical fiction. | Novels.
Classification: LCC PS3623.A3595516 H54 2024 (print) | LCC PS3623. A3595516 (ebook) | DDC 813/.6—dc23/eng/20231017
LC record available at https://lccn.loc.gov/2023046550
LC ebook record available at https://lccn.loc.gov/2023046551

Printed in the United States of America
Publishers Printing

10   9   8   7   6   5   4   3   2   1

Chapter One

GRAHAM

London, England

1813

"This one is ambitious, Graham," Tom said, eyes fixed on the papers he held as he walked beside me. My closest friend from our days together at Cambridge, he was a head shorter than I was, stout, with a hairline that had already admitted defeat. "Are you certain of success?"

I gave him a look full of all the exhaustion I felt. "As certain as one can be in any investment."

I'd hardly slept last night, instead going over the numbers, drawing and redrawing the plan, practicing the speech I'd give Mr. Lane when I asked for his partnership. My mind would not relent, poring over every minute detail, looking for that one thing I might have forgotten, misplaced, miscalculated.

"This could be the one time you're overconfident," Tom muttered. My friend doubled as my banker and financial adviser, so my success was his success as well. I brought him investment proposals, some riskier than others, and he'd advise me on whether or not I could manage them. Sometimes we disagreed on whether I *should* though.

Passersby were trickling home, leaving the easternmost edge of Hyde Park quiet save for a solitary laugh in the distance, the crunching of boots on gravel. An older woman crossed our path, and I stopped short to keep from colliding with her, holding out an arm to catch Tom, whose focus was so complete he'd have walked himself off a cliff. Her primped little dog yelped as it struggled against its leash, trying to chomp at our boots.

Tom grunted. "Half the payment, you could manage. But all?" He shuffled the four pages in his hands, mind working behind his eyes. His voice lowered. "After all this time, you're finally secure. You are comfortable. Why risk that now? Think of your mother. Your sisters."

"I *am* thinking of them, and of their futures." The investment had fallen so neatly into my lap, it was the first time I'd considered believing in fate. It was exactly what I'd been searching for. What I *needed*. An investment that would pay out for the rest of our lives. "I realize I cannot afford to buy the land outright myself," I said, so he'd know I had considered all the options. "I haven't come to London merely for *your* opinion."

Tom furrowed his brow, mumbling to himself. "Half, yes. Half. Or better, your usual quarter of a whole, if he's willing."

Would he be? None of what I did was a one-man job. Finding the right pieces to the puzzle had been key to my success. Tom, my family, and especially Mr. Lane. That familiar sick feeling from talking about money twisted my gut. Not of fear, though. Over the years, Mr. Lane had become a mentor, a good friend, and I respected his decisions. It was the feeling I got when I needed something important, desperately, but I wasn't sure I could have it. The feeling had followed me my whole life.

"Half," I repeated.

Tom nodded curtly, shuffling again. The crease in his brow deepened as he focused on the numbers. "If you want it—"

"I want it." Grabbing his arm, I directed him around a hole in the path, toward Mayfair and the most elite townhouses in London.

He looked up from the papers, nodding to a passing gentleman. "I'll move some things around. You're due a payment from the Bradley account, but your earnings from the Bristol investment ought to cover you until then." He held up a page, always checking, then rechecking.

We crossed the street, and there it was, just ahead. The Lane House. Standing tall, sweeping, as white and fresh as it must've been the day it was built. Even the front door, shining and sleek in the sunlight, reeked of money, and I both loved and hated the smell of it.

Too little and you'll starve to death. Too much and you'll drown.

"I daresay Miss Lane isn't going to like this." Tom studied the grand house as we approached, our footsteps slowing.

"She'll recover." I glanced at the top right window and straightened my cravat. Tom, as though on instinct, smoothed his coat and lifted his chin. Everyone who was anyone stood a little taller when they passed the Lanes' house.

"Have you heard"—Tom cleared his throat, busying himself with organizing the papers a final time—"if she might be attending Frank's assembly?"

My brows rose. An incredibly intelligent man such as himself couldn't possibly be so daft. Anna Lane had dozens of suitors every Season, but not even the richest, highest ranking of them all were good enough. The latest rumors had her on

Alexander Lennox's arm, which only confirmed my opinions of her. "I have not heard. Nor would I encourage you to seek her out. The woman is poison, Tom."

He bristled. "She is no such thing. Why, just this afternoon she—"

"She is a snake hiding in the bushes, waiting for a man to put out his hand so she can strike."

Tom laughed outright, then slapped a hand on my shoulder. "Not Anna Lane. She is an eternal Diamond of the First Water."

In Society's eyes, perhaps. But what did Society know? "She's a shrew."

Tom grinned as though he understood something I did not. "You would know better than I." He tipped his hat, handing me back my papers. "Send notice, and I'll be ready to adjust your funds."

"Thank you." I nodded back. Tom retreated, and I drew in a long, steadying breath.

Facing the grand entrance, the tall mahogany door framed by white stone columns, I took off my hat. *He won't pass this up. He can't.* Of all the investments I'd brought to Mr. Lane over the past three years, this one dwarfed them all. As I took the four steps, I rustled a hand through my flattened hair and licked my lips. Before I could knock, the door opened.

"Mr. Everett," Lyons said, clearly surprised to see me. "We thought you'd removed to Brighton for the fortnight."

I gave the butler an easy smile. Polite. Amiable. Business. "Indeed, I had. But circumstances required an urgent return. Is Mr. Lane at home?"

"In his study." Lyons opened the door wide. "Do come in."

Chapter Two

ANNA

"More butter," I said to Mrs. Devon, licking my finger after sampling the French beans. "I need everything just a little bit . . . *more* tonight." I squinted at her, and she nodded in understanding. Her features were wrinkled with age and wisdom. Our cook loved a challenge, but more, she loved getting things just right. I suspected she loved helping me butter up Papa too, which I needed tonight, desperately.

I needed out of London.

"And the lamb?" she asked with patient eyes, hands hovering above the platter of perfectly sliced meat.

"Oh, the lamb is divine." I reached to pinch off another piece, but she shooed my hand away, her humor evident in the way she held back her pleased smile.

"You'll dirty that lovely gown before dinner," she muttered, handing me a rag to wipe my fingers.

Mrs. Devon was so good to me. So good, I often found myself at her little table belowstairs. Coddled with a slice of late-night pie or a plate of buttered bread, listening to the quiet sounds of servants chattering happily together as they cleaned and prepared for the next day. I envied their comradery. The family they'd created. Papa had become so busy of late.

Through childhood, I'd have said our lives were near perfect. Papa was all I had, but he was all I'd needed. In London, he saw to business and his many holdings. But every summer, he'd take me to Lyme. Just the two of us. He'd say, "Where shall we go, Annie?" and I'd beg for sand and shells and the chance to unearth treasures. He'd bring his book and a few blankets and pillows with us to the seaside, and I'd explore.

Looking back, I couldn't help but wonder how he survived those trips. He endured my ceaseless questioning about fossils and bones and oddly shaped shells, my temper when I'd forgotten to eat or drink, and then my half-drenched form splayed across his lap for an hour's nap halfway through the day. No matter if I was an utter devil to take home by nightfall. He'd smile. Again and again for a fortnight by the sea.

As I grew older, I'd hunted less for treasure, more satisfied to sit alongside him and read. Instead of questioning him about shells, I'd question him about Shakespeare and Aristotle. I'd wonder about life and what I might do, where it might take me. And Papa would challenge my thinking, encourage me to consider different points of view. I never felt too young or silly or inadequate. If I lacked knowledge, he'd simply point me in the right direction to find it. And most certainly, if I needed him, I only had to ask.

We'd last been to Lyme three years ago.

And unfortunately for me, finding Papa when I needed him—for anything more than a passing conversation or private dinner—was proving to be a difficult task.

Mrs. Devon brought over the butter dish and sliced several thin pieces to lay over the French beans. "Your father would put butter on his butter if it was all we had left to eat."

Indeed. With this spread, I'd certainly have Papa's attention tonight.

"Miss Lane." Lyons approached, holding a massive bouquet of roses in his arms, a small card attached. "For you. Where shall I put these?"

"I should think that depends on who they are from." Mrs. Devon frowned, her gaze flicking toward mine. She was the only one I'd told.

Lyons looked at the card. "Mr. Alexander Lennox."

My jaw clenched, muscles seizing to run as though the man himself was about to turn the corner. The nerve of him, sending me flowers after what he'd done. He'd taken my hand, led me around a turn in the garden, and spoken such lovely words that I'd let him kiss me before my maid, Mariah, caught up to us. I shook my head, remembering how thin and dry his lips had been. The whole experience had been as lackluster as a paste diamond. I should have known to abandon him then. But some of us did not have mamas to teach us the ways of men.

"Throw them out," Cook ordered with a raised finger. "We've no use for dirty roses here."

Lyons looked utterly confused. "But they're from—"

"Do throw them out, please," I insisted, then softened the directive with a smile.

"And the card?"

A card? What more could he possibly say? I inhaled deeply and huffed the air out with a wave of my hand. "I am certain it is filled with a thousand apologies, pleading for forgiveness—nothing he has not said already. But I do not wish to hear from nor see him again." Which was why I had to leave London by week's end before he returned from Bath.

Oh, I'd made a grand mistake trusting Alexander Lennox. The worst of all.

"Out with them!" Mrs. Devon swiped at the air between us. "Can you not see she is overset? That man is a rake and a scoundrel, Mr. Lyons, and we don't need reminding!"

Lyons's eyes grew wide, and his back straightened. "Immediately, Miss Lane." And he was off.

I blew out another breath, my shoulders sagging. The Season had been a disaster. When I'd confronted Mr. Lennox about the woman he'd secretly proposed to, he'd admitted everything. He'd been engaged for months, but the arrangement was *not to his liking*, and he *did not love her*. Not like he supposedly loved me. He *could not bear* to lose me. *Would do anything* to earn my forgiveness.

Then I learned that Mr. Lennox—handsome, charming, amiable Mr. Lennox—had spent his inheritance and needed more. Apparently my marriage settlement was worth far more than his intended's. What he loved, it turned out, was not me but my father's money.

I shook my head, as though the motion could rid me of the past month's memories. I regretted every flutter of my heart; in fact, they made me ill to consider. The very idea that I'd given that man an ounce of my affection turned my heart as cold as stone. Were all men liars? Greedy, self-centered, and callous? I was beginning to believe so.

"Thank you, Mrs. Devon," I said, touching the wooden table between us. "For dinner. And for everything."

"Not at all, dear," she said with an affectionate smile. "All will be well. You'll see."

She couldn't know how much her words meant to me. How dearly I hoped she was right. I swallowed hard against the thickness brewing in my throat and blinked through the burning in my eyes. I hadn't loved Mr. Lennox—how could I? I hadn't truly known him, just the façade he portrayed. But I had trusted him. I'd given him my time and my dreams. And now I felt like the grandest fool.

How was I to face the whispers that were sure to come once news of Mr. Lennox's entanglement spread? As much as I appreciated Mrs. Devon, her pies and buttered bread could only help so much. I needed to be away from London for as long as possible. I needed to go to Lyme with Papa—just the two of us.

I nodded to Mrs. Devon and turned toward the stairs.

Lyons waited for me at the top, standing tall and resolute.

"Where is Papa?" I asked, glancing at myself in a mirror in the foyer. I winced at the pale girl staring back and pinched my cheeks. My dark hair, curled and pinned, had come from Papa, but my honey-brown eyes were, I was told, from my mother.

Lyons wrung his hands together, then promptly shoved them behind his back. "Mr. Lane is in his study."

I checked the clock on the mantel. "By now, he should already be dressed for dinner. I shall go and—"

"Allow me." Lyons stepped back. His features were more wrinkled than usual, not defensive, but also not welcoming.

Why should he care if I wanted to see Papa? I tilted my head and blew out a little laugh. Perhaps, as Papa often claimed, I was reading too much into nothing. "I should like to remind him of the promise he made to be punctual," I said with a playfully raised brow.

"Of course." Lyons cleared his throat. "Only, Mr. Lane is entertaining at present."

My spine went rigid. Father did not entertain at this

hour. There was only one person who had an open-door invitation to come and go as he pleased. One man who'd been a catalyst for all my problems, for everything had changed after he'd first shadowed our door three years ago.

But *that* man had quit London two days ago.

Indeed, *that* man made Alexander Lennox's attempts to charm look tame in comparison. He'd swooped into our lives with gleaming opportunities, and before I could blink, he'd stolen Papa's time and attention, and left me with the wolves.

Yes, the mere thought of *that* man made me itch all over.

I took a few even breaths despite the nerves collecting in my stomach. No, no. It couldn't be him. He'd been excited to leave London. Happy to spend extended time with his family. I vaguely recalled choking out a laugh at some stupid joke he made as he waved goodbye, giddy with the pleasure of seeing him go. Papa's caller couldn't be him.

Then, who?

I offered Lyons a tight smile. "At this hour? The matter must be quite urgent. Who has come to call?"

Lyons's shoulders sank as he heaved a great sigh. "After the flowers, I wish not to disappoint you again, Miss Lane."

No. Not tonight. Not when *I* needed Papa most.

"Don't say it, Mr. Lyons. Don't you dare say his name."

He was shaking his head. I knew he'd heard me rage belowstairs to Mrs. Devon more times than I'd care to admit, in such an unladylike manner my cheeks grew warm just thinking on it. Because of that, he knew I'd need preparing. So he lifted his shoulders once more, met my gaze with firm resolution, and said, "Forgive me, Miss Lane. But Mr. Everett has indeed returned."

Chapter Three

GRAHAM

"She's invited me back to Bath," Mr. Lane said. His sturdy wooden chair creaked as he leaned back, clearly trying to fight the grin that lifted the creases in his face and brightened his eyes. "I feel half my age again."

I crossed my arms, fighting my own grin. I'd never seen my friend look both so unraveled and alive at the same time. Happier than he'd been when we'd first met three years ago and made a small fortune together. At first, he'd intimidated me beyond reason. Everything about him bled sophistication: the golden fob watch dangling on a chain at his hip and the way his hair grayed primarily on the sides. His light-blue eyes pierced straight through a person, and he spoke with such confidence as though he were the cleverest man in every room. Most of the time he was.

But now, three years into our partnership, I leaned back in my seat, crossing my arms loosely, and examined the easy way the skin around his eyes crinkled as he spoke of Ms. Peale.

"She seems taken with you," I said, encouraging him. We'd met her at the Pump Room at the beginning of the year while investing in a new theater in Bath. She'd eyed Mr. Lane right away and joined us on many outings every time we visited to oversee progress. "And she is handsome."

"*Beautiful,*" Mr. Lane said with feeling. He shook his head, and a light flush colored his cheeks. "But I cannot go."

"Nonsense. Of course you'll go."

"You are young," he said pointedly, as though I needed reminding. "You do not yet understand the complexities of marriage. Nor do you have a daughter as obstinate as mine."

I hoped I never would. "Miss Lane will understand."

He rubbed his temples, clearly at war with himself. "I made her a promise. Years ago. I won't remarry until she is married and settled."

I reeled back, then quickly tried to steel my surprise. We rarely spoke of Anna, keeping family and business behind their respective, distinctive lines. But even still, I knew Mr. Lane wouldn't have made such a promise without the utmost care. He loved Anna. He endeavored to put her first above all else. But he deserved happiness too.

"I know, I know." He looked away with a laugh. "I'd thought she'd find someone at eighteen. There are certainly plenty of respectable gentleman in London vying for her attention. But here we are. She's nearly one-and-twenty, and while I love her"—he gave me a look as though he needed me to remember that singular fact—"I do not wish to remain alone for the rest of my life."

I nodded, feeling compassion and determination to help my friend. "If she won't marry, find something to keep her distracted," I said. I thought of the woman whose dog had barked at Tom and me in the street. "Get her a pug or a terrier."

Mr. Lane smirked. "Speaking of distractions, what do you have for me this time, Everett?" he asked.

My stomach flopped like a fish on dry land as the necessary details pushed to the front of my mind. This opportunity felt like a turning point in my life. A crossroads where one path led me to success, and the other kept me stagnant forever. I hated being out of control, but hopefully, after this, I'd never need anyone's help ever again.

I cleared my throat and looked Mr. Lane straight on, unflinching. "Land in Brighton. Fourteen acres to develop. The seller means to move north to live a more private life. Because I'm well-acquainted with the family, they've offered me the first opportunity to buy."

I watched him carefully for any reaction, any outward indication of his thoughts. Mr. Lane was a first-rate player. When it came to business, the man gave nothing away. If you wanted his partnership, you had to earn it. And the fact that I had earned his favor so many times still astounded me. Perhaps I would find out today that I'd become too confident. Too bold.

Moments passed, and still he did not blink. He was the same man who spoke about love and family, who'd encouraged me to visit my home for a fortnight instead of seeking out more investment opportunities. But the business side of him was more serious. More firm and intimidating.

"That much land would be a great undertaking," he finally said. "Brighton's popularity may not last. Especially with how fickle the Regent can be."

Confidence. I nodded. "I believe it will last. The Marine Pavilion is unlike anything you've seen. Rumor has it, he only means to improve it. Doctors are traveling to the sea with their patients, and tourism brings wealth and industry. As with any venture, there is always risk, but I cannot imagine the land will depreciate. The profits, should we divide and hire builders, are substantial."

Mr. Lane dipped his pen in ink, his hand hovering over a blank page. "Tell me your plans."

I pulled out a paper from inside my coat upon which I'd neatly sketched the land and my plans, unfolded it, and slid it across the desk to him. *Always be prepared,* Mr. Lane had said when I'd first come to him years ago. *Know every detail.*

I pointed to the small rectangles I'd sketched inside the larger drawing. "We could divide the land into forty-three parcels and hire an architect to assist in building the homes," I said. "And if we sold each plot at, say, fifteen hundred and seventy-five pounds . . ."

He took the page, then drew a long rectangle with his pen and wrote out a calculation.

I arranged the same numbers in my mind, as I had a hundred times last night, seeing them as though they were written on the wall behind Mr. Lane. "Sixty-seven thousand, seven hundred and twenty-five," I said.

Mr. Lane looked up, furrowed his brow, then continued writing on his page.

My gaze caught hold of a little painting on his desk. A young girl with smooth brown curls dangling over her shoulder, soft eyes, and a smile that brightened her features. Anna. She looked happy. Content, even.

Perhaps the artist had been generous.

The truth was, Anna Lane had impossible standards. No man living could possibly meet them and, having seen for myself how often she waved off suitors, what little admiration

I'd initially harbored upon meeting her evaporated. Too much time with Anna and her blistering remarks left a man feeling as unwanted as an empty ink jar. Luckily, I did not need her good opinion to befriend her father.

"Sixty-seven thousand," Mr. Lane announced, then cleared his throat. "Seven hundred and twenty-five pounds. Quite a profit margin."

I nodded, no less sure of the numbers than I'd been before, and he raised a brow.

"Well, the profit certainly looks good," he said. "But does the land?"

That was the question. Our investment, like the many other opportunities we'd taken together, depended on the smaller details as well as the larger. "In my opinion, yes. The soil is prime for building and only a short distance to the sea. I own property not far from it. My mother and sisters live there now."

Mr. Lane scratched his head and sniffed. "With what you've presented, I'd be a fool not to invest alongside you. But what exactly are you offering, Everett?"

Finally, the point. Typically, we split profits twenty-five percent to seventy-five in his favor because, while I could find the best investments, he had the money and connections. He'd been so generous with me over the last few years, largely, I assumed, because of his friendship with my late grandfather.

Never had I been so bold with Mr. Lane. Would he think me overstepping to ask so much of him? I'd finally reached a place financially where I could afford to take big risks; I just needed someone with a large enough purse to make that risk bearable. If I landed this deal—if I made as much money as I intended to make—I could afford to present my sister with a dowry full enough to tempt a decent husband. I could offer my mother a comfortable living for the rest of her days.

And I could expand my holdings and provide for a family of my own eventually. Modest, of course, all modest in comparison to Mr. Lane's lifestyle. But compared to how bleak things had seemed for me when I'd left Cambridge, I would be living like a king.

I braced myself, infusing my voice with the confidence of a man twice my age and experience. "You and I will go in as even investors." I met his eye firmly and was surprised to see not a flinch of disregard in his. "I will stay with my family in Brighton for the foreseeable future to oversee the work, and you would lend trusted builders and architects."

A soft knock sounded on the door.

Mr. Lane watched me appraisingly, then said, "Come in."

Lyons entered. "Forgive me, Mr. Lane. But Miss Lane once again insists you join her for dinner before the food grows cold. She said to tell you"—the poor man cleared his throat, wincing with mild embarrassment as he continued, determined—"that she will march down here herself to retrieve you if you do not come at once."

Spoiled woman. What did she think we were doing, playing a game of spillikins? These were important matters— money and business and securing futures. Honestly, I'd rather be home spending time with my family, but this investment could not wait. I would not be here otherwise.

Mr. Lane looked at me, any embarrassment of his own masked by a polite smile, and I remembered my place. Though I'd come to appreciate the inner workings of the Lane household, and admittedly felt close with Mr. Lane, I was not a member of his family. Another line, distinct and firm.

"One moment more, Lyons, thank you. We have just finished."

Finished? A weight dropped to the bottom of my stomach. I'd considered the possibility that Mr. Lane would not wish to invest. This one in particular was a long game. We likely would not see profits for at least a year, and that was after extensive work on my part. But investing alone meant tying up too much of my carefully acquired savings. My family had waited long enough to live their lives without fear of poverty, without having to tread as though the ground beneath us could break at any moment.

More pressing, the time I'd been granted to present enough funds to purchase the land was expiring. I needed an investment partner, and now.

The door closed behind the butler, and I waited with bated breath. I would let him speak first.

"You mentioned a short timeline," he said, standing and shuffling papers around on his desk.

I stood to match his height and moved around my chair. "I have one week before the seller moves on to other interested parties."

He blew out a breath and raised his brow. "I should like to see the property myself first, but I don't know how I'll find the time. With Ms. Peale's invitation to Bath, and Anna, here . . ."

What could I say? My adamant assurances would do the man no good. It was either he trusted me, or he didn't.

He rubbed his jaw and turned thoughtful. Serious. "You know I respect you, Everett. You're every bit as honorable as your grandfather was."

I clasped my hands behind my back. "Thank you, sir."

"But to invest such a sum without having seen the land myself . . . I worry that to trust any man so fully would be a fool's errand, and I do not wish to set such an example for you."

My stomach sank. But I nodded. "Of course, sir." Where would I find another partner on such little notice? Let alone convince him of my plan?

"Still, I cannot imagine passing up what seems to be such an obviously good investment. Land of that size is so rare an opportunity. Not to mention the profits, and you offering to oversee the work."

My gaze settled back on his, firmly and resolutely, as the gates parted for one last chance to convince him.

"Mr. Lane, if your hesitation is solely set upon the land, I assure you—"

The door burst open, and our attention pivoted.

Anna, in the doorway, dressed in an apple-red gown like some forbidden fruit. Dark brown hair cascaded over her shoulder from a coiffure at her neck, dangling above her exposed collarbone and smooth, porcelain skin, enough to drive a man mad with every breath she took. I gave myself a full second to appreciate the vision that was Anna Lane before reminding myself of her poison.

Her honey eyes met mine accusingly, like she knew I'd let my gaze wander, creating the strangest ripple effect in my chest, then she scoffed and looked heavenward. The vivacity with which she had opened the door seemed to drain out of her.

"Good evening, Miss Lane," I said, but my voice had lost its confidence.

She parted those full lips and enunciated each syllable in my name with painful precision. "Mr. Everett."

Why did I ever think her response would be different? That her features might soften upon seeing me like they so often did in ballrooms with her friends.

The line had been drawn, and she was decidedly on the other side of it.

And thank heavens for that line, for the woman hated me. She was like fire: unrestrained and scalding if you got too close.

But just like fire, she was captivating. Some unexplainable part of me loved to watch her temper ignite. Loved to see her fuming with frustration. A pretty little thing, Anna. Especially when a man knew the right words to say.

Tilting my head, I watched her with exaggerated appreciation. She *hated* when I complimented her. "Might I say, what a *stunning* dress."

"You may not," she said flatly, not hiding her disregard. It stung; it always did. But I would never fire back.

"Annie, Mr. Everett only means to pay you a compliment," Mr. Lane said as he tucked in his chair. "You must learn to receive them graciously."

My lips twitched. "I am more than happy to help her practice. There is so much to compliment."

Her father moved around his desk and pressed a kiss to Anna's temple, but her eyes stared daggers at me. "You must be hungry, Mr. Everett," she said as her father pulled back and stood between us.

"How kind of you to worry, Annie," her father said.

I crossed my arms, steeling myself. This would not be a

gracious invitation to dinner. Anna did not care one whit if I starved to death at her feet.

Still, I played my part. "I am indeed."

She placed a lace-gloved hand upon her hip. Amusement infused her plastered smile. "A dinner basket, then? For your walk home?"

She wanted to be rid of me without displeasing her father. Well, I wouldn't make it easy on her, brilliant a move as it was. I shot back an amiable grin and sweetened my voice to a sickening measure. I might be forced to concede, but not without poking at her embers first.

"How thoughtful of you, Miss Lane. Your father speaks often of your generous heart, but I am overcome with gratitude to be a firsthand recipient. You are truly a diamond among women. As beautiful inside as out."

Anna stepped nearer. Tauntingly. "In that case, I shall have Cook add extra portions of the goat cheese, which I remember you are so fond of."

I hated goat cheese. But I smiled. "So generous. So kind."

"Heavens, I hope I am not interrupting business." She smiled at her father. "But Papa, you did promise to be punctual this evening, as we have something very important to discuss. And we cannot have the food getting cold."

His eyes sharpened. "Yes, of course I remember. Everett, forgive me. I shall have to cut our meeting short."

"Need I remind you of our time restraint, Mr. Lane?" I hurried to say. "Did you have any further questions before I go?"

He looked between us and took in a long breath that lifted his weary shoulders. He seemed to think it through, then exhaled, and said, "A life lesson for both of you: Never make important decisions on an empty stomach." He turned to me with an encouraging smile. "The hour is late. Come, Everett. Dine with us."

"Papa," Anna chided.

Her surprise mirrored my own. Not for being invited to dinner, which I often was, but because I'd been invited into what felt like a *private* conversation.

Either he was unaware of his daughter's intentions for the night, or he disregarded them entirely. "I am not appropriately dressed, sir," I said.

"Nor I," he said with another sigh. "But you'll forgive us this casual dinner, won't you, Annie? Shall we?"

Anna's cheeks blossomed pink, but not out of embarrassment. She was angry.

Clearly, she wanted something.

Mr. Lane motioned for me to follow him out of the study and in to dinner, so I offered Anna my arm.

True to form, she turned her nose up at me, took her father's arm, and smiled the most innocent and gracious, helpless and hopeful smile that could turn any man's heart to utter mush.

A smile that would one day trick some poor hapless man into marrying her.

She spoke something softly in her father's ear and he laughed, then she glanced over her shoulder and frowned at me.

I smiled back, if only to play the old game we always played.

Who would win her father's attention tonight?

Chapter Four

ANNA

Graham Everett *knew* he was not wanted tonight.

I'd given him every clue, every opportunity to excuse himself, and yet still his footsteps clomped behind.

Were all men this careless about a woman's desires? Or were they simply daft?

He'd come with another investment opportunity; I could tell merely by looking at him. His coat wrinkled, trousers dusty, and his sandy hair a matted mess. Judging by the number of times he swiped his hand through it, something was clearly troubling him.

Not that I cared. Graham could take his greed elsewhere. From the very first moment he'd set foot inside our home, he'd charmed Papa with his intelligence and scheming. He was the grandson of one of Papa's old friends, which had apparently warranted Papa taking the man under his wing.

I'd tried everything I could to dissuade Papa from inviting Graham to every outing, introducing him to every associate, every connection, every friend we had because even then I could tell that Papa's time and attention were shifting by the day. Less for me, more for Graham and conversations fit only for men's ears. What I had tolerated in the beginning grew into something utterly vexatious, and before long I found myself belowstairs with Cook. Far enough away not to hear the clinking glasses and boisterous laughter in Papa's study.

Indeed, Graham had kept Papa so busy over the past few years, I'd lost count of the weeks I'd been left home alone while he sought out some venture or another. He'd only just returned from Bath!

Whatever new investment scheme Graham Everett proposed this time, I'd thwart at any cost. At present, *I* needed Papa.

In the dining room, Papa helped me into my chair at the head, then patted my shoulders before moving to his spot at my right.

I straightened my silk skirt comfortably under the table and pretended not to hear the screeching of the chair to my left. I could feel Graham there, tall and wide and filling the other space beside me.

Pea soup was poured into my bowl, then my glass filled with wine.

"I am very fond of pea soup." Graham aimed his comment to Papa.

I cleared my throat and glared.

"No more than I," Papa laughed, lifting a spoonful to his mouth. "Another commonality we share, Everett. Thank you, Anna. Your thoughtfulness brings me great pride."

I forced a pleased smile, for naturally I had planned Papa's favorite dinner for tonight, for a new beginning. Had I known Graham was attending, I would have served raw turnips.

Graham leaned closer to his bowl as he finished his soup. Comfortable, much too comfortable at our table.

My appetite waned, but I politely sipped my soup, watching Papa's progress to ensure the evening went according to my plan. After soup, he'd want more wine, which I signaled for. Then soon after, I motioned for the soup bowls to be taken away.

"More favorites." Papa grinned at the fricassee of lamb, green beans, potato pudding, and spinach cakes that arrived at the table. "A surprise to be sure. And much needed after the day I've had." His eyes focused, and a crease between his brows appeared. "What is the occasion? Have I forgotten a celebration?"

The opposite, actually, but how could I tell Papa of Mr. Lennox's betrayal with Graham sitting *right* there. I tried for a smile. "I've missed you, that is all."

"Don't be modest, Everett," Papa said, motioning to the platters situated in front of us. "Help yourself."

Graham looked to me for, what, approval? I set my jaw and stared back. If he thought I might allow him to serve me, he would be greatly disappointed. I gave him my best smile. "Yes, Mr. Everett. Please do not be modest on my account. You've always had quite the appetite when you come to our table."

A muscle in his jaw ticked as he watched me. He tilted his head to hide his annoyance, and it was too good. He had to know how dearly I despised him. I broke our stare and held my breath to keep from laughing.

Papa served the green beans and lamb, and the room grew quiet, all nicking forks and slicing knives.

Then, "Mr. Lane, would you mind passing me the goat cheese?"

I stopped chewing. *Do not react.* Graham was baiting me.

"Delicious, is it not? Try it with the lamb." Papa passed the little plate to Graham, who took it in his wide hand. "Keep the plate near you, I've plenty."

"Excellent. Thank you," Graham said, catching my gaze. The smile he gave me was nothing short of taunting, as though he wanted to prove that nothing I said or did bothered him in the least.

Well. We'd disprove that, would we not?

"I imagine your mother was not pleased to hear your excuses, Everett," Papa said. "Were you able to see her at all before you turned back?"

"For all of seven hours, sir. And no"—he stifled a laugh—"she was not pleased, to say the least. But I shall return directly."

Papa turned his attention to me. "I always forget how quiet the streets become as Society retreats. Don't you, Anna?"

"Indeed," I agreed.

Our home had been bustling with callers all Season, Mr. Lennox regularly among them. A few suitors had quickly met with Papa's disapproval and were promptly discouraged from returning. Others found worthy matches elsewhere, and I could scarcely remember their faces. The remaining had sent flowers, taken me on rides, or escorted me to dinner parties. From their numbers, I had free rein to choose. Unfortunately, I had chosen poorly.

"Although I do not miss entertaining," I added. "I fear I am still recovering from a near constant rotation of new faces and the latest news of who matched with whom. To say nothing of late nights and dinner parties. I daresay, I am envious of those who are retreating from Town." I forced a little laugh, measuring Papa's reaction.

Papa became intent upon his plate. "I have not seen Mr. Lennox come to call in several days. Has he quit Town?"

My cheeks flushed with embarrassment. How I wished I could cut all ties to that name. To be so openly pursued by a man who'd already promised his hand to another . . . Things had advanced so far, my own father had started to wonder about his intentions. But admitting that I'd been charmed and tricked by Mr. Lennox, let alone wounded, was not a topic of conversation I would broach with Graham present. He would likely go home and laugh himself silly. If I could just get Papa away, I could tell him everything, things would settle, and I could try again next Season.

I set my fork across my plate, my appetite lost. "I believe he had business in Bath. In truth, I would dearly love some time away myself."

"Time away? But we have everything we need right here in London," Papa said.

"Perhaps a little too much of everything," I muttered. I waited until his eyes found mine, then added, "And perhaps not enough of you."

Papa's innocent smile faltered, and he took a bite of lamb. When he finished chewing, he said, "I have been away more often than usual this past year. Distracted, I'll admit."

Knowing Graham sat silently, listening to my every word and judging me behind those light brown eyes was almost unbearable. I looked up from my plate to see him lifting a forkful of lamb slathered in goat cheese. For the slightest second he hesitated, then brought the bite to his lips.

Would he never relent?

Graham frowned down at his plate as he took a deep gulp of wine to chase down the tart flavor of the cheese.

I clasped my hands in my lap. "Careful, Mr. Everett, else we run through the entire cellar tonight."

Papa stepped gently on my foot. He'd lectured me many times before on acting the part of a lady around his friend. "To where are you dreaming of visiting, Anna?"

A servant poured Graham more wine.

Here was my opportunity. Luckily, I knew my father. He thrived on detail and was more easily swayed by concrete plans, so I met his gaze straight on. "Lyme. A quaint cottage by the sea."

Papa raised his brow and exchanged a glance with Graham. I wanted to scream at how Papa always looked to the man for support. As though *he* might have something to say about my liberties. But Graham would never admit what he truly thought. Only what he knew Papa wanted to hear.

"You wish to visit the seaside?" Papa sliced a bite of spinach cake, his eyes faraway and thoughtful. "It has been some time since we have visited Lyme."

My heart picked up speed, and I turned toward him. "Though it feels like just yesterday. A good book and the sea at our feet. Remember when I was girl, how I'd dig for fossils and bones until the sun fell?" My life had been so full, my heart content. Just the two of us, Papa and me, safe and happy, and the hardest decision I had to make was which color dress to wear.

Papa's smile warmed, and he reached out and took my hand. "Some of my fondest memories," he said. "Everett, have you ever visited Lyme?"

Instantly, my face turned cold. Graham's cheeks had pinked from the wine, and he did not look away when I met his stare. Uninhibited, with his eyes focused so intently upon me, I remembered why half the women from the Season had asked me about him. Why they concocted plans to fall into his path and throw their calling cards at his feet. He was handsome in a natural sort of way, a man who had to do nothing but smile halfway to get attention. It was maddening.

Slowly, he turned his gaze to Papa. "I cannot say that I have, sir. With every respect to Miss Lane, Brighton has outgrown Lyme in popularity in recent years. I daresay the entertainment found there rivals even London."

I scoffed. The man couldn't pass up an opportunity to debate me. "How so?"

He set down his wine glass. "For one, the Marine Pavilion and its gardens are second to none. There are yacht races, water parties, the Level, the Steine, a prestigious theater—"

"Indeed?" Papa's expression moved from surprise to growing interest.

No, no. I would not let Graham's opinions overshadow mine. I did not want Brighton. I wanted Lyme. I wanted Papa and time away where things moved slow, where people conversed simply for the sake of conversation with absolutely no connection to Mr. Lennox or the whispers that followed.

"Lyme's history is superior to Brighton in every way," I said. "We could visit for a fortnight, Papa. We could leave . . ."

". . . truly must visit to experience the town for what it is." Graham was droning on. Papa's gaze warred between us, and desperation caught hold of my will like an iron trap.

"Tomorrow!" The word burst from my lips, silencing the room, and I flinched at how utterly ridiculous the suggestion was. Calculated, planned—that was Papa. Spontaneity was as rare as an early rose.

Graham's lips parted. That irritating crease in his brow deepened as he watched Papa with as much confusion and curiosity as I.

"Dearest," Papa said to me softly, laying his cutlery on his plate. So much said in that single word.

I fell back into my chair, my shoulders drooping. What more could I say to convince him? I couldn't tell Papa how foolish I'd been. How I'd trusted Mr. Lennox, believed his charm to be genuine care, and thought myself falling in love. The truth was I hadn't known anything about him. Not really. Because all men were glorious charmers, all aiming lovely words at their latest ambition. The only man who'd never wanted anything from me was Papa, and it seemed even he had other priorities of late.

Graham shifted in his seat. Then he placed his napkin to the side of his plate. "Perhaps I should leave you for—"

Papa lifted a hand. "Not at all. Finish, and we shall have port."

A rejection. Good heavens, how it burned my heart. It welled in my throat and pooled at the corners of my eyes. "Then I shall excuse myself," I managed to say.

But just as I made to stand, Papa grasped my arm. "Annie, sit," he chided. "I have an idea. One that I think will be pleasing to us all."

I caught Graham's gaze, but he quickly looked away. At least he gave me the decency of composing myself.

"It may not be Lyme, but Mr. Everett is right. Brighton is flourishing. He has an investment deal he'd like me to consider there, but I find myself in want of time. One can never have enough, it seems. Everett, I hope you understand, but there is no one in this world I trust more than my daughter."

I looked at Graham, who mirrored my confusion. What was Papa planning?

"I trust her opinions," he continued, "and her knowledge on the trends of London Society. If you could convince *her* of Brighton's worth, and of the land you wish to invest in, then you may also have my good opinion, and we shall have a deal and contract to sign upon my return."

Graham went as pale as the goat cheese on his plate.

Papa turned to me. "Anna, dearest. Do this for me— determine if Brighton is worth an investment, and afterward we'll find our little cottage by the sea in Lyme. Hmm?"

I tried to make sense of what Papa had just said. There was a business venture brewing between him and Graham, and somehow, by some strange turn of luck, *I* had been granted decision-making power.

But most importantly, Papa had agreed to my proposal. He'd take me to Lyme.

The investment noise would last a few days at most. Then we could rid ourselves of Society, Mr. Lennox's pursuit, and the gossipmongers. We'd have no one to worry over but ourselves, just like old times.

I could not temper my grin. "I would not mind at all, Papa."

Papa grinned in return. "This is an excellent plan. Everett, if I may prevail upon you, Annie will leave with you tomorrow, and I shall follow shortly after the . . . *meeting* in Bath I told you about."

My jaw went slack. *"What?"*

Graham cleared his throat. "I—of course," he said, shifting in his seat. He blinked hard several times, and for once in his life, the man looked terrified.

I shook my head. "I'm sorry, leave *with* him?"

Papa could be oblivious to some of our interactions, but he was not daft. He knew Graham and I were not fond of each other.

"Everett's family lives in Brighton," Papa said to me. Then he turned to his friend. "She need only stay with your family for a few days—five, if I can push the horses and reach my destination in good time. A week at most."

"A week? Papa," I started to argue. "Do you not think that improper? I can certainly wait a week for your return."

"Or perhaps, sir, you could rearrange your meeting in Bath and take Miss Lane *after* seeing Brighton," Graham argued.

"I cannot go to Bath," I blurted, gripping the arms of my chair. Mr. Lennox was there, and I would rather perish than be forced into his company so soon. "I simply cannot."

Papa nodded, considering. "Well, I have been summoned, and I must go. I would trust Mr. Everett with my life, Annie. I certainly trust him with yours. You'll take Mariah with you. His family will await your arrival."

Graham sat back, speechless, which was entirely unhelpful, but he could not want this arrangement any less than I.

Papa glanced between us. "This plan will be perfect for us all. And, in truth, a little time together might do you both some good."

What, did he think we could reconcile our differences? Graham and I were like a fox and a hound. Some personalities did not mix for a reason.

"Then we can finish our business, yes?" Papa raised his brows, then turned back to me. "You help me with this, do a good, thorough job of determining Brighton's potential, and when I come to claim you, Annie, we shall find a perfect view of the sea and spend a full fortnight away together. Just us. There is much I fear we have missed in each other's lives of late, and I do not wish to make a habit of continuing to do so."

He nodded, either satisfied with the plan or oblivious to our reluctance, or perhaps both. My mind was whirling, dizzy. My shallow breaths inadequately compensated for the shock pulsing through my heart.

We'd leave tomorrow. Graham and me. The two of us . . . together. Without Papa.

What would we even *say* to each other?

Graham nodded, agreeing again to the plan, and I swallowed at the thought of staying under his protection for a week. We *hated* one another; neither of us had made any secret of our opinions. But alone, and out of my father's view, how would he treat me?

Indeed, I almost wanted him to treat me poorly. Papa would expect a thorough report to support my opinion of Brighton, and part of that would be proving Graham's poor judgment. One false move, and I'd tell my father every step out of line the man took. I'd write it all down so I wouldn't forget. And we would not be alone. He had a mother and a sister. Perhaps two sisters? I could not recall. Were all the Everetts as arrogant as he?

One week was all I had to sacrifice. A temporary arrangement in exchange for a fortnight of healing with Papa. Away from the consequences of a foolhardy decision. Away from pretending. I'd let Graham charm himself in circles. Perhaps I might even enjoy a view of the sea from a different shore. But first, I'd disprove everything he thought he loved about Brighton.

I sat back in my seat. This was all fine. It would be awkward, undoubtedly. But what choice did I have?

I imagined an evening in Graham's drawing room. Him, sitting by the fire with a book and an evil smile, and me, starved from the paltry dinner he'd served to pay me back for all the goat cheese.

He wouldn't. He needed my good opinion as much as I needed his, and, judging by the fear etched in his every feature, he knew it. All would be fine. Absolutely, perfectly, wonderfully fine.

Yes?

I looked up, meeting Graham's darkening expression. I refused to let him see my fear. For the first time in our acquaintance, *I* had the power. His aim would be to please me.

"I shall be ready early. I imagine we shall take an extra stop or two, since you'll be traveling beside the carriage on *horseback*." My smile, at last, was genuine. Never in a million years would I share a carriage with that man for so long a trip.

His nostrils flared the tiniest bit. He wouldn't refuse me in front of my father, especially when he wanted an investment. I could read the man like a book, and I relished in every sign of his discomfort.

"I wouldn't have it any other way," he said with a tight smile.

"Good man," Papa said. "Now . . . port."

Chapter Five

GRAHAM

I checked my pocket watch for the fifth time in two minutes. Where was she? We were set to leave a half hour ago, and I'd been standing outside by the carriage awaiting the *five more minutes* Lyons had promised six times over.

Typical of Anna to keep someone waiting. What was she doing in there? Adjusting her hair? Pinching bites off a crumpet? Either way, I was powerless. Forced to bend to her wishes now that she had the final say in my investment.

My stomach twisted, but I wouldn't give in to the fear. I'd faced impossible odds before. I could do it again. I could win this game.

I'd merely have to charm the devil.

The door opened, and Mr. Lane jogged down the stairs. "She's coming," he assured me with a smile. "So sorry for the delay. She's gathering things in her satchel."

"Not to worry, Mr. Lane." I gave him what I hoped was an amiable smile, just as a servant brought out another trunk the size of a tea cart to add to the carriage helm.

Mr. Lane laughed heartily and slapped a hand on my shoulder. "Don't look so terrified, Everett. She won't bite."

"I am not so certain," I muttered. "Perhaps you should speak with her about Ms. Peale before you leave. She might change her mind about Bath."

His chuckled but scratched the back of his head and winced. "I do not think that is wise. Not until I speak with Ms. Peale and make my intentions known. With all sincerity, I cannot thank you enough for agreeing to host Anna on such short notice. I trust you with my daughter, Everett. She is my world. Keep her safe. Keep her happy. Should anything go wrong—"

"It won't, sir." I straightened my spine. Safe, I could promise. As her guardian, I'd fight off any foes, give the woman my own lifeblood if I had to.

But keeping her happy? That was an entirely different beast. I'd aim for *content*, and Mr. Lane would have to be merciful. My main goal for the week was to show off Brighton. Its beauty, its charm, and its people. If I could not win Anna over, perhaps they could.

He nodded once, his features firm and serious. "Safe travels, then. I shall meet you in Brighton."

"Until then, sir."

I watched as he hopped into his carriage, a servant closing the door behind him. And he was off.

The front door of the house opened again, a footman standing at attention, and Anna emerged with a satchel in hand. Her hair was silky and shiny and practically glowed in the sun. Soft curls bounced as she took the steps, her dress swayed with each movement, and something low in my stomach clenched. Gads, she was beautiful. Too beautiful.

"Good morning, Mr. Everett," she clipped.

A peace offering? "Miss Lane. You are—"

"Where is your horse?" She stopped a few feet in front of me, crossing her arms around her satchel and staring hard. "I am ready to depart, but it appears you are not."

Lud, she was fierce. She truly thought she could oust me from my own carriage, speaking to me like I was nothing more than dirt beneath her boots. That might have been true when we first met, but I'd worked hard for my place. My riding or not had nothing to do with Brighton, and no reasonable sway on her opinion of the investment.

"It looks like rain," I lied, staring back.

She raised one delicate brow. "It absolutely does not."

"It does," I continued, moving aside to allow her access to the steps leading into the carriage. "You would not wish for me to catch cold. For then I would not be able to show you Brighton, and you could not accurately form your opinion for your father. Indeed, by the time I recovered, your father will have returned, and your opinion, lacking as it shall be, will be irrelevant. He will wish to form his own. With me." I finished with a happy grin, which she returned with a fiery glare.

Thinking on it, catching cold might actually be worth a seven-hour horse ride. "So if you insist—"

Anna brushed past me, not waiting for assistance. She braced herself against the carriage doorframe as she climbed inside, followed closely by her lady's maid. Surprised, I took that as my invitation.

"Good morning." I nodded to her lady's maid, taking my seat opposite the two women.

My carriage was small but sturdy. I'd bought it from an older gentleman who'd profited from one of my investment opportunities. He'd given me an unfair advantage on the price— I'd assumed from gratitude at our success—and I'd not argued.

I knocked thrice on the roof, and my driver urged the horses forward.

Anna drew in a long breath. Then another. Then she rifled through her satchel and pulled out a small brown notebook and charcoal pencil.

She opened to the first page, then her gaze met mine. "Day one," she muttered.

Besides her maid, who had perfected the role of an invisible servant, Anna and I were alone. And that was a strange feeling. "Writing in your journal?" I tilted my head, leaning back in my seat.

Anna barely spared me a second's glance. "Something like that."

This was going to be the longest ride of my life. I crossed my arms, trying to get comfortable, but my mind was fixed on this week and what it meant. Convincing Anna to appreciate Brighton enough to allow her father to invest with me would be no small feat. I needed her to love Brighton, which meant I'd have to appeal to her heart, if she had one. But what could Brighton offer a woman whose every need was met at the snap of a finger?

"I think you'll find the Steine particularly diverting." I watched her pencil scratch along the page, then tried again. "Brighton comes alive at night. People often gather in the evenings to socialize. I shall take you tonight and you can see for yourself just how happy the people are."

Again, silence. What in the blazes was she writing in that little book?

Knees swaying close to mine, she lifted her head, her keen eyes studying me. "I shall be tired after a long day of traveling. I shall have dinner in my room. We shall start tomorrow."

I clenched my teeth. Devil take it, I was *trying* to be civil. "My mother will be very disappointed if you take dinner in your room tonight." Ginny would be, too, if nothing more than having something to gossip about to her friends.

She continued writing, focusing on her page as she spoke. "Papa said one week. Excluding traveling, we shall have about six days." She flipped a page in her book, angling it so I could see. "One." She pointed to where she'd written, then circled the number. She flipped the page. "Two," she said, working in the same fashion before flipping the next page. "Three. Four. Five. Six."

I swallowed.

"Six days. I will approve every outing, and I promise to be fair in my opinions. My decision will be made from my general opinion of Brighton, the land you wish to acquire, and . . . well, *you*, after staying in your home."

"You've outlined the entire week already."

"My father has taught me to be very thorough."

"Indeed, with such thoroughness, I am surprised you do not already know the outcome."

She shrugged one shoulder and gave me an eerily even smile. "I am quite certain I do."

We held each other's stare. I forced myself to breathe evenly despite the growing urge to clench my jaw. She wanted me to fail. She hated me so much, thought me so low and beneath her, she wanted to see me suffer and break. Little did she know, people like me knew how to rise from the dust and keep moving. We knew how to prove malevolent naysayers wrong. I had already come so far, earning the respect of so many people who'd assumed the worst of me. I would not let a woman with an unfounded opinion be the end.

I leaned forward, elbows on my knees. "I am truly glad you feel that way, Miss Lane. I dearly love a challenge."

The flicker in her eyes dulled for the shortest second. Fear? Worry? She always seemed so confident, so brash and condescending. Perhaps somewhere deep down within her, Anna was not so confident.

She said nothing more as she closed her notebook, then tucked it away in her satchel. She removed her gloves and laid them on her lap, idly examining her fingernails.

I turned my attention out the window, thinking hard.

Six days.

I had to make them count.

The streets of Brighton were noisy with shuffling shoppers, carriages creaking, and the clip-clop of horses' hooves as we slowed to pass through town. Gigs were stopped along both sides of the road in front of the row of shops leading down to the seaside. Tourists were everywhere.

How anyone could disregard this growing town baffled me. I'd loved Brighton at first sight. I loved the bustling streets, the energy that seemed to flow as naturally as the sea. I loved the fishermen coming in with their daily catch. The pungent smells had repelled me at first, but now, they'd become home. They tasted like success and victory. The rocky shores with brilliant coloring. The English Channel stretching out in browns, greens, and blues as far as the eye could see.

Men found their livelihoods in those waters, while others found healing, hope, or adventure. When I'd first visited, I'd spent hours watching the fishermen lay out their nets to dry, listening to their boisterous conversation and seeing the life in their eyes despite how exhausted they were from the night's work. I wanted that light. Not only for myself, but for Mother and my sisters too. They deserved reprieve after being trapped with nothing for so long.

I glanced over at Anna, crumpled against the carriage door in sleep. The moment I'd been dreading had arrived. We were nearly to Highcliffe House, but with such short notice, I hadn't had time to warn my family of my own arrival, let alone our guest. And I couldn't shake the feeling that I'd returned to have my entire world be engulfed in flames. Life had taught me to expect the worst. Perhaps I ought to with Anna Lane in tow.

Brighton's stables came into view, and I knocked on the carriage roof, loud enough to jolt Anna awake. The driver pulled over to the side, and I opened the window, calling out, "Hire a horse for me, please, Brunner."

Anna squinted, holding her hand above her brow to shield her eyes. "Have we arrived?" The curls on the left side of her face had been smashed from where she'd leaned against the window and dreamed, and there was a crease along her cheek. The sight would have been endearing on any other woman.

"We are nearly there. I shall ride ahead and prepare my house for your arrival. My driver will bring you safely behind."

"Is your home not always prepared?" She looked annoyed, but her voice was still soft with sleep. *Almost* endearing.

I drew in a steadying breath through my nose. That barb would be aimed more at my mother, and I'd love to see Anna spar with *her*. But this visit was work, and my home was not ready to be examined with such a critical eye. Anna would expect perfection—a fashionably decorated home, spotless guest room, lavish meals, and rooms to wander through and relax in. The reality was, she'd find a modest home decorated only with the barest necessities which we'd acquired painstakingly over time, from investment after investment, much like we had our staff. We lived comfortably and simply and without a care for anyone judging the scarcity in our library, the age of our furniture, or the condition of the blankets we slept under.

But we could pretend. Mother could make things appear better than they were. She'd done so my entire life. She just needed time.

"I'd like to see that Highcliffe House is in order and ready for your arrival," I repeated, opening the door and stepping out.

Anna leaned forward, then reached for the door and shut me out.

Well, then.

Brunner handed me the reins to a horse from a stable house across the drive.

"Take your time," I said after he'd resituated himself upon the driver's seat. "Be slow on the turns."

The man nodded his understanding and, after I'd mounted, he urged the horses into a slow trot.

I set my sights ahead. The sea stretched for miles, and I would follow it down, cut left, and meet it just outside the populated part of town.

"Faster, you." I nudged the horse's side, and he obeyed. Wind blew all around, buffering up my coat and ruffling my hair. My entire household was about to be thrown into similar commotion. The least I could do was give them as much warning as possible.

Down the bend and across the expanse, I led my horse

off the road and gave him his head, and we cut the usual ride in half. His sure-footed pace was exhilarating. My heart pounded in my chest. Highcliffe House stood a distance away, just as I'd left it a fortnight ago, and I let out a breath of relief.

Home.

At the top of the drive, I quickly dismounted and climbed the stairs.

Roland opened the door. "Mr. Everett, is everything well?" he asked, looking past me. "Is the carriage behind you?"

"We've a guest," I said as I caught my breath. "Mr. Lane's daughter."

Mother stepped out of the front door with wide eyes and a hand on her throat. "Graham, what has happened?"

"I have agreed to host Miss Lane for the next week, Mother. Forgive me, but I need—"

"Ready the balcony room immediately, Rebecca." Mother spoke over me. "Harriet, alert Cook. I shall add to the menu at once. And Ginny!" She turned back into the house, calling for my sister. "Tidy the drawing room, then the music room, and for heaven's sake, fix your hair!"

All at once, the house came alive. All three of our servants—my man, Roland, and our two maids, Rebecca and Harriet—swooped out of sight. Voices sounded, bangs and dings and shuffling echoed off the walls.

My shoulders relaxed. "Thank you, Mother. This whole trip was thrust upon me. I could not object. And worse, Mr. Lane has given Anna the power to approve or deny my investment proposal. Everything must be perfect this week, down to the letter."

"Then we mustn't waste a moment's time." Mama looked

out at the lawn, focused and composed despite it all. "Where is Tabitha?"

Tabs. My youngest sister. Arguably the loudest and most eccentric child in all of Brighton, and that was saying something. She needed a governess badly, but I hadn't yet considered our budget against the necessity of it. Mother had taught her to read and write, but unfortunately much of her education came from running freely around the estate. She was likely covered in dirt and practicing the latest slang she'd read in one of Ginny's novels.

Her manners were not yet polished enough for a woman like Anna.

"Find her." I rubbed my face with my hands. "And send her to the vicar's for the week."

Mama reared back and furrowed her brow. "She is your sister, Graham. You cannot hide her away like an animal."

"Can't I?"

Mother smirked and tugged me inside the house that had become our refuge these past few years. Imperfect and plain, but a great deal more home than Father's. I wondered what he'd think if he saw us here. He'd made his choices, and we'd made ours. Wherever he was, I could almost guarantee we were better off than he was.

We strode down the front hall, searching for my sister in rooms and closets to no avail.

"Miss Lane's visit must run smoothly," I said to Mother, who peered down the servants' stairwell. "My investment depends upon it. This life we've built depends—"

"This life is *our* life. *Our* family." Mother closed the door behind her. Her once-thin face had rounded out, but her gaze could still look sharp when she needed it to. "We are who we are. I grow tired of running from the truth. We cannot change the past nor alter who we have become because of it. We must embrace it."

Her words were wise, but embracing the truth would not put food upon our table, nor would it provide my sisters with dowries and security. "Not yet. Not when we are so close to standing on our own feet without another man's name to support us."

She raised a hand and gently thumbed my cheek, then drew me into an embrace. She smelled like lavender and ginger. "We are all grateful for Mr. Lane's support, but *you* are the one who brought him such lucrative investment deals. You made the connections, found the resources, and finalized the plans. That man was a bag of money, nothing more."

"I owe him much more than that," I said. The lessons I'd learned by working with him had built me into the man I was.

"Perhaps, but he owes you just as much. I am so immeasurably proud of you, Graham. Look at what you have done for your family. There is a roof above our heads, clothes upon our backs, food on our table, and the most beautiful views right outside our doors. *You* built this life for us. We have all we need right here. Anyone who sees anything but the most admirable of men in you does not deserve your time."

I sighed, letting my shoulders rest for a moment. I was grateful my mother had found reasons to be content, but it was my duty to provide better and more, and I would. I would not stop until we had it all.

"What do I do with the embroidery?" Ginny stood in the doorway of the drawing room with a basket over her arm, loose, colorful threads dangling everywhere, even about her shoulders as though she'd bathed in them.

"Genevieve," Mother chided, striding toward her in a rush. Her hands were a whirlwind as she worked to untangle Ginny. "What have you done?"

"My reticule required several different colors!" she trilled.

"Every color in the rainbow?" Mother's voice raised an octave.

"It is all Graham's fault!" Ginny screeched. "I've never needed to be organized before! Why have you given us only five minutes' notice to prepare for that beast of a woman?"

"I've hardly had five minutes to prepare myself," I said, shaking my head. "Her father has run off to Bath to court that woman he met several months ago."

My family knew all about the Lanes, about my professional relationship with Mr. Lane, and my less-than-happy interactions with his daughter.

"The carriage is coming up the drive, Mr. Everett," Roland announced from the front door.

"Blast, blast, blast," I muttered, pacing from room to room. Where was Tabs? The dining room was spotless, library decent, and music room nearly dust-free thanks to Harriet's quick work. Mother had insisted we furnish the room at the end of the hall on the second floor as a guest room. Unfortunately, Anna's lady's maid would have to double up and sleep with Rebecca or Harriet.

"Go now, Graham," Mother said, rushing past. "I will tell the servants to find Tabitha and send her straight to her room. She and I will review manners and propriety before bed."

"Thank you, Mother." I would worry about all that later. For now, I looked in the mirror on the wall opposite the drawing room and adjusted my cravat, then smoothed out my hair and rubbed a bit of dirt from my jacket. I would play my part to perfection.

Roland, who acted the part of butler, footman, and valet, as well as every other job we needed of him, rushed past me to retrieve the steps for the carriage. I followed him down the front stairs to the drive just as the carriage rolled to a stop.

A deep breath of sea air calmed my nerves. Perhaps the doctors in town actually knew something about the sea's medicinal properties. When I'd asked Mother where, in all of England she'd want to live, she'd chosen Brighton. At first, I'd dragged my feet, imagining soggy boots and sand in every crevice. But the salty air had made her smile again; perhaps it could grant me a similar balm in the coming days.

Roland laid the steps under the carriage door, then opened it as I approached. Mariah descended first, and Roland directed her to the servants' stairs around the house.

Then Anna appeared, steadying herself within the doorframe. Our eyes met for the briefest moment, just long enough for her to get her bearings. Her hair had been readjusted, her hat pinned back on, cheeks perfectly rosy, and full lips set.

"Welcome to Highcliffe House, Miss Lane," I greeted her, holding out my hand. She grasped my wrist instead, leaning more weight on me than I'd expected as she struggled down the stairs. "Are you well?"

"Your carriage needs realigning," she muttered, releasing my arm and rubbing her hand on her skirts. She scrunched her nose. "And you smell like horse."

"Thank you." I held out my arm to lead her into the house, where my mother and sister no doubt watched from the window.

She forced a tight smile, then turned and strode toward Roland, who'd moved to open the front door. I stretched out my neck. She could not talk to me like that. Not within earshot of my servants. And especially not in front of my mother.

Roland stood still as a statue at the door. Good man. I nodded my appreciation as I followed Anna toward the house.

Chapter Six

ANNA

I could taste the sea.

Salty, humid air filled my lungs as I drew in one last deep, sullen breath before taking the few stairs up to Graham's front door. Highcliffe House, modest in size and painted a creamy white, stood against a speckling of trees in every direction. Weather-roughed potted bushes trimmed into spheres stood on either side of the door where his man waited.

Never had I imagined where Graham lived or what such a place would look like, *feel* like. From the front drive to the front door, the house was simple and plain, but also clean and tidy and somehow elegant. The latter I'd attribute to his mother's hand.

Most importantly, Highcliffe House was far removed from Society's eye. Far enough that anyone looking to appease their curiosity regarding my current state after what Mr. Lennox had done would be hard-pressed to find me. Perhaps, by the time Papa and I returned to London, something or someone else would have already overshadowed his transgression.

I caught Graham's eyes watching me as I stepped inside

the house. Though he tried to hide his thoughts behind a firm mask of polite manners and amiability, Graham disliked me as much as I disliked him. As per usual, his efforts were made strictly to win more of my father's money. I was merely a pawn in his game.

". . . such a happy surprise." A woman's greeting echoed from the hall.

"My mother, Mrs. Julia Everett," Graham said as a petite woman strode toward us. Her light-brown hair was pinned into a simple knot atop her head, a more casual look that reminded me I hadn't been expected as a guest. I held steady, firm against the awkwardness that swelled in my chest, to keep my nerves from overcoming me as Graham said, "Mother, Mr. Lane's daughter, Miss Anna Lane."

"You have a lovely home, Mrs. Everett," I said with a curtsey. "I cannot thank you enough for hosting me on such short notice, and for so long."

"Thank you, Miss Lane. How kind of you," she replied, reaching out to squeeze my arm. "May I introduce my daughter, Genevieve."

A girl a few years younger than I stepped forward. She was a mirror image of her mother, but all sharp edges. "How do you do, Miss Lane?"

I gauged from her piercing gaze and clever, pursed smile that she was not impressed with me. What had Graham told her about me? She was pretty, well-dressed in a wispy muslin, with a forced politeness she'd no doubt learned from her brother.

"I'll admit, the Brighton Road is not an easy one to travel, all twists and turns and hills, but I am happy to be away from London for a time," I said.

Miss Everett harrumphed a smile, and Graham shot her a weighted glance; then, as though on cue, his sister clasped her hands together and turned her gaze to mine. "You must be in want of tea, Miss Lane. Shall I ring for some?"

"I would dearly love a cup," I said.

Miss Everett nodded stiffly, then turned on a heel. I noticed a stack of papers half-scribbled on and creased on the desk just outside the drawing room, and as though he'd been watching my line of sight, Graham swept a hand across them and shoved them inside the drawer.

"Please don't let me interrupt your day," he said to his mother. "I have a mountain of paperwork to see to."

"But you've only just arrived," his mother protested, a look of longing aimed at her son that I understood all too well. She missed him. Like I missed Papa. Men like ours were never around long enough.

Graham cleared his throat and gave his mother a warm smile. So warm, I almost did not recognize him. "I have a busy week, and I must prepare."

I wanted to laugh. He could prepare for a lifetime, and my answer would still—would always—be no.

"But you will join us for dinner, won't you?" his mother asked.

He leaned in and kissed his mother's temple. "Of course. I shall be in my study if you need me." Then he turned to me, and there was a decided lack of warmth. "You as well, Miss Lane. You are the object of my attention this week. If there is anything you need—"

"Do not trouble yourself, Mr. Everett," I said blandly. We both knew his good manners were only for show. "I am quite capable of taking care of myself." I briefly met his gaze, then turned, angling away from him. By the looks of things, his family was eager to have him home. I'd be doing us all a service by rejecting his investment offer.

He frowned, then bowed before stalking down the hall to some shadowed room.

His mother took my arm and laced it through her own as she led me toward the drawing room. "Forgive my son, Miss Lane. His mood comes and goes depending on the load he carries. After a good night's rest, he shall be back to his cheery self."

Cheery? I squeezed her arm tightly. Her son was a beast, but she was delightful.

The Everetts' drawing room was quaint, well-kept, and clean. It was very simply furnished, save for the back corner, where stood the most exquisite and ornately carved harp. Lovely, but almost out of place against the dated carpets and the settee with its wooden arm chipped with age. None of it seemed to bother Mrs. Everett, though. Indeed, she seemed genuinely happy to receive me, and I was surprised by how instantly comfortable I felt in her presence.

Miss Everett took a seat beside me on the settee just as a servant came in with the tray, and Mrs. Everett, satisfied that we were settled, slipped out of the room.

Back straight, poised and purposeful, Miss Everett would not meet my eye as she poured the tea. "Do not feel obligated to eat, but our cook prepared a small service."

"Thank you," I said, helping myself to a little cake. My stomach rumbled; between my rushed morning and that horrible road, I hadn't eaten a thing all day. "My father tells me you've not been in Brighton long. How do you find it?"

"We've lived here for almost a year," she said, handing me a cup, then serving herself.

I got the distinct impression she would rather be somewhere else. Probably because of something Graham had told her about me. "Your home is very comfortable. Last I remember, you lived just outside of London. Did your brother drag you all the way out here?" I tried for humor, then took a sip and smiled warmly at her.

She patted her lips with a napkin, then stared at me with thinly veiled scrutiny. "My brother *led* us here. He has worked tirelessly to make Highcliffe House what it is. Indeed, I daresay every book, every blanket, every flower is evidence of his effort and care. We are not among those who are given anything and everything they desire, so we are very grateful for our modest and *comfortable* home."

Oof. I'd offended her. I swallowed, then set my cake down. She did not like me. Not at all. "I see," I said.

"Do you?" she said with a wry smile. Again, she tilted her head and gave me such a look, I almost thought I was in a London ballroom vying against her for the most eligible bachelor.

I set my tea and plate aside. Best to get straight to the point. "Miss Everett. I am not sure what your brother has told you about me—"

"My brother's happiness and success mean a great deal to me. He works exceptionally hard—ten times as hard as other men—to get the same result. Whether you approve of him or not, his home is more than sufficient for the likes of you."

My eyes widened, then hers did too, as though she just realized how forward and rude she'd been. I could have taken offense, were I not easily able to respect and discern her intention to defend her brother at all costs. He'd likely whined about me, told his entire family how horrible I was. But why on earth would she care if I approved of her brother? Disliked him, yes, but my approval of him did not matter. And I'd complimented his house! The girl rebounded my every word as though I'd smeared her brother's name among the *ton*. My dislike of him was no secret, but hers of me seemed entirely unfounded.

Mrs. Everett strode into the room, replacing her initial look of exhaustion with one of happy ease. "How do you find your tea, Miss Lane?"

"Perfectly warm," I said amiably, then met Miss Everett's tight smile and muttered, "Though a touch bitter."

"Sugar?" Miss Everett showed her teeth, spooning a healthy portion into my cup.

Her mother did not notice; she was glancing about the room as though expecting to find something out of place.

A door closed hard from the floor above. Feet stomped, and voices carried loudly. I angled my ear, but I could not make out the words. A woman's voice, and someone much younger.

"Ginny, darling, why don't you play the harp for Miss Lane?" Mrs. Everett raised her brows. We'd only just met, but I wondered if her tone was a bit frantic.

Miss Everett—Ginny—tensed. "Must I?"

"The harp. *Forte*." Mrs. Everett muttered the last word. "Miss Lane, if you'll excuse me, I must see to my youngest daughter."

I started to stand, to offer to join her and save myself from the thrashing of Ginny's hot and cold temperament, but Mrs. Everett was already at the door. "Dinner will be set around six. Ginny can show you your room whenever you are ready. Do rest, and please enjoy our home as if it were your own." She waved a hand and was gone.

Ginny was placing pages on a little stand in the back corner of the room beside her exquisite instrument. Her eyes focused, her elbows comfortably tucked as she positioned her fingers upon the harp's strings to play.

Then the most beautiful sounds infused the air. Ginny's fingers drew the strings into a melody of soft, moving music. Was I more surprised that she was so proficient or that such an angry person could make such beautiful sound? Either way, her music captivated me, and I found myself with plate and cup back in hand.

My shoulders started to relax. My stomach settled. I'd always assumed Graham's lifestyle was akin to Papa's, but his home was nothing like ours. A harp instead of a pianoforte. Bare walls save for a few amateur paintings. A sister whose temper gave way to free speech, and another hidden away upstairs. So much to write down in my notebook.

After a few songs, and a few too many sweets, Ginny's voice broke my peace. "Shall I show you to your room?" She swiped up her music pages and set them on a nearby table in a swift movement, then strode toward the door without a backward glance.

I set down my plate and cup and hurried to follow.

"We've two additional floors," she said, leading the way up the polished wooden staircase from the foyer. "The first is our library with beautiful windows overlooking the sea, designed and reconstructed by Graham. There are two other rooms for studying, and a smaller guest room. And the second floor is our rooms. *Mama* wanted you to have the balcony room with the best view." She emphasized the word as though her mother was indeed the only one so generous.

I'd be near the family. The walls were not that thick. Would we hear each other? At the top of the staircase, to the left, was a set of double doors that opened to a wide wall of windows, though I could not make out the view. A brief glance revealed shelves of books with a few comfortable-looking chairs facing them. A scarce selection, perhaps, but enticing. We climbed the second, shorter staircase to the right of the library, up to the top floor.

"Mama sleeps here," Ginny said, pointing to the only room on our right, set apart from the others. "I am here." She pointed to the room in front of us. We walked a few paces to the left. "Graham here."

I paused, staring at the dark door, following the patterns of wood grain down to the bronze knob. Sunlight stretched from under his door, and I imagined the curtains pulled back. I wondered what Graham Everett kept inside his room. Was he tidy? Did he sleep with a ledger book under his pillow? Perhaps he stuffed bank notes under his mattress.

"And this is my little sister Tabitha's room," Ginny said, pointing to the next door. "Though she often sneaks into Graham's room to sleep. You might hear her fretting at night."

"Does she often have bad dreams?" I asked, still half glancing back at Graham's door.

"Almost every night." Ginny walked to the end of the hall, where a door stood ajar. "This is yours."

Ginny opened the door wide, and instantly the dark hall filled with sunlight. The room was generously sized, considering the entire size of the second floor. Wispy curtains framed the double doors that led to a balcony straight ahead. We stepped inside the room, and I turned in a slow circle. A small bed was situated against the right wall, with a little writing desk beside it, and an armoire on the opposite wall. Beside the hearth was a small table with a white washbasin.

Ginny waited at the door, arms crossed. "To your standards, it might be plain, but—"

"It is perfect," I said, noting my hairbrush beside the washbasin. Mariah had already unpacked my things. My notebook was likely inside the writing desk.

Ginny, for once, seemed pleased. Proud. "As my brother said, if there is anything you need, please tell us. We want your stay to be as *comfortable* as possible."

I raised a brow, and she smirked. Clearly. They'd likely given me the best room in the house. What had felt comfortable turned sour. Graham's family were generous hosts, but not because they wanted to befriend me. They wanted my money. Well, my father's money. They wanted this investment as badly as Graham did, even if just to please him. And I did not blame them.

I always had the best. The front and center placement at every function. Why? Because I had Papa's name and money to back me. We were not titled, but we were old money, and Papa had acquired many holdings. Mamas like Mrs. Everett wanted me to be friends with their daughters and to be courted by their sons, but not because they particularly liked me.

They liked what I could offer.

"Take your time preparing for dinner," Ginny said. "We shall meet in the drawing room."

I nodded my thanks, and she shut the door behind her.

Finally, a breath.

I'd survived the drive. Survived tea. And now all I had to do was survive dinner at Graham's table and I'd be one day closer to the other side of this disastrous Season.

Papa would help me fashion a life for myself. Help me choose a suitable husband I could be happy with, be myself with, build a life with.

Most girls had a mother to fret over such things, and while I sometimes longed for one, I did not truly know what having one felt like. I did not feel the *need* for a mother, because I'd always had Papa.

He had always been enough.

I took the little key sitting atop the writing desk and unlocked the drawer. My notebook waited for me there, alongside a quill and inkpot.

Inside my armoire was a pretty green silk dress that Mariah had set aside for me for dinner, which I approved. I stepped out onto the balcony into a light, salty breeze. A smooth stone balustrade had blocked the view, but Highcliffe House was closer to the sea than I had realized. Greens, blues, and browns colored the water that crested on a rocky shore not far below. The water was endless, moving with life as it met the marvelously blue sky above.

I leaned my elbows on the balustrade, admiring the view and enjoying the sounds of birds chirping overhead. For a moment, I thought of Lyme. A memory flooded in of Papa sitting beside me on a wide, smooth rock. He, with his book, and me with my bucket of treasures, cuddled up beside him to watch the sea.

At nearly one-and-twenty, I still needed him. Of late,

more so than ever. I could not afford to make another mistake like Alexander Lennox.

If Papa meant to invest his time with anyone, it would be with me.

And nothing Graham could say or do would change my mind.

Chapter Seven

GRAHAM

Try as I did to bury myself in work, I could feel her movements.

The sounds of Ginny's harp and the clinking of their cups on saucers. A creaking of the floorboards above my head. My home—the halls, the drawing room, even somehow my study—now smelled all wrong, richly infused with the cherry blossoms and jasmine of the Lane household. In London, she avoided me with precise calculations. But, here, in my home, she was everywhere.

At my table. In the place of honor.

Anna unfolded her napkin and smoothed it upon her lap, frowning, then nodding politely at something Ginny said from across the table. Mama's shoulders were tight with the weight of performing for a guest. From the head of the table, as the hostess, she motioned for Roland to bring out wine.

I felt like a fraud sitting at the other end, considering that every prior time we'd dined together, Anna had directed the course of the evening. In my family, Tabs joined us every night for an informal dinner. I smirked, thinking of the fit she must've thrown learning she'd be excluded tonight. Normally,

Ginny would whine for a new dress or new ribbons, and Tabs would turn Mother green with stories of dissecting some odd creature she'd found washed up on the beach. We'd laugh too loud, not worrying if we dropped our napkins on the floor, and slouch in our seats as our stomachs filled.

I glanced over as Anna took a small sip of wine. Her keen eye took in the place settings, the tablecloth, even the servants, and she measured and weighed it all. No doubt judging my family for how we lived and what we lacked.

Intertwining my fingers, I watched her smile briefly, fleetingly to Mother. She was uncomfortable. It had to be strange, this shift of power in our dynamic, though I had to admit I enjoyed watching her writhe a little in discomfort. But this week, I needed her in good spirits.

"I am so happy to have you home again, Graham," Mother said with a smile. "I do hope you can stay a while longer this time."

"For how well you do without me, I scarcely believe I am needed," I teased.

She raised her chin. "Needed is different than wanted. And you happen to be both."

I looked down at my empty plate as Roland, Harriet, and Rebecca uncovered platters of food on the table. My mother's words were nice to hear. I had almost fulfilled what was needed by my family. To be wanted by them was a privilege, an honor, that not everyone could claim of their relatives. I knew firsthand how painful that sort of rejection was. And I never wanted to feel it again.

I glanced over to find Anna's gaze, which she promptly flicked away, lips pursed. This might be the hardest weeks' worth of work I'd ever done. But it was time to get to it.

"Miss Lane," I prompted, offering her a scoop of salted asparagus.

She raised a brow, and despite not having her expressed approval, I started to serve her. Asparagus, rice casserole with truffle and foie gras, sauteed potatoes with parsley—Cook had outdone herself.

"How do you find Brighton thus far?" I asked Anna.

"The few moments walking between the carriage and your house, Mr. Everett, are not enough to form an opinion on the whole. Your home, however, is lovely. I suppose I have your mother to thank for the generous welcome and more than adequate accommodations."

My mother beamed.

"And your dear sister for her beautiful musical display."

Ginny shrugged at Anna but grinned proudly at me.

"Of my first day, I shall write a good report to my father," Anna said.

I finished her plate with a slab of soft, flakey cod and a spoonful of sauce.

Polite. Compassionate. Content? Who the devil was this woman?

I took a cautious bite of fish. What was I missing? Had she already laid a snare to trap me in my own home? I'd have to sleep with my eyes open. I'd tread carefully. Slowly.

"I am glad to hear it," I said, watching her. Her gaze was as straight and unreadable as ever. Even though this was my house, my table, she knew she held power here. I knew it too. I took a deep breath before trying my luck. "Miss Lane, I would love to take you for a tour of the town tomorrow, if you are willing."

She smiled, slowly chewing her bite, swallowed, then said, "Forgive me, but that sounds dreadfully boring."

Ah. There she was.

Ginny bristled, back straight. "Brighton is anything but dull."

I gave her a warning look. She'd have to simmer her temper; it would do us no good to rise to Anna's verbal sparring.

If she didn't want a tour, then devil take it, what did she want? I turned my attention to my plate, finishing my fish and vegetables in a few swooping bites.

"Graham tells us you used to travel to Lyme with your father?" Mother graciously broke the silence.

"They are some of my fondest memories," Anna replied. She touched her lips with her napkin.

"Then you must be fond of the sea."

"Very much."

Mother gave me a pointed stare. As though she'd parted the seas and now it was my turn to walk through.

I drew in a long breath through my nose, then gave Anna my most charming smile. "There must be something you're interested in seeing here in Brighton, Miss Lane."

She took a slow drink of wine. "I rather like the view outside my window."

Frustration simmered in my chest, and I gritted my teeth, somehow still managing to hold my smile. We only had this week, and she wasn't even going to make an effort.

I tried again. "As I said earlier, the Steine is a popular social spot. I can introduce you to our local society there, as well as make new connections with the tourists." And I could show her how thriving our little town had become. The market, the lending library, the bustling seaside would all be steps away. All overlooked by the Marine Pavilion, which, if nothing else, should impress Anna.

"I am from London, Mr. Everett. I do not travel to socialize. I travel to be free of Society." She set down her fork, as though to punctuate her standing.

"Others certainly do. Surely you wish to make an informed decision for your father's investment for the whole of his investors. Not just those like yourself."

She blinked, then slowly met my gaze. Her lips parted as she huffed out an exhausted puff of air. "Not tomorrow. The next day perhaps. Tomorrow . . ." She mused, looking blankly down at the table. She took in a breath, a faraway look in her eyes that relaxed her features. She was lovely when her countenance softened. Then, gently, but determined, she said, "Tomorrow, I should like to take a walk on the beach."

Mother dabbed her lips with a napkin. "Would you like to sea bathe?"

"Heavens, no." Anna laughed. "The water must be frigid."

"That is the point. It's exhilarating," Ginny argued defensively.

"In Lyme, we dipped our feet in, and that sufficed." Anna took another lazy drink.

"A walk it is, then," I said, determined. I would find the best view. Something private, secluded. Superior to Lyme in every way, so that the only things she'd have to write about in her little notebook were positive.

Dessert came and went, with talk of the comings and goings of Brighton tourists. Anna listened politely, commenting on a few names she recognized from London. By the end of dinner, it did not seem so strange to have her at my table. She spoke mostly to Mother and Ginny, only giving me a rare word now and again.

At long last, Mother rose. "You must be exhausted, Miss Lane. Might we get you more comfortable?"

"Thank you," Anna said with a little sigh. "I do have a bit of writing to do before I retire. Thank you again, Mrs. Everett. Miss Everett. Mr. Everett." She clipped my name, as per usual, and I could've sworn she smirked at me.

"Good night, Miss Lane," I muttered, settling back in my seat, eager for the larger than normal glass of port I'd have upon their departure.

I looked up to catch a swoosh of her green silk skirts as she walked out the door.

Decidedly, finally, blessedly alone.

Chapter Eight

ANNA

I'd been dreaming all night. Something happy and comfortable. As awareness started to trickle into my consciousness, my limbs still felt deliciously heavy, as did my head pressed into my pillow. The heat of my body had warmed my blankets, and I did not wish to move, despite light coloring the back of my eyelids.

I yawned, rubbing my eyes. Oh, but I did not wish to get out of bed. Back home, I slept as late as I desired, especially when Papa was traveling. I should not feel this comfortable in Graham Everett's home, but goodness, I'd slept better than I had in ages. I'd written everything down in my notebook, every strange interaction from Ginny's lecture in the drawing room to Graham's obvious wheedling at dinner, before falling fast asleep.

Part of me was eager to hear the rushing sea and watch the tide roll in, but an equal part of me simply wanted this week over and done so I could enjoy the view with Papa instead. I hated how forced and tense things were with the Everetts. How delicate every matter was, and how desperately they wished to please me. If Ginny's outburst was any indication, and Graham's constant attempt to rush me through Brighton, they all hated me and would rather be rid of me. After they got what they wanted, of course.

Graham had proven *that* fact long ago.

My wooden bedframe creaked, and I froze, eyes still closed. Pressure shifted on my mattress, though I remained still as a board.

The movement ceased. Had I imagined it? Was I still dreaming? I almost believed I was, until little breaths sounded from above me. A sniff. Had an animal climbed onto my bed?

I opened my eyes to slits and peeked through my eyelashes; I was facing the door, which was slightly ajar.

Another small movement, pressure on either side of me like whatever it was, it had braced itself over me.

I turned and looked up, meeting a pair of sea-green eyes.

Sucking in a breath, I felt a scream already in my throat, when a little hand covered my mouth.

"Shh," the tiny voice said. "Don't scream, or she'll catch us."

I pushed up, scrambling back until my head hit the bedframe. "Who are you?" I croaked, my voice still rough with sleep. Was I being robbed? I looked around the room for the bellpull.

The little girl stared, her thick blonde curls springing out in every direction. An untidy sprinkling of freckles raked across her cheeks. She glanced back at the door.

"Who *are* you?" I breathed, snatching my blankets and covering myself as best I could.

"Tabitha." A toothy grin appeared. She must've been seven or eight for the large teeth and gaps between them. "I'm your new sister." The pride in her voice was unmistakable.

"My new *what?*"

The little hand shot back to my mouth, the girl's eyes growing wide. "I would've come down for dinner, but Mama said you and Graham needed time alone." Tabitha wiggled her eyebrows. Her eyes dashed to my trunk, then to my things that Mariah had laid out on the desk and bedside table.

"Graham is your brother?"

"Mm-hmm."

This was his second sister? "How old are you?"

"Eight and a half," she declared. "How old are you?"

"Almost one-and-twenty."

For some reason, that fact seemed to encourage her. She scooted closer. "Mama said you were someone *really* special, and that I was not to interfere with Graham's business. Did he propose last night?"

Propose? The girl was deluded. Were all eight-year-olds so out of touch with reality? "Your brother and I are absolutely *not* engaged, and never will be."

She frowned, pouted, grunted. "Whyever not?"

"Because—" I stopped myself from saying, *because he ruined my life,* and instead finished with, "He is very disagreeable."

Tabitha blinked, her frown still creasing her brow, then shrugged as though she couldn't argue me. "He works a lot for us, so he can be quite grumpy, but I imagine he'll be happier with a wife. And you're very beautiful." She gave me another toothy grin. "Can I have that golden brush on your table?"

I followed her gaze to my hairbrush. "No."

She pouted again. "Why are you here then? If not to marry my brother?"

"He and my father are investment partners." *Why* was I still talking to this girl? I glanced to the door. Where had I laid my robe?

"Your father . . ." Tabitha touched her chin. Then, "Oh." She looked at me with wide eyes. *"Ohh."*

I leaned over, and with one foot on the floor, reached for the bellpull and tugged. Mariah would rescue me. I'd tried to maintain my modesty with an armful of my blankets, but Tabitha did not seem to care in the slightest.

"You're that Lane woman."

It was my turn to frown.

"He talks about you. But usually not kindly." She turned thoughtful. "He says you harp upon him without end."

I raised a brow. A smile itched at the corners of my lips. Graham had said that, had he? That explained Ginny's attitude. Well, it was time for the truth to out. "You are mistaken, Miss Tabitha. It is your *brother* who harps upon me."

"How so?" She sat back on her knees, crossing her arms, as ready to fight as a girl her age could be. She'd defend her rotten brother to the end, and I instantly respected her for it.

I drew in a deep breath. I had to remember that my audience was his sister, and a child. "For one, he teases me beyond reason. He'll say one thing, but I *know* he means the opposite."

She raised her chin. "That is just who he is. He likes to tease, but he doesn't mean it. You just have to get him back."

"Oh, I do," I assured her. "But he also comes over to my house uninvited."

Her eyebrows rose a half-inch.

"He comes to dinner informally in the dirty clothes he's worn all day. Talking business at the table. And he has the nerve to comment on my daily activities, as though he has a say in what I should or should not do."

Tabitha reared back dramatically. "How incredibly rude."

For the first time in weeks, I smiled sincerely. "I wholeheartedly agree."

Tabitha shook her head slowly, looking about the room, pondering. "Then again, I cannot think of another woman my brother has ever spoken of, kindly or otherwise. He leaves us for London and spends all his time with *you*."

"With my father," I amended.

"But he speaks more often about you."

Good gracious, what was wrong with this girl? "I highly doubt that," I said flatly.

Her eyes went round, sincere. "Mama says when a boy likes a girl, he'll sometimes act strangely. Like when Tommy Bates pinches my arm in church."

"No, no," I started, stumbling over my words. "No, Miss Tabitha. That is not—"

"Miss Lane?" Mariah knocked on the cracked-open door, before pushing it open further. "Are you unwell?"

"Yes—" I called at the same time Tabitha said, "She's well!"

"Tabitha?" A man's voice—Graham's?—called from down the hall.

The girl slammed her hand over her mouth, shock in her eyes, and scrambled to my side like I might protect her from an incoming foe. "Drat," she muttered between her fingers.

The door opened, and Mariah stopped short at the sight of Tabitha half on top of me in my bed. "Get off her at once." Her voice was stern.

I pulled my covers closer, and a moment later Graham,

disheveled and hair frumpy like he'd just hopped out of bed, stepped behind Mariah, hovering at the door. Our eyes locked for the shortest second before his mouth fell open in shock.

"Tabitha Elise, what are you doing!"

"Meeting your *someone special*." Tabitha wiggled her brows suggestively.

Graham's cheeks turned cherry red, and the whole thing was *almost* worth it except that I was *in bed* and Graham was *right there*!

I touched my hair. *Still in curling papers.*

"Get out—!" we all said in tandem.

"—of Miss Lane's room *at once*!" Graham bellowed before stepping back and out of sight.

Tabitha looked heavenward and slid off my bed like honey pouring out of a pot. "I shall come again," she whispered, taking her time to straighten herself. "I will speak to him about manners and courtship, and this time he'll get it right. I think you and I shall be fast friends."

Reeling with embarrassment, I watched her skip away.

Mariah closed and locked the door, then rushed to my side. "Are you all right? I've heard stories about that girl belowstairs."

I touched my cheeks, my temples. "I should like to hear them. I cannot decide if she's a jester or a menace."

"Both." Mariah pulled out a blue cotton day dress and rummaged around in my trunk as I slid from under my covers. "But most of all, she's trouble, downstairs at least."

Mariah helped me dress, telling me everything she'd learned about Tabitha's waywardness, how she often stole treats from the kitchen and tracked in dirt and sand from outside. The worst, perhaps, was her hidden collection of dead sea creatures that the servants would find in the most awful of places.

"Their maid Harriet said she opened Miss Tabitha's armoire and found a large rotting crab hidden on the bottom shelf."

"Good heavens." I half laughed, until the thought of how a rotting crab must have smelled sobered me.

After dressing, I took a quarter of an hour to write down the morning's events in my notebook. The adamancy of that little girl, the stealth. Papa would have been mortified had I ever behaved that way as a child. We seldom had visitors when I was young. Papa had been an only child too, so our little family stayed small. Interacting with mother's family proved too painful, so apart from an obligatory visit once or twice a year, he avoided them.

The more I wrote, the lighter I felt. That girl with her wide-toothed grin. Completely unaffected by life or the opinions of others. She seemed so comfortable in her own skin, so carefree and open with her thoughts. She did not, for one moment, change who she was, how she spoke, or what she said according to whom she was addressing.

Childhood ignorance, to be sure. But when did one outgrow the ability to speak freely, openly, without thought of what might be lost or gained in the exchange?

The more I thought on it, the more I adored that little girl, properly behaved or not. The more I felt a sense of protectiveness over her fierce, free spirit. I did not want her to grow wise to manipulation like her brother.

Speaking of whom . . .

I sighed, stepping out onto the balcony of my room.

Birds cawed from a distance, swooping down to the water and back up again. A person could get used to this view. I leaned forward on the balustrade where sunshine warmed the cool stone. I was excited to go down to the shore, be near the water and just . . . sit. But I also felt a rising anxiety at spending the afternoon with Graham, who'd no doubt fill my ears with nonsense and ruin the entire outing. Best to get it over with. Perhaps I could sneak down another time alone.

I peeked my head around my bedroom door, finding the way empty and quiet and safe enough to depart through. But I'd no sooner stepped foot in the foyer, when—

"Oh, Miss Lane." I turned to find Mrs. Everett at my right. Her cheeks were rosy, her whole demeanor flustered. She wrung her hands together. "Miss Lane, I am mortified to hear that my daughter Tabitha intruded on you this morning."

"Please, think nothing of it," I assured her. "Honestly, after I realized she wasn't going to murder me in my bed, she was quite entertaining."

"She is wild and cares far too little for the opinions of others," Ginny said, following her mother out of the drawing room. "She was very excited to meet you."

I raised a brow. "She seems to have quite the imagination." I still hadn't recovered from the poor girl's misconstrued idea of who I was, and especially who I was to Graham.

His heavy footsteps carried from a room around the staircase. "Mother," he said, breathless, as though he'd run back and forth a hundred times and still had not prepared himself for the day. He looked fresh out of a bath, and I wondered, if, when he'd come upon me with Tabitha, he'd been just out of bed as well. Heat flooded my cheeks. He fretted with both his cravat and his damp, wavy hair as he stepped into the foyer, all musk and citrusy. "Ginny. Miss Lane." His eye caught on my notebook and stayed there. He frowned, then bowed to the three of us, stern and serious. "A thousand apologies, Miss Lane—"

"Unnecessary," I muttered, suddenly unable to meet his gaze. He'd seen me in my *nightgown*, with my hair still in curling papers! How would we get through this day, let alone five more, if every encounter was as tense and rigid as this one?

Graham frowned, holding his hands behind his back.

"Would you like to break your fast?" his mother asked me gently. "We've a small spread laid out in the dining room."

"Or if you're ready to explore Brighton's coastline, we can leave now," Graham said. He waited like a butler at attention.

Amiable, all of them. They walked on ice to please me.

They'd give me anything I wanted, and why? For what? Money. Opportunity. Absolutely nothing to do with merely wanting to host and befriend me. My mind started to snap, like the final threads in an old rope worn too thin. For once, I just wanted to be treated like someone who had nothing to give.

I cleared my throat of a sudden thickness. What good would it do, wishing to be anything other than I was? I couldn't change to whom I'd been born. And honestly, despite it all, I did not want to.

"Thank you," I said, lifting my chin like I always did when I felt uncertain. A trick Papa had taught me. "Yes, I shall break my fast." Then the perfect plan formed in my head as though the devil himself had concocted it. I turned to Graham. "And afterward, I would like Miss Tabitha to join us on our explorations. Please do see that she is ready."

"Oh, no," Mrs. Everett said—pleaded, almost. "Tabitha must rest. She is quite out of sorts this morning."

Was she out of sorts? Or was she exactly as she should be? I held my gaze against Graham's, who'd gone pale. "I should really like her to join us."

He swallowed, his nostrils flaring with what surely was frustration at my adamancy. He did not wish for his little sister to cause a fuss. But I wanted the company of someone who did not treat me like a polished thing. Someone who would speak their mind and opinions openly and truthfully without thought to consequence, and certainly without back-handed, two-faced kindness.

Graham nodded. "I shall have her prepared to leave at once."

I hugged my notebook close. "Perfect."

Chapter Nine

GRAHAM

Harriet had earned her wages twice over with how presentable she'd made Tabs. Her face was clean, her blond hair elegantly curled and trailing down the back of her freshly pressed brown day dress. On the outside, she looked as fancy and well-behaved as any nobleman's little sister.

But on the inside . . .

She'd taken Anna's hand and smiled up at her with the innocent look of a child, and Anna had allowed it, strolling along beside her with the ease and comfort of a sister, which she was most certainly not. Their straw hats were unsettlingly similar. Both laced with blue ribbon and white flowers like they'd been paired together on purpose.

My shock from this morning still lingered, of seeing Anna sitting up against her bedframe, hair messy and tangled, with Tabs on her bed, completely oblivious to propriety and social etiquette. I rubbed my temples for the millionth time, as though doing so could erase the sharp edges of how I'd stood there like an utter fool, desperate to hide within the deepest hole but forced to wait out Tabs's slow retreat from Anna's bed.

Anna's *bed.* I shouldn't know what she looked like, cheeks warm and eyes still soft from sleep, all wrapped up in her covers. I could hardly look at her without picturing that moment and wondering things . . . things an honorable man shouldn't.

Why would she invite Tabs? What game was she playing at? She'd clearly seen Tabs at her wildest this morning, so I could only deduce that Anna meant to encourage my little sister into even worse behavior. More gossip to write about in her notebook, more stories to tell her father upon his return, more reasons against investing in Brighton. I could still sense her disapproval from this morning. With every interaction, she looked at me with disdain, her responses curt and annoyed. I might never gain her approval, but I'd give her no reason to think less of my family. Especially my youngest sister.

A few steps behind them, I strained my ears to listen to their conversation.

". . . beautiful day. The sun should warm us up nicely," Anna said.

Tabs gave her a wide grin. "What do you imagine has washed up on the shore?"

"I could not begin to guess. What are you hopeful for?"

"A dead prawn?" Tabs side-eyed Anna to gauge her reaction. "Or perhaps a live adder."

But Anna did not miss a beat. "I used to long for those same things when I was your age. But now I am rather afraid of adders. If we come upon one, we should make your brother capture it for us."

"Graham? He is not brave enough to catch an adder."

"I beg your pardon," I interjected.

Tabs looked over her shoulder at me with a lazy flick of her eyes, still put out with me for the lecture I'd given her for

76

intruding on Anna this morning. "What is it?" She feigned ignorance.

I cleared my throat, trying to regain some control of this strange outing. "Should there be an adder, or even a dead fish, we should steer clear of it and focus on the purpose of our day, which is to show Miss Lane Brighton's beauty."

"What isn't beautiful about an adder?" Tabs argued. "They are colorful and sleek and move so gracefully. Don't they, Anna?"

"*Miss Lane*," I corrected her.

Tabs rolled her eyes at me from a half-hearted turn of her head. "I have permission, obviously, brother."

Anna squeezed Tabs's hand and laughed her musical laugh. "You do indeed. And I agree. How can you truly know a place without seeing its creations firsthand? If we come upon an adder, we shall certainly examine it."

I leaned my head back to stare at the heavens. If God took me now, it would be a mercy.

I drew in a slow, steadying breath. We were nearly to the cutoff where we'd start a careful descent of a hidden pathway that led to the most private, unadulterated view of Brighton's coast. There would be no fishermen here, no bathers, no tourists idly walking by. If it was privacy Anna truly sought, she'd find it here. Only those of us who'd lived here for more than a year knew of this place, and we kept it a closely held secret.

Anna looked over the tall, yellowing grass at the wide sea stretching out to the horizon. Was she impressed by the view? Was she impressed by anything? As someone who never lifted a finger, who was granted anything her heart desired without a second thought, would she truly appreciate so simple an afternoon?

I'd sent our servants ahead with blankets, food, and a few parasols should the sun continue to be as unyielding as it now was. I had given thought to every detail, granted every wish. I could only hope it was enough.

"Do *you* play the harp?" Anna asked Tabs.

"Oh, no. Not yet. It is so dreadfully tedious."

"You should consider learning while you are young. That way, when you are your sister's age, you will have talents to display. The harp is a very respectable instrument, and I daresay when you are older, you'll be grateful for a skill to use when times get *truly* boring."

Tabs looked down at her feet. She was likely bored right now. Perhaps if Tabs showed an interest in playing the harp, we could hire out. After this investment was secured.

"Oh, look, the gulls are sunning!" Tabs tugged Anna to the right, pulling her through tall grass to the edge of a hill toward the sea.

Anna drew in an audible breath but followed. The two of them peered down at the rock-covered beach where a dozen or so gulls were resting on boulders. Our servants were a few paces beyond with everything set up just as I'd asked.

"Come, Anna, we are nearly there!" Tabs said.

"Wait a moment," I called. "I shall go first and help you both down."

"We are able!" Tabs called as they rushed forward. I shouldn't have let them, but Anna was grinning. Something about the sea air was working within her. For now, I'd be grateful, but we'd only been gone a half hour. How much longer could Tabs continue without a fuss?

Anna had stopped at the top of the descent, though Tabs was already halfway down.

"May I assist you, Miss Lane?" I asked as I approached. It would be awkward, taking her hand and supporting her down, but I'd do it.

"No," she replied firmly. "I can manage."

By the looks of her hesitation, I doubted it. "I am happy to help, if you'll just take my hand." I stepped ahead of her, securing my footing on rocks that were half buried.

"I said no, thank you. Walk ahead." Her lips were pursed, eyes focused on the ground.

I waited for her to move, but she seemed to be taking half steps or less at a time. She would surely fall without proper support. My jaw clenched. Why was she always so obstinate? So unconventionally persistent. Did she act this way with everyone, or was I alone allowed that singular pleasure? More likely than not, she thought I was not good enough to aid her. I had no doubt she thought me lower than a servant.

I watched her take another cautious half step, but just as her foot came down, the dirt shifted, and she started to slip. Her hands flung out, mouth opening wide in surprise.

My senses seized, breath stopping in my throat, and I reached out. I nearly grabbed her, until she found her footing on a dried patch of grass between rocks.

"Take my arm," I commanded. Anxiety trailed through my veins, pumping into my chest. If something happened to her, I was a dead man. Mr. Lane would never forgive me. "I shall help you down."

But the blasted woman stepped around me; this time, somehow, surer of herself. "I have it," she said through her own flexed jaw.

I kept both hands out, ready to grab her, to catch her if she fell either way, only taking a breath when she finally reached the bottom of the hill. But even then, we were still several paces away from the picnic spot my servants had laid, and this was no sandy beach. Brighton was all unforgiving rocks that shifted as you walked. In boots, I could manage, but even I had miscalculated and slipped once or twice.

Anna took a few steps to feel it all out, and I could see the determined frustration in her countenance. She would roll her ankle before allowing my assistance, and even then I wondered if she'd prefer the pain to a moment of my attention.

Tabs had already settled on the blanket ahead with a crumpet in hand. She waved to Anna. "Come, sit, Anna! There are crumpets! And jam!"

"Won-wonderful," Anna called back. Then, "I would have appreciated wearing boots, Mr. Everett."

She was right, but I had to pick my battles with her. Shoes were not on the top of the list at present. "Yes—well, you look so lovely this afternoon, I cannot say I have given notice to your shoes. I shall have to beg your forgiveness."

The words were bile in my throat. I did not mean them. She *did* look beautiful, of course; she always did. But if I were to compliment a lady, I would never be so disgustingly obvious as that.

She seemed to know it, but, like always, she refrained from calling me out. That was not how proper society did things. All that mattered was one's intentions, or their supposed intentions. Which was how Anna and I had become so good at pretense with one another.

She muttered something under her breath, and my lips itched to smile.

I added, "And might I comment on the view. The day is

so brilliantly sunny, if you look hard enough, you might be able to make out the coast of France."

"Indeed?" She shaded her eyes with her hand, then dropped it and stood still, peering out with critical focus for a moment longer. "I think you are toying with me."

"I would not dare, Miss Lane."

She crossed her arms, still staring hard in the distance, then Tabs called, "Anna, I've a spot just for you!"

I knew better than to ask if she'd saved one for me. But I followed anyway.

Anna sat down beside Tabs, facing the shore, and took a crumpet from the basket between them. She placed it on a plate, then spooned out a little raspberry jam from a jar. "This smells heavenly," she said.

I took the opposite side of the blanket, sitting a healthy space apart from them.

"It's my favorite," Tabs said with a grin. Her two front teeth had come in with a wide gap between them that I hoped would never close, for it was very decidedly Tabs. She had a speckling of auburn freckles across her cheeks and over her nose. Seeing her wild curls so tame did something paternal to my heart that made my throat tighten. I'd been at school when she was born and missed her first few years of life. Now, every time I returned home from a business trip, she'd grown an inch.

"What do you think of the shore, Anna?" her little voice asked. For all the rotten things she'd done, especially the surprise she'd pulled on Anna this morning, I could forgive her anything when she spoke so sweetly. Especially because she asked the very question I wanted Anna to answer.

"It's different," Anna said, dapping a napkin at the crumbs on her lips. "Much rockier than I anticipated."

"It's better if you remove your shoes and stockings," Tabs insisted, pulling her foot up and tugging at her shoe.

Blast. *Here she goes.* "No, Tabs. Let's not today," I said. Heat tinged my ears, and I hated it. I hated that Anna had forced this on us. Tabs did not understand the impropriety of the situation, nor would she easily be swayed against it, and I would look like a fool trying to stop her.

"But we always do," she whined, continuing to take off one shoe, then the other.

"We have a guest. Let's not today," I repeated more firmly.

Anna reached for another crumpet, likely trying to give us a moment to find peace. These were the times when I realized that Tabs dearly needed a father, which was a role, as her brother, I could never adequately fill for her.

She was resolved. Stockings removed, she shifted to her knees, scowling. "I shall be quick, Graham. I want to show Anna how easy it is to walk with bare feet."

I leaned toward her and said in a voice I hoped was both quiet and gentle, "Tabs, this is improper. Please sit back down, or I shall have the servants take you home. Miss Lane does not wish for such familiarity."

"I'm sorry?" Anna sat up straighter and set aside her plate. "I doubt *you* have any idea what I wish, Mr. Everett."

Tabs's scowl eased. She looked Anna up and down, then mimicked her raised brow and crossed arms before facing me again. "Yes, indeed."

Ugly, impolite words hovered on the tip of my tongue that I wished I could let free. Because of course, just to spite me, Anna Lane *had* to oppose me. She had to get *her* way.

"You—" I started, but my voice was too cross. *Keep her happy*, Mr. Lane had said. I stretched out my neck, drawing in one calming breath, then tried again. "Of course, Miss Lane." I waved a hand, dismissing my hold over the situation, my pride, my opinions, everything disagreeable. "Whatever you wish."

Anna turned to Tabs. "I should love to watch you explore the shore. After I finish my crumpet and cake, perhaps I shall join you, and you can show me all that you have found."

Tabs practically glowed. "You'll join me?"

"In a bit, yes," Anna said with a laugh.

"Watch me," Tabs said as she stepped out on the rocks toward the shore. "You just have to have good balance."

"I see that," Anna called. "You are very, very good."

I settled back down, working hard to calm my frustrations. What did Anna Lane know about hardship? I was on my own here, taking care of an entire family, trying to parent my littlest, wildest sister, and she thought a day out would solve Tabs's blatant disregard for propriety?

Oh, how I wished I could loose my tongue and tell her exactly how wrong she was.

One day.

With each deep breath, I remembered my goal: Business first.

Chapter Ten

ANNA

Tabitha—Tabs, as Graham called her—walked carefully upon the rounded rocks like she was as familiar with this shore as she was the floors of her own home. Her little feet and thin form moved, crouched, even sometimes hopped to and fro over the bigger rocks. She was beautiful, kind, and just ornery enough to keep life interesting.

I missed my younger days with Papa, when I could speak my mind and the adults would either take me seriously or laugh congenially at my silliness. A girl as free-spirited as Tabs should not have to fear taking off her stockings at the beach.

"Careful, Tabs," Graham called, despite a servant walking behind her. "Not too far from us. And not too close to the water. The rocks are slick."

I groaned internally. Did Graham have to control every second of every day—what it looked like, felt like, smelled like? The man needed to let loose. "She is only having fun," I muttered.

He tensed but ignored me.

Tabs shrieked as the tide swept in and splashed the brown,

earthy rocks at her feet, and I laughed at her joy. She was being herself, and it filled up the deep crevices of my heart.

"Brighton's other beaches are similar," Graham said with a sideways glance and a frown. "Others have the society and economy tourists crave, so there is something for everyone here. This particular shore has a little rougher terrain, but it is more private, as you'd desired. And I believe the sea is a little greener here because there are not as many fishermen, nor boats, to stir up the water. Altogether, this beach has a more natural and calmer feel."

Would he *never* relent? Did he think of nothing besides his precious investments? I sighed. "Please do not ruin my view by telling me how I should feel about it, Mr. Everett."

He startled, taken aback. "On the contrary, Miss Lane. I merely wish to share it with you."

I gave him a look. His pretense was not lost on me. Flattery, always with the insincere flattery. After Mr. Lennox, how could I trust any man who wanted to dip into my father's pockets? Graham was tolerating me just as I was tolerating him. Without Papa here, why did we have to pretend otherwise? Why did we have to converse at all? And if we did, why could I not speak as freely as Tabs? Bitterness took hold of me, and I said, "Perhaps you should keep your thoughts to yourself and stop trying to control mine."

Well, that came out cross.

I risked a glance at Graham. His brows furrowed, and his nostrils flared as he took a breath. "Have a care with your words, Miss Lane. My sister is near." Frustration colored his tone.

I'd bristled him, hit a tender nerve. I felt the heat of embarrassment from being chided burn up my neck, but I did not give it notice. "Then please do not try to bend my ear for the next five days while I experience this town. I have a sound mind all on my own."

He shook his head. A bit of him unraveled as he said, "I did not mean to suggest otherwise. I was merely . . . having a conversation."

"A conversation?" I laughed half-heartedly, looking over at his shoulders hunched, lips pursed. He truly did not see it. "A conversation with an intent to bait or persuade my good opinion is not one I am interested in having."

He motioned toward the sea. "I assure you I had no motivation by stating that the water appears greener here."

"Everything you say has a motivation." My lips twitched, happy to release the words I'd been dying to say. Graham would never tell Papa of my impertinence. He wanted everything to be perfect—or at least he wanted things to appear that way. "I know for a fact you hate me as much as I hate you. At least be honorable and admit it."

"*Hate* you? What the devil are you talking about?" His cheeks reddened, and he raked a hand through his billowing hair, like a kettle about to blow. A war seemed to rage in the thoughts behind his eyes. Clearly, there were things *he* wanted to say, but he fought to hold them back. After a moment, he said, "You are the daughter of a man I revere. A man I engage with regularly in matters of money and business. Out of respect for him, I try to be polite. To be amiable toward you."

I looked back out to the sea and shook my head, frustrated with Graham's denials and growing too emotional so far away from home. Polite and amiable. Exactly as I'd feared. How could I ever make a match, keep a genuine friendship, when everyone—including myself—hid behind a mask? I clamped down my feelings and looked away. "You are the biggest fraud I have ever met."

He reared back and squinted his eyes. "Why? Because I think through what I say before I say it? Some would call that wise."

"Or cunning." I pursed my lips.

He scoffed and looked at the sea. "I am *cunning* for trying to have a conversation."

I scoffed right back. "Oh, please. If you truly want to have a conversation, then say something genuine for once. I dare you."

There was silence for a beat, save for the restless sea and the birds flying above in the distance.

His jaw ticked as he ran his hand through his hair again. "Something genuine?" He looked at me. His eyes were blazing, but his features were smooth, revealing nothing. "About what, precisely? As always, Miss Lane, I am entirely at your service."

I let my lips form a smile. "Sarcasm suits you better than false flattery." Indeed, even his countenance seemed more genuine. More relaxed. I doubted he was capable of relaxing into himself fully. Would I even recognize him if he did? Still, I cast the bait. "Very well, then. Tell me something personal. Something that . . . embarrasses you."

His fiery eyes watched mine. "So you can write it down in your little notebook and use it against me?"

I tried unsuccessfully to bite back my humor. Surprise, perhaps even shock, made my heart stutter. Graham had never spoken so openly with me. He'd never shared exactly what he was thinking outright. In the subtlest way, he'd turned my bait against me.

I wanted this game. I wanted to play, and desperately. "I won't."

He faced the sea again. "I have a hard time believing you."

"I do not blame you. But I'd rather like to hear what you have to say. I won't write it down."

He eyed me carefully, cautious and obviously wary of my promise. "Very well."

We looked away from each other, anticipation warming the space between us on the blanket. What would he say? If it wasn't embarrassing or strange . . . if he said something just to charm me again . . .

"I . . ." Graham shook his head, then crossed his legs.

I waited with bated breath. Whatever he was about to say pained him, and stupid as it was, I'd never wanted a secret more. Graham was a gossip paper. A mystery to unfold. Waiting for his words was like unearthing a fossil on a beach in Lyme.

He drew a very long, very deep breath that he huffed out. "I wear . . . spectacles. To read."

I threw up my hands. "Oh, for heaven's sake, is that all?" What a show he'd made for something so common. To think I'd thought him interesting for a half a second.

A crease formed between his brows, confusion writ upon his features.

"Put them on, then. Let's see them," I said. He owed me that much for ruffling me so. *Graham Everett* in spectacles. I could not picture it.

"No, thank you," he said. "I do not like to wear them."

"But you have them on your person?"

He shifted uncomfortably in his spot. "Of course. I need them to read."

I widened my eyes, waiting. This was perhaps the longest conversation we'd had in a solid year.

"Must you always have whatever you want?" he muttered through evident frustration, patting around the chest of his tailcoat and waistcoat. Then he undid a few buttons of his coat, reached in to what I assumed was a little pocket, then pulled out his hand, and there they were.

His spectacles were round, bronze circles. The sides were the same color, stretching out and forming a curl at each end. I shrugged. Why did they embarrass him so? "Those look like my father's. Put them on."

He tossed them into my lap. "*You* put them on."

I let out a laugh. "Saucy, are we?"

But Graham just shook his head and watched Tabs fill up a little bucket with shells. "I won't be made a fool."

"Oh, you do that already without the spectacles." Perhaps that barb was too far. Too mean. But honestly, how boring could he be? Business, business, business, and never any fun.

I unfolded the arms of his spectacles. His lenses were thin and unscratched and clearly well cared for.

Was this odd? Me, trying on Graham's spectacles? Surely *he* was the odd one, always so rigid but playing sweet and oblivious. Why would he hide such a silly thing as wearing spectacles?

Let him think of me what he would; at least I could say I hadn't anything to hide. I curled the edges of his spectacles around my ears and pushed the frame up the bridge of my nose. They were too large for my face, so I leaned my head back just enough to hold them on. Everything turned blurry.

"Ah, yes, the view is much improved. I much prefer

Brighton from this perspective." I pushed them down to the tip of my nose and glanced at Graham.

He was watching me with a raised brow, humor evident on his quirked lips, but he swiped the smile away with a hand. "Are you satisfied now?"

I pretended to pout. "No words of flattery? With how freely your prose flows, I should think you had a whole book of poetry at the ready for such an occasion." I took off his spectacles and handed them back to him.

"I am honestly at a loss for words," he said, pulling out a small square of cloth and wiping his spectacles down as though I'd tainted them.

I rolled my eyes as he carefully placed them back inside their secret pocket. "I do not have disease, Graham."

I realized my informal slip a second too late, but Graham did not miss a beat.

"Let's hope not, *Anna*."

My name in that low voice of his felt like a trap—too sweet and somehow beguiling. I slapped my hands on my thighs. "Well, as delightful as conversation with you is, I think I shall engage with your sister for a time." I straightened, then pushed myself to my feet.

Chapter Eleven

GRAHAM

That was the strangest thing I'd ever witnessed. Anna
Lane wearing my spectacles. I looked at the skies, half await-
ing them to turn completely black or for stars to start falling.
Perhaps even the sun would turn red.

But nothing happened.

My spectacles weighed heavily in my pocket. No matter
that I'd wiped them clean, she'd touched them, worn them.
And it was strange. Even though she was Anna Lane, she was
still a beautiful woman, and the familiarity she'd shown me
was uncharacteristic, at least according to how she usually
treated me.

But what she'd said about us hating each other, about
how ingenuine we were with each other . . . I'd hardly believed her words. I'd known she didn't like me, though I *had*
wondered why. But to hear, to see, how much I *bothered* her
was more than the exchange of fiery words. This was deeply
rooted within her, and to be the cause of it was unsettling, to
say the least.

Over the years, Mr. Lane had taught me how to speak to
people, how to put them at ease, how to compliment them,

charm them, convince them to trust me. Connecting with people was part of investing. I'd always felt so at home with him, I'd never had to *work* to connect with him. I could always be myself. Unless Anna was around.

Of late, she darkened every room. Always shooting witty retorts to trip me up, make me feel unliked and unwanted. Who could charm their way out of that?

Cunning, calculated, cross. *That* was Anna Lane.

But everything she'd just said, how ridiculous she'd let herself look with my spectacles on . . . Was that girl—that outspoken, teasing woman—who she *really* was?

She'd stood up and was walking toward Tabs on the rocky shore as though nothing in the world bothered her. There was no rigidness to her shoulders. No heaviness to her step.

How could I keep her that way—as content as Mr. Lane had asked for? She did not want me to engage her with business matters. What could I do? By the end of this week, I needed Anna to love Brighton enough to approve of her father investing with me. But I also needed to succeed on Anna's terms.

Mr. Lane expected details, information, numbers. But Anna did not need those things. She already knew her father had agreed with my assessment. She sought an experience. One that might rival her childhood travels to Lyme. How could I give her that?

Anna and Tabs were standing at the edge of the shoreline, water lapping up on the rocks by their feet. Tabs pointed down, and Anna looked back at a large boulder nearby. The two walked over and sat down together, and Anna started tugging off her slippers.

I bolted to my feet, gesturing for my servants to clean the

picnic, and paced to the boulder. "Anna," I started, and Tabs gave me a mean look.

"Miss *Lane*," she corrected. The little urchin.

Anna's grin split her face. She looked up at me, considered for a beat, then said, "He has permission. *For now.*"

Tabs turned her back on me, and Anna added, "We are just dipping our toes in, *Graham*. Do not fret."

I liked the sound of my name much less when she was annoyed with me. "I most certainly will fret. Your father has entrusted me with your protection. These rocks are too unstable. You might slip, and if you do—"

"You will be right behind me, I am sure. My knight in shining armor come to save me."

She gave me a look full of sarcasm, but decidedly lacking in disdain, and I stood still, completely unsure of everything. She deposited her folded stockings on top of her shoes, which were set together on the boulder. Then she reached out her hand to Tabs, who grinned and took it.

"Can we take off our hats?" Tabs asked innocently.

I furrowed my brow. "Absolutely n—"

"Of course!" Anna said over me, reaching to unpin her own. "Just for a small time, though. We wouldn't wish to burn."

I spun around in place. The servants were working, but the three of us were otherwise quite alone. The last thing I needed was a rumor traveling about town for Mr. Lane to hear upon his return.

Anna stepped forward, unsteady despite Tabs holding fast to her side to balance her. Her foot was so small and smooth. So strangely *intimate*. And her smile stretched from ear to ear.

This was her childhood, I realized. And she was experiencing it all over again but in a new way.

"Oh my, the rocks are so smooth." She laughed. "You are right, Tabs. Walking is much easier without slippers."

"Graham, you should remove *your* shoes!" Tabs said with wide, innocent eyes.

"No, thank you," I muttered. Had the world turned upside down?

The sea came in small waves, lapping up and splashing gently. Tabs let go of Anna and dipped low to reach in the water, pulling out a smooth, bright pink shell. "Look at this!"

"Goodness," Anna said, hobbling close, but not quite in the water. "That is a lovely shade. Where is your bucket?"

"I shall retrieve it!" she called, rushing past us. "Watch for more! Pinks are my favorite."

The tide was rolling in, and Anna stepped out on the wet rocks. My stomach rolled, muscles tense with anticipation. She might fall or twist her ankle, and then what we would do?

"It's so quiet here compared to London," she said, eyes focused on where the sky met the sea.

It took me a full ten seconds to realize she was talking to me.

"Yes," I agreed quickly. I was standing a full step behind her, just far back enough that the water could not touch me. "Is that . . . bad?"

"No," she said, looking over her shoulder toward me. "It is a good quiet."

She spoke as though she knew the difference. "Peaceful," I offered. We never spoke so easily like this, without effort.

She nodded, then turned back to the sea. "Do you come here often?"

Was this a trick? Another way for her to find fault in me? I waited a beat, considering. Her shoulders were relaxed, loose tendrils of her hair wisping softly about her neck in the breeze. The thin muslin of her dress, growing damp from sea air and the laps of water licking her hem, swayed around her, betraying every perfect curve. Her hips, her waist. My mouth went dry, and I swallowed.

"When I am home, we always come here for an afternoon. Just the four of us."

"With how busy you are?" Anna looked back again and met my gaze, surprised. "Do you honestly?"

"Have you found any more shells?" Tabs called, taking quick but careful steps closer.

Anna hurried to look down, then crouched low to pluck one from the water. Her entire hem drowned, and when she rose up, a foot of her skirts was soaked.

The strangest thing was, Anna Lane—proud woman that I knew her to be—did not seem to mind.

Tabs hobbled on her last step and fell into Anna's side, both of them laughing as they steadied one another.

"Here, I've just found this," Anna said, pressing a shell into Tabs's open palm. It was brown and plain, but to my astonishment, Tabs grinned and added it to her collection.

Anna lifted her skirts and followed Tabs, splashing down the shoreline.

If only she'd acted like this, wild and carefree and understanding, life for the past few years would have been much more enjoyable.

"Graham," she called, startling me out of my wondering. "Our bucket is growing heavy. Carry it for us, won't you?"

Before I knew what I was doing, I reached out my hand

and took the handle. I did not know whether to believe Anna's show of friendliness, for she certainly did not *like* me any more or less than usual, or if this was just a way for her to get through the week until her father came to claim her. I followed Anna and Tabs, receiving every shell and occasional rock sent my way, enthralled to see how my wild little sister had befriended the proud and prickly daughter of my business partner.

Until the tide rushed too near my boots, and I scuttled sideways.

"Oh, for heaven's sake, take off your boots, Graham." Anna's shoulders sagged as she watched me and shook her head. "Is he always like this?" she asked Tabs.

"Mama says he cares too much what other people think."

I shook off the few droplets that had succeeded in wetting my boots. "When you are in the business of investing like I am, the opinions of others are important."

"Well, I for one would not wish to do business with someone so uptight. I much prefer the playful sort." Anna's steps turned slow, lazy.

"Uptight?" I blew out a laugh. "You are one to talk."

"I beg your pardon?" Anna's brow creased in that familiar way, but her smile was new. Almost like she knew I was taunting her, and for once, she liked it.

I straightened, determined to play this new game she'd started. What could it hurt? Her father would never hear of it, as neither of us would ever tell him. And I was already so low in her opinion, I doubted I could fall much further no matter what I said.

"I have never seen you leave your house in any sort of disarray. Indeed, I hardly recognize you today." I motioned to the whole of her.

"That is very rude," Tabs chided me, and I could not help but laugh. She was right, but Anna had started it.

"I am quite at my leisure, Graham. You should try enjoying the view now and again instead of focusing on its investment potential." Anna raised her haughty little nose in the air and turned away.

Tabs, the little devil, mimicked every motion, scoffing dramatically as she, too, turned away.

Lands above.

Anna was turning my own family against me. She drove me absolutely mad. One minute, she was still and quiet and beautiful, then the next she was irking me to no end. Uptight? I could relax, play, have a good time; Tabs knew it, too. I was not some titled or newly inherited well-to-do chap who dawdled about looking for the next round of entertainment. My family depended on me.

I sat on the rocks, set the bucket down, and wrestled with one of my boots. I'd show her how to have fun. I'd show the both of them.

One boot off, then the other. I threw them aside. Then I tugged off my stockings through muttered curses and threw them in the pile as well.

Anna and Tabs had left me behind, but all for the better. I rose to my feet, yanking an arm out of my coat. If they wanted me playful, I'd give them playful. I'd be as entertaining as any young buck strutting around London. Tossing my coat aside, I navigated the familiar rocks with careful steps. I hurried up behind them, unexpected, then, for the last few measures, bolted into a run.

I caught Tabs around the waist, and she shrieked so loud

the gulls took flight. I twisted her little body over my shoulder. "How's this for playful, little sister?"

"Put me *down* at once!" Tabs hollered, pounding my back with her fists. But I could hear the laughter in her voice. The happy fear.

I laughed, stepping knee-deep into the frigid water. "Did you not say this morning how dearly you wished to sea bathe?" I tickled her sides, and she writhed, half laughing, half screeching.

"Anna, help!" she cried, and I turned.

Anna had her arms folded, her face aglow. "Your brother has gone mad," she said, laughing. "It is the most fearsome sight I have ever beheld."

"He won't hurt *you*. Save me, please!" Tabs called.

Anna looked happy. Wishful, almost. The sight of her so open, so rustled by the wind, made my breath catch and my heart pound in my ears. A reckless idea took hold of me. Poorly thought, I knew, but I wanted it. And when I wanted something . . .

I whispered to Tabs, "I'll let you free if you help me get her."

"Deal," she whispered back, breathless.

"What are you whispering about?" Anna asked. Slowly, she uncrossed her arms.

I understood her hesitation. We did not let down our walls with each other. This part of me, like her sea-drenched hems, was something new.

But instinct told me to try.

Just as slowly, I slid Tabs down my shoulder to the ground. "You go round to her back," I whispered. "I'll chase her straight on. On my mark."

"What are you doing?" Anna started backing up, hands up in surrender, looking between me and Tabs. "Why did he let you go, Tabs?"

Tabs shrugged, grinning like a jackal as she rounded on Anna. "Dunno!"

When she'd moved far enough away, I shouted, "Now!" And Tabs took off.

Anna shrieked, struggling down the rocky shoreline.

Tabs with her nimble steps reached her in seconds, when I had only just begun to chase after them. "I have her!" she called, arms holding fast around Anna's waist. "Get her, Graham!"

"He wouldn't dare," Anna said, half-heartedly struggling against Tabs. She eyed me with a fierce but playful glare. I knew her well enough after three years to know she was not truly scared. She was testing my limits. Wondering how far I'd dare go.

I stopped in front of her, face to face. "Good work, Miss Tabitha. I've wanted to make this woman pay for her crimes for a long time."

Anna snorted. "My crimes?"

"That dinner basket you offered me back at your house wasn't the first time you've tried to turn me out, was it? Your feigned politeness is like sugared poison."

"Sugared poison?"

"Indeed, you are so polite. I recall your sweet concern over the scuffs on my boots upon our early acquaintance, and so pointedly in front of your father."

"You could've been a thief, for all we knew." She raised her chin, smirking. "I do not regret it."

"Oh?" I stepped closer, until she and I were a breath away.

A low ache settled deep in my stomach. This was the closest I had ever been to Anna Lane. We'd been in the same room more times than I could remember, but I'd never counted her breaths, never noticed the little scar above her brow. Up close and unreserved, Anna Lane was a new creature. Though, still, she had that fiery look in her eyes. And that tantalizing scent. Jasmine. Cherries. And the sea. "You will."

I wondered what she thought of me, seeing me like this. At home. Relaxed. Tabs wanted me to play as I usually did, and apparently so did Anna.

Dare I?

Anna's lips turned up, her shoulders relaxed like she knew I'd given up, and I took it like a challenge.

In a breath, I lifted her in my arms, cradling her close to my chest, then bolted toward the sea. She held fast to my neck, kicking and shrieking and begging for Tabs to save her.

"You wretched man! Let me down!"

My heart flew into my throat, beating fast through every limb. "This is for the goat cheese!" I said, tightening my hold against her efforts. "And that horrible little notebook you write in!"

I splashed into the sea, and she sucked in a breath, fingers digging into my neck. Her smooth hair brushed my jaw, and I swallowed in the sweet scent. Confound it, how could a woman be so overwhelming in every way? I'd danced with a hundred and not one of them had felt this good. This instantly familiar.

What am I doing?

"I swear, Graham, if you throw me in that water—" Her voice turned desperate, but she'd stopped squirming, her face still tucked into my neck.

"We could have been friends you know, three years ago when I first met you. But *you* decided I was your enemy. That perfect, hateful little smile you always give me—"

"It makes you mad, doesn't it?" She was just as breathless as I.

"Furious," I corrected her, taking a few more steps. My muscles seized with the shock of the cold water rising with my every step. "I hate the way you smirk at me. You know *just* how to be frustrating."

"Throw her overboard, Graham!" Tabs called.

"And what of your condescending flattery? Hmm? 'How stunning you look, Miss Lane,'" she mimicked me. Rather perfectly. "Just last week! What was it you said? 'What a lovely gown. So *flawlessly* altered. You glow as though Aphrodite herself kissed your cheeks with envy.'"

I bit my tongue to keep from laughing. The sea moved all around us, gulls squawking in the distance, the cool breeze rustling, and I stood knee-deep in water, holding her in my arms like it was the easiest thing in the world. "Every woman deserves to be complimented."

"*Sincerely.*" Her eyes bored into mine. They were so light brown they were almost golden in the sun. I blinked, but I found I did not want to look away. Not from her eyes. Not from the curve of her nose. Not from those round lips that parted perfectly enough to be kissed.

I blinked.

Anna Lane.

Mr. Lane's daughter.

Had I gone entirely mad?

I did the only thing I could think of. The necessary thing.

I dropped her in the water.

Gently, of course, as a gentleman would. To her credit, she fell gracefully, feet first, uttering something between a shriek and a gasp. The water soaked her nearly up to her waist. Slowly, she found her balance, her mouth forming a very shocked *O*, and lifted her furious eyes to mine.

Blast.

I turned on a heel and bolted back to the shore.

"You devil, Graham Everett!" she shrieked, splashing from behind me.

Tabs cackled, clapping her hands together with a gleeful look, chanting, "We got her! We got her!"

I'd just stepped foot on dry land when slim arms encircled my waist. Slim, but strong. Strong enough that I stumbled backward, and those same arms pulled me down flat on my rear at the same moment the freezing tide rushed in. Water crashed into my back; my muscles seized with shock, breath tight in my lungs.

Anna came round, standing above me and wiping her wet hands on the dry spots of her dress.

She tilted her head, clearly pleased with herself, then walked away.

Chapter Twelve

ANNA

That scoundrel. He'd *actually* dropped me!

I struggled to catch my breath, seized by chills and shivers as I strode toward Tabs. My mind raced in a million different directions. Graham holding me. Tabs shrieking in joy. The way he'd lifted me up, and how I'd so easily wrapped my arms around his neck. How warm his chest was. His neck. He'd smelled of oat soap and leather and the slightest hint of tobacco. I'd wanted to stay right there.

We could have been friends.

But then he'd gone and *dropped me.*

My legs were numb from the cold sea, but the rest of me was on fire. Angry at him for actually throwing me in, but also some level of embarrassment that I'd let my guard down for the slightest moment. I'd let him carry me. And I hadn't hated it.

I kept walking forward, though every instinct in me wanted to glance over my shoulder at Graham. He was too sharp around the edges for that sort of fun. Too rigid and set upon formality. While I appreciated rules, I did not feel the obligation to live by them wholly, especially when away from Society's eye. But he did.

Didn't he?

Hands trembling, I bunched up my skirts, squeezing out the water that had soaked the fabric from my waist down to the hem.

"You got away so easily," Tabs said, crouching down to help me wring out my skirts. "He should've walked you out farther. He threw me out in the deep once, and I had to swim back."

Little traitor. I fought a laugh, attempting a serious frown. "You betrayed me."

"But you got him back good! Just look at him. Completely drenched."

Graham, drenched? I swung around to find him sopping wet, cravat removed, waistcoat undone, stepping out of the water. He brushed a wet hand through his hair like some battle-worn hero who'd just swum miles to shore from a shipwreck. Then he twisted a handful of his shirt to wring out the sea, exposing his glistening chest and a lean length of his stomach.

Good . . . heavens.

"Well done," Tabs said, and I spun back to her. "He shall have to sun all afternoon."

I swallowed hard, squeezing my eyes shut for no good reason at all. "I hope your servants brought towels." A lot of them. Several to cover up Graham's legs and arms and chest and face.

Why had I sought out anything that might change our formal relationship? He was so good at irritating me. Making him admit what I'd imagined all along, that our dislike was mutual, that he played just as hard as I did to keep it a secret, to test the lines we'd drawn for each other, was less satisfying than I'd hoped.

Because now I was forced to look at him in a new way,

from a new angle. To admit that there was more to Graham than a thirst for money. He was a person with secrets, just like I was. He laughed and had opinions and played with his little sister.

"Come, let us dry off in the sun." Tabs handed me my hat. "This is always my favorite part. More food, watching the sea. T'so much better than lessons at home."

The servants seemed to have expected as much, having laid out towels and a new spread of queen cakes and fruits, which drew Tabs like a fly. I dried off my legs and skirt as best I could, then arranged myself on the blanket beside her, accepting a plate of sweets and a cup of lemonade from a servant.

Down several paces from where we'd wandered, we again faced the sea, warmed by the sunshine. I took a small bite of my queen cake.

"A towel, please," Graham said from somewhere behind me, and my nerves seized. A quick glance assured me he'd covered his upper half, thank the heavens.

"Thank you," he said to his servant. His voice sounded the same, but for some reason, hearing it made me feel different inside. Nervous. Anxious. Like something was both gnawing at my insides and tickling my skin.

Our relentless bickering and underhanded politeness, even his feigned flattery, had never seemed more comfortable nor more welcome than now. Could we just pretend this afternoon hadn't happened and go back to the way things had been?

I took a sip of lemonade, then set my cup down upon my plate. How early, exactly, could I say I was ready to depart? But even then, if we went home, to *his* home, would we sit in the drawing room all afternoon?

I listened to the rustling of his hands and towel, the

shifting of rocks beneath his feet, all mingled with the rushing of the sea and the birds overhead and the pounding of my heart in my ears.

"Blanket?" he asked, and I finally looked up. His cheeks were flushed, full lips parted, and his eyes seemed to study every inch of my face. Like I'd changed too. He held a soft, red blanket in his outstretched hand.

I swallowed and cleared my throat. "Thank you."

Instead of handing it to me, he unfolded it, then laid it over my lap. Tabs whined, and he chuckled, taking another blanket and doing the same for her.

With a queen cake in hand, he laid out his towel beside us and sat down, resting his elbows on his knees. We sat in silence for a time, while Tabs, full and lazy, sprawled out on her belly and picked at the rocks in front of her.

"I'd say something about the view, but we both know how well my last attempt was received," Graham said.

I cast him a sideways glance. He was baiting me. More straightforward than usual, but still, that comfortable bitterness. So I gave it right back to him. "Tabs, darling, your brother is annoying me. What can I do to silence him?"

Graham grinned down at his cake, sending a prickling sensation all through me.

Tabs rolled to her back, stretched out, and rested her head on my leg. I startled at first, unsure what to do. Should I rest my hands at my sides, or place them on her back? The breeze blew a strand of her curly blonde hair in her face, so I tucked it behind her ear. She smiled, so I smoothed the rest.

I caught Graham's gaze, which was solemn and serious, just before he looked away.

Tabs yawned. "Tell him you think he's handsome and

you'd like to marry him. That should send him running back to his study."

I blanched, my breath stopping altogether, and Graham must have swallowed a bite of fruit at that precise moment, for he choked, then coughed in a fit.

At least we both agreed on *that* point. "There, there, Graham. You're more likely to win a thousand pounds in speculation than ever hear those words from me."

"I wasn't"—he coughed again, voice hoarse—"Tabitha, you cannot say things like that."

I shrugged. "I did ask for her advice. And judging by your reaction, she's excellent at giving it."

Graham looked over at me, cheeks flushed, but eyes all business. "All right, then. Tabs, how can I convince Anna to love Brighton enough to allow her father to invest?"

I shook my head, unsurprised by his persistence, and snatched up my cake for a hearty bite.

Tabs grabbed my free hand and placed it back atop her head in motions that insisted I continue to smooth her hair. "Have you asked her nicely?"

"Yes," Graham said.

"You have not!" I exclaimed through a mouthful of cake.

Graham handed me a napkin, amused, and turned his voice to honey. "Please, Anna, will you love Brighton and allow your father to invest with me?"

Allow my father to give all his time and attention to Graham when I needed him most? With Mr. Lennox and gossip abounding? As soon as word spread that I'd been duped by a man already engaged, that I'd been second best, I'd never be taken seriously by a worthy suitor ever again. I'd be pitied and gawked at. Allow my father to invest with him? "No."

He threw his hands up. "Did you not enjoy today? I gave you exactly what you wanted."

"You threw me in the sea!"

"You practically dared me."

"And I shall be writing all about it in my notebook."

"Wonderful," he muttered to my delight.

We were silent for a bit, save for the sea. Then he turned to face me. "I am not ignorant, Anna. So I know you've already made your decision. But if I have to beg, I will. I *need* this investment. What can I do to change your mind?"

Tabs's eyes closed, and I sighed. "Graham, can't we talk of this later?"

"All I'm asking for is a chance."

"I told you. I will do my best—"

"A *fair* chance. Sitting on a beach all week is not Brighton. Let me take the reins. Let me give you a real tour, a real Brighton experience. Then you can make a *real* decision based on your impression of this place, not your opinion of me."

"Don't forget to say please," Tabs added sleepily.

Graham smirked, then tilted his head. "Please."

He hadn't been horrible today. But an investment of this magnitude would require meetings, decisions, more time apart from Papa. I might as well be asking him into our family for the next decade with how focused Papa's attention would be on him. And I needed Papa beside me now most of all after Mr. Lennox's deceptions.

Panic stuttered my heart into motion, wrapping around my throat with a strong hand. I imagined news had already started to spread. How long would it take to reach Brighton? If I handed Graham this investment, how could I be certain I would ever have Papa's attention again?

Unless . . .

I thought for a moment. "Say I do give you a real chance . . ."

Graham straightened, eyes alight. "I'll make this trip unforgettable. Exciting. I won't ask you to do anything you're uncomfortable with."

I nodded once. "Then will you swear, after I've followed you along all week, that no matter what I decide, you'll leave my father alone after this venture? No more investments. No more random evening calls."

He drew back, brows furrowed, frowning. "You speak as though I am some unwanted horsefly. Your father and I are friends."

Friends? My father was twice his age. I started to laugh. "Honestly, Graham—"

"*Honestly*, Anna." He was serious. Offended. "I count your father in the highest regard. Indeed, he may be the only person alive I confide in fully. Investments aside, I will not forsake a friend who has become essential in my life just because his daughter throws a fit."

My lips parted, and I drew back, armed with the most hateful retort on my tongue.

But I stopped short, surprised to see Graham's jaw set, his face reddening and a boyish pain shadowing his features. Like I'd wounded him somewhere deep where few people could reach. Tabs stirred in her sleep, and I placed a hand on her shoulder. "It would appear you are the one throwing a fit at present," I muttered instead.

He cleared his throat, rubbing a hand over his face as though he could wipe away his feelings. Facing the sea, he said, "So it isn't Brighton, then. It's me. You don't want your father to invest with *me*."

"I don't want my father to invest his time with anyone." Anyone but me.

Graham's gaze fixed on Tabs. He watched her, then picked up a small rock and smoothed it over with his thumb. His voice came out serious, low. "Will this agreement eventually terminate? Say, upon your marriage?"

I considered his offer, imagining myself a lonely spinster, too weakened and embittered by gossip to try her hand at love again. I couldn't let Mr. Lennox be the end of me. I would rise above this embarrassment. "As long as it takes."

"You are asking me to abandon a close friend for the mere possibility at an investment that I dearly need. You hate me that much?" Graham's eyes flicked to mine with a vulnerability I'd yet to see in him. He wanted to know, but he also didn't.

I leaned in. "Do you know who escorted me through half the Season while my father was away in Bath with *you*?"

His brows furrowed.

"My great-aunt Agnes. We left every ballroom early. I took callers while she dozed in the corner. I had to send regrets to dinner parties when she took ill."

"She sounds like every young woman's dream."

"Oh, I enjoyed myself." I smiled. "But I assure you, all the finest gentlemen were taken halfway through the Season, and I did not appreciate that fact until it was too late."

Graham sighed, rolling his shoulders like I'd placed a new weight upon them. Guilt tugged at my heart, but his friendship with my father was not permanent. One day, he'd marry, have children, and build a life full enough that he'd forget about my father and our little corner in London. He had no blood ties to us. Only forced ones that could be clipped with no lasting damage.

"If this is your condition, then I agree," he said quietly, and my heart flew into my throat. I'd won. My goodness, had I just won? "But," he continued, "you will allow me to read your notes before you give them to your father, so I can feel certain that you did the work you promised you'd do."

"You might not like what I've had to say so far," I said dryly. But what did I have to hide? I'd written with my father in mind, using a professional, factual tone with only the barest hints of gossip.

Well, perhaps there were a few notes I wasn't proud of.

"After three years with you, Anna, I am certain I can handle it. Can we agree?"

I shrugged. Why not? One week more, and either way I had what I needed. "Very well, then. We've a deal."

Graham nodded, swallowing hard. His mood was more somber than ever. "Wonderful."

Chapter Thirteen

ANNA

Besides the ticking of a little clock on my desk which read five thirty-seven the next morning, Highcliffe House was without a sound, but I was awake. Alert. Unable to sit still.

Not long after Graham and I had made our deal, we walked home, Graham carrying Tabs until she was awake enough to stumble down the path and chase the wind. He hadn't said much, but I knew his mind was at work planning out our week.

As promised, the notes I'd made in my notebook after dinner were straightforward, perhaps tinted in favor for the way the sea had relaxed me. I'd mentioned how easily I could see families picnicking there, chasing one another, perhaps tossing an unlucky member in the sea. Knowing Graham would read it later made me laugh. I ended with a final assessment: Brighton was no better than Lyme; worse, if one considered how rocky the beach was. Therefore, nothing had convinced me that its popularity might last long enough to warrant a grand investment.

Let Graham argue that point.

I'd yet to call for Mariah and decided to simply enjoy the

view. As I opened my balcony doors, salty sea air and sunshine assaulted my senses. Just above the line of treetops rose the sea, blue and green and sparkling brilliantly at the start of a new day. Leaning against the cold balustrade, I untied my curling papers and watched the waves roil from far out. The sea was musical, soothing as it welcomed the morning. Five more days until Papa came for me. My future looked brighter than it had in some time. I tugged on a few crooked curls.

Then a man coughed.

I lurched backward, crouching low, not wanting anyone to see me in my nightdress. On my knees, I peeked through the pillars in the balustrade.

Graham.

Dressed in a white shirt and brown, worn breeches, he carried an armful of wooden poles hefted over his shoulder, heading downward on a trail toward a little white building partially hidden behind a copse of trees. What was he doing?

Perhaps I had seen wrong. Perhaps I was still groggy, and I'd mistaken a servant for my host, but I'd known Graham for years. I wished I could deny it, but his angles and features were frustratingly familiar.

I glanced back to my notebook and pencil resting on the writing table beside my bed. Then at my already half-tied stays and pink-and-brown-striped cotton pelisse folded in a chair. And before I knew what I was doing, I was sloppily dressed, tiptoeing down the stairs and out the front door.

Following him.

The air became more frigid the closer to the sea I traveled. I moved slowly, for the trail Graham had followed veered to the right before continuing toward a grassy area and the little building where by now he'd surely stopped. Stone barriers as tall as my waist lined the path on either side as I drew closer. They veered out and connected with a wooden fence that surrounded the little stable house.

Was it a stable house?

Graham owned several horses, but I'd assumed, seeing as he lived in a sea town, he housed them elsewhere. He couldn't possibly fit them all in that small building. The wooden poles he'd carried now leaned against the shaded side of the building. What was he doing here, so early and in such informal dress?

I took careful steps, peering around each side of the building until I'd walked its entirety. No sign of him. Not a single rustling of leaves.

He'd gone inside, then. What could he possibly be doing? Building something? Worse, hiding something? Whatever it was, I *had* to know. I'd come down all this way from my bed. I hadn't even arranged my hair.

I lifted my chin. If not for my sake, for Papa's. In one swift movement, I slid the door open.

And there he was. Sitting on a stool. With a pail of milk under a cow.

He looked up, his neck bare from his loose shirt, then blinked down to the cow and looked up at me again. Then he jumped up, knocking over his stool. "*Anna*? What are you—"

My jaw hung open, eyes racing from the cow stepping forward then back over a sloshing pail of milk to Graham's parted lips, his eyes growing wide with alarm. "Are you . . . *milking a cow*?" Where were his servants? I could count on my hand the ones I'd seen so far.

Graham took the bucket and swung around, setting it on a little table across from the cow's stall. One cow. No horses.

A brown-and-white tabby cat zigzagged around Graham's boots.

"It is very early. You should be in bed." His cheeks were ruddy, but the rest of him was entirely pale. He grabbed a rag and wiped his hands, then pushed the cow back into her stall. "You should not be wandering about on your own."

I was still in a state of shock, but I managed, "I saw you from the balcony, and I wondered what you were doing, and I . . . *Why* do you have a cow? In the middle of Brighton."

Graham shook the cat off his boot. "Get off, Constantine. Go on."

My eyes trailed his clothes—clothes that he clearly reserved for *working* in.

"We have a lot to see this afternoon. A lot of walking. You should return to your room and—"

"I find I am wide awake."

We stared at each other. Graham, filthy. Me, without so much as having splashed water upon my face.

"We brought them with us," he muttered. His brows drew together as he looked anywhere but my face. "When we moved here from the country. We couldn't stand to sell the cow, after everything. And Tabs loves this stupid cat." He shook the creature off his boot again, and I found myself reaching out to—what?—help him? Help the cat? Who was this man? This version of Graham was so hesitant and serious and unsettled. In London, he walked with a sure gait, a steady pace, an intimidating confidence. This man could hardly look me in the eye. He closed the cow's gate and brushed past me, out the door.

I didn't know what to say, but I could not stay there, so I

followed him and said the thing running circles in my head: "You are milking a cow. By the sea."

"It's not that unusual, Anna. If we didn't have her to milk, we'd be buying it. And we already had her, so . . ."

"But—" Oh, it would be rude to ask him outright again. Ruder than I already had been by following him. There was something he wasn't saying. Something he didn't want to say, judging by how ready he was to abandon me. He gathered the wooden poles and trudged to the fence line. Despite the gate a few paces down, he hopped over the fence, then hoisted the wooden poles over his shoulder and turned toward the pasture.

"Graham," I called as I strode to the gate, my shaking fingers working to unlatch it.

I nearly skipped to match his quick pace, but he would not offer more than a grunt until we finally reached the other side of the enclosure, and he dropped the wooden poles. The fence encompassed a small plot of grassy land, a pasture for the cow. Though I'd tied my hair back, it was a mess of curls along my shoulders. I wiped my brow with my sleeve, very unladylike, then placed my hands on my hips. I was not finished with this conversation, but I'd have to tread carefully to get the answers I wanted.

"The cat I understand. But the *cow*? Why did you not just sell it and buy a new one?"

Graham huffed out a breath, looking along the fence line. Then he bent down and picked up an axe that had been left leaning against a spot on the fence. "I purchased that cow when I returned home from Cambridge. When my family needed her most, she produced more than a cow should. And she was halfway through her third pregnancy when I purchased Highcliffe House. Selling her when we left would have felt like a crime after all she did for us."

"*Left?* But why would you leave your childhood home?" I swallowed. This was none of my business. Indeed, I'd inserted myself into Graham's private affairs without cause or necessity, and here I was, asking for more, but I had to know.

"Home?" Graham reared back, brows furrowed. A look of disgust passed over his features. "That place was not a home."

I furrowed my brow. Not home? What, then, caused his family to leave? Graham never spoke of his childhood. Rarely allowed a glimpse into his life before London to anyone. If he had, I'd have heard something by now. To Papa, he'd spoken of his mother, his sisters, but never . . .

"Do you mean it was not a home after your father died?" I winced. So forward, and so brash. But there was something Graham wasn't saying, something that pained him beyond words, and we were teetering on the precipice.

Graham was silent, watching me carefully, with sweat on his brow and specks of dirt on his unshaven jaw. Then he drew in a steady breath and tilted his head, thoughtful. "My father did not die, Anna. He left us. I have not seen him in almost nine years."

My features froze. No, that could not be. A father leaving his family was unfathomable. The greatest dishonor. I thought back over everything Papa had told me and every piece of Graham's life story I'd gleaned from random conversation over the years. "But that cannot be. You've a country house just outside of London. And I swear someone told me you lived with your grandfather in the summers."

"Yes. My grandfather cared for my education. He did everything he could to account for my father's lacking." He gripped the axe naturally, and without his waistcoat or jacket, he seemed somehow bigger, stronger. Lines of muscle were taut with strength from his neck down into his arms.

Graham.

Graham Everett.

He turned to the fence and swung down upon a wooden pole lining the fence. It busted too easily, and I realized the wood had rotted. "My father traveled in the summers, seeking easy money to maintain the façade he showed Society, while my mother stayed behind with Ginny."

He swung again, and five wood panels broke away. Mesmerized by his strength and how easily he managed his axe, I watched his back as he kicked at the remnants, pushing them away with his boot.

"He left you all." My voice was small, quiet with remorse and disbelief.

Graham picked up a long log and set it in the same fashion the others had been placed. Then he turned the axe over to the flat side and started hammering the wood into the supple earth. "Grandfather hired tutors for me, then sent me to Cambridge on his own account when I was sixteen. I attended for nearly two years. When he died, I went home to mourn with my family, only to realize that the happy letters my mother was sending me were all pretenses."

I waited while he set another log against the others. "Something was wrong?"

He grunted, then started hammering again. "My father had not returned all year, and our funds were as nonexistent as our food. My mother managed the house and tended the garden alone because, without pay, our servants had found better employment. I used my meager savings to buy a cow—*that* cow—and the last necessities we needed to get through the winter."

I stood there gaping like a fish, trying to decide what to say. All the time I had berated him both in my mind and through that stupid game we'd played tormenting each other, Graham had been struggling to support his family?

"Graham, I had no idea."

He reached out, pointed to a smaller wooden pole at my feet, and I quickly lifted it, tilting it toward him. Before turning back, he stopped and looked me straight on. "You didn't know?"

Brows raised in shock, I puffed out a breath and shook my head. "Forgive me. I suppose I made assumptions based on . . . Well, I thought your father had died. I assumed you'd inherited a house. Land. A living."

He watched me carefully for a moment, holding fast to the wooden pole and axe. "I thought you knew. I was sure your father had told you, and that was why—" He stopped himself, heaved a great sigh, then turned and placed the log beside the other. "You should go back inside. Dress properly."

"You thought that was why *what?*" I took a step toward him. My mind warred with my heart. I had not necessarily felt bad for tormenting him because he'd tormented me right back. His circumstances did not change the fact that he'd invaded our home and stolen Papa's attention. Except, apparently, he'd done it out of dire need.

Ignoring me, he swung the flat side of the axe several times, until he was satisfied that the wooden fence was secure. He leaned his weight against it, testing its hold.

I waited, unmoving, until he faced me, more confident

and sure of himself than he'd been all morning. "I thought that was why you hate me so much."

I scoffed. "I don't hate you."

His gaze moved to just above my shoulder. "You treat me rather poorly. And I seem to remember you saying just yesterday—"

"Well, I had *no* idea of your circumstances yesterday."

"You would have felt pity for me, if you had?" He smirked. "Don't, please. I've managed just fine on my own. It was all for the better. Stop looking at me with those sad eyes. Please, do go back to hating me again."

"I *don't* hate you," I repeated, but my feelings were starting to blur. Hatred felt an awful lot like compassion of late.

"Say something genuine, Anna. I dare you." He mimicked me from yesterday. The nerve!

But he was right. I could be honest about how I felt without being cruel. He'd spoken honestly with me yesterday, and with how vulnerable he was now, I owed him that respect, however small. "I just think you're . . ."

He stood there, without turning away, and crossed his arms in a show of patience.

"You're a little too . . . put together."

"And what, pray tell, does that mean?"

"Oh, come now, Graham. You're always with your perfect manners in London, perfect smile, all amiable and easy to please."

His lips twitched into a smile, eyebrows raised in a show of surprise, and he ducked his chin. "And *I'm* the one with a book of poetry?"

I frowned. "On second thought, I take it all back. I do hate you."

He laughed outright, and I tried desperately not to join him. "I think we both know how to play our hands well when we need to," he said, and the way his eyes trailed over my face made my skin come alive.

Who was this man? I shook my head. "And why were *you* milking your cow?"

He shrugged. "My staff is overworked this week, and I was awake. I learned how to milk her back when I first bought her. It calms me."

I crossed my arms despite the lightening mood between us. I felt eighteen again, thinking back to when Graham and I had first met. How harshly I'd judged him and his scuffed boots. How he'd aimed to charm us. And how I'd thrown it all right back in his face. Of course he'd hated me right back, how could he not? I rubbed my burning cheeks. What a mess I'd made—first with Mr. Lennox, and now with Graham. I was the very worst judge of character.

He seemed to read my mind, like he knew how it felt to be standing there, stripped of any illusions, unbearably honest in front of another person. He shifted, leaning back against the now sturdy fence at his waist, elbows resting on the wood, still watching me. Then he said, simply, "I like your hair down like that."

My hand immediately touched the curls over my shoulder. "It's a mess."

"That you would come outside so unkempt. I like that about you too. You don't care about the opinions of others. Not to say you are not normally, otherwise, perfect in every way. But you do it so effortlessly."

What was he playing at? There had to be an underlying meaning to his words. But these compliments did not feel like his usual flattery. These felt real. An uncomfortable lump raised up in my throat, and I did not know how to respond to Graham's kindness.

Kindness I so clearly did not deserve.

"I'm going to walk you back to the house," he said, straightening. "When you're dressed, if you're desperate for more time with Tabs, she can show you around this morning, if you'd like. I have plans for us this afternoon."

He wanted solitude, and I could give him that. Especially after all he'd just given me. I walked beside him back toward the little barn. "And what of you?"

He smirked. "Well, the chore I need to do next is not fit for a lady's eyes or sensibilities. But it must be done. And then I must finish working on a formal proposal for a potential investment."

"Always business."

"If I could survive by sitting on piles of inherited coin, believe me, I would. But that is not my lot in life."

My heart betrayed me. I had the sudden urge to take his arm, to comfort him, to *compliment* him on the hard work he'd done to save his family despite what that had meant for my dynamic with Papa. I hadn't the slightest idea what sort of disarray Graham had gone home to after his schooling. And directly after his grandfather's passing. Nor the years between then and when he'd knocked on Papa's door. All because the one man he should've been able to trust had left him.

"Do you know where your father is now?" I asked.

He held open a gate on the other side of the barn. "Not precisely. And I couldn't care less. He came back only once, to gather a few things, making empty promises as usual, then nine months later we had another mouth to feed."

"Tabs?" I asked as I passed through the gate.

He smiled. "Tabs."

We shared a moment's humor, imagining a world without that girl. Then another ache squeezed my heart. Tabs did not know her father. Graham had taken that role as well. How very strong he must be to carry such a load. As angry as I was at him, a little piece of my heart softened. "Thank you for telling me."

He latched the gate, turning slowly to face me. When our eyes met, he seemed surprised that I'd thanked him. He offered me a gracious smile in return and said, "Thank you for asking."

Chapter Fourteen

GRAHAM

She hadn't laughed at me.

Nor had she taunted me, been cruel or biting about how I chose to spend my morning. It hadn't always been a choice.

In that split second when she had pulled open the door, standing there with utter bewilderment on her face, I expected her to turn on her heel and leave. A show of shock, pity, perhaps even disdain. She'd certainly given me scowls for less.

Instead, she'd stayed.

She'd looked surprised, but more curious than disgusted. She'd walked with me out in the field in her thin nightclothes covered with an equally thin pelisse. And my mind was still reeling from it.

On mornings such as this, I scrubbed the muck and dirt off my hands so thoroughly, no trace was left for anyone to see those parts of me. Likewise, I took great pains to bury our past. We left behind Father's crumbling estate, relocating far enough away to live a quiet life. But no amount of scrubbing could erase the callouses and scars on my hands, nor the worries that kept me up at night. The parts of my past that weren't worthy in the eyes of Society. I'd thought Anna knew some of where I'd come from. But now she knew everything.

That afternoon, I paced slowly, cautiously, down the hall and into the quiet, empty foyer, feeling like a fraud yet again. My clothes, the silver pocket watch on my fob, the shiny new boots I'd purchased not long after Anna had first berated my old ones—it was all an illusion. A means to an end. One day, after I'd secured us financially, I could strip myself of all finery and finally rest.

My carriage awaited us in front of the house, ready to transport us to the heart of Brighton. I planned to take Anna and my family around the town, stopping to visit both the lending library and marketplace, so she could see how lively and welcoming the people were.

After yesterday's conversation, it seemed we'd formed a truce, but after this morning, I had no idea what to expect from her.

The drawing room sat empty, so I took a seat on the sofa, knees bouncing, facing the three paintings Ginny had painstakingly perfected over the last year. They brought color to the otherwise dull brown room. I'd not inspected my home with such a critical eye in some time, but now I noted the worn arm of the sofa, how the fabric had started to wear almost to a tear. What did Anna think of this room? Had she noticed the imperfections and stayed despite them?

Footsteps sounded in the foyer, and I jumped to my feet.

"Graham," Mother said, Ginny and Tabs on her heels. She wore a wide-brimmed hat with roses bunched at the front that matched her pink-lined dress. Never once, not even in our dreariest of times, did she fail to impress when she wanted to. Because of my mother, no one knew how terribly we'd suffered.

"My husband is unwell," she'd begun saying years ago. It was better than, *"My husband does not want children, nor a wife, nor any responsibilities, and has decided to try his life over again in America."* Among other truths.

She kept the girls home, tutoring them herself. Having prepared for the worst, she'd had a meager savings. That, plus a small storage of goods, kept us alive until my first invest-ment—funded by a small inheritance my grandfather left me in his will—paid out. If anyone saw the truth buried beneath my mother's careful falsehoods, they were too polite to ask. And now we were well enough off to bury the past for good.

Why had I told Anna the whole of it? She'd seemed so willing to listen, and the more she asked, the more she *waited*, the more the words had flowed. And she'd stayed.

Mother frowned. Always aware, always measuring. "What is the matter?" she asked.

"Nothing." I raised my brows, instinctively defending against whatever ruffling she saw in me. She couldn't possibly know that I'd told Anna everyth—

"Good afternoon," Anna said at the doorway, and we all turned. Her cheeks were flushed, those thick, silky curls rearranged from the wild mess of the morning into a loose, delicate bunch atop her head. She held her hat in her hand.

Tabs swooped upon her, saying something that made Anna's smile grow wide. Then her eyes met mine. Her smile started to fade as she examined me, and I her.

"Mr. Everett," she said, then she did the strangest thing yet. She curtseyed.

My lips parted, red heat burning up to the tips of my ears. A curtsey was nothing more than a social courtesy, but from Anna, it felt like the world on a platter.

Chin lowered, an easy, warm smile grew on her lips as she rose. "Are we ready?" she asked the room. "I am eager to see this place that you all have grown so fond of."

Mouth dry, I could not speak. It was as though my senses had betrayed me, and every intelligent thought I'd once possessed had abandoned ship.

Mother drew her brows together and gave me a questioning look. "Yes," she answered for me. "The carriage is waiting. And I see you have your things, Miss Lane. We shall have luncheon on the seaside."

"Won't you sit by me in the carriage, Anna?" Tabs tugged on her arm.

Anna held her close. "If you'll have me."

"Perhaps I should stay in, with the carriage so full," Ginny said with a sigh. Strange, seeing as though she'd normally beg for an outing. Any chance for a glimpse at her latest blade, Mr. Anderson.

"You'll join us," I directed, but the words came out weak. What was wrong with me? Was I catching cold? I cleared my throat. "Shall we?"

I motioned to the door, and Anna stepped aside to let me lead. She was letting me *lead*. I nodded, walking past, acutely aware of the scent of jasmine and cherries permeating every space, then nodded again as Roland opened the door.

Steps had been laid at the carriage door, and I stood beside them, offering my mother a hand, then Ginny, then Anna, who'd pinned on her hat. Something in my chest constricted when she took my gloved hand with hers. Her long brown lashes, the peak of her upper lip, the smooth skin on her neck were like sparkling treasures, rare and priceless, as was the feel of her fingers as they softened their grip and then pulled away.

She situated herself on the bench opposite my mother, leaving space between herself and Ginny. She touched the curls framing her face. If she permitted, I could sit right there, beside her.

"Ahem."

I looked down to find Tabs, hands on her hips with one of her little eyebrows raised. Foot ready to stomp.

"You're acting strange."

Ah. How could I forget? "Well, *someone* woke me in the middle of the night," I said, offering her my hand, which she took as she stomped up the stairs.

"I had a bad dream. Likely from all your harassment of late." She cast me a disparaging glance over her little shoulder, then huffed and plopped between Anna and Ginny.

Well. I tempered my humor as I took my seat, then knocked on the roof and set the carriage in motion.

"You'll wrinkle my skirts," Ginny whined, shoving Tabs to the side.

"No more than they already are," Tabs retorted, pinching Ginny's leg.

Anna started to smirk but seemed to think better of it. "What shall I expect today, Tabs? My gracious host has yet to inform me."

Anna flicked her eyes to mine. Again, I struggled to think. She was looking at me. *Really* looking at me. Me, despite knowing everything. And she was teasing. Smiling. My heart stammered in my chest.

"Anything. Everything," I said.

"I believe," Tabs enunciated, "she asked *me*."

Anna and I shared a look so full of the same thought, we burst out laughing.

"Forgive me, Your Highness," I said, rolling my eyes.

"We shall start at the haberdashery," Tabs said matter-of-factly, "where my brother will buy me three new ribbons."

"And me!" Ginny added brightly.

Still laughing, I said, "We most certainly will not."

"*I* want three new ribbons," Anna said with a beguiling look that always seemed to work in her favor.

I cleared my throat, my smile waning. Anna wanted me to buy her something?

"You will love the lending library, Miss Lane," Mother said, and soon the four of them were absorbed in conversation of books and stories.

Soon, the edge of the Steine came into view. Situated at the heart of Brighton, the Steine was a wide, expansive, and fashionable green lawn, along which an L-shaped row of shops bustled with customers. One could find just about anything desired, as well as one of the finest lending libraries in all of England. At the head of the Steine, the Marine Pavilion loomed over all. I could just make out its edges. I hadn't yet received an invitation to one of Prinny's parties, but perhaps after I secured this investment . . . I'd longed to see inside those walls.

We stopped at the southernmost border, and while Mother quietly whispered reminders to Tabs about proper behavior and propriety, I advised Brunner of our afternoon plans.

"Come, Graham!" Tabs tugged on my arm. Distant music, merry and cheerful, from across the Steine carried on the wind as we made our way toward the shops.

And I wasn't proud of it, but somehow, the three of them wore me down, much to Mother's chagrin. Our first stop resulted in a rainbow of ribbons, which all three girls let fly in the wind as we walked down the footpath.

The afternoon crowd bustled in every direction, some on horseback, others in gigs or phaetons, many by foot. I noted every man who tipped his hat at Anna. Per my duty as her host, of course. Not smiling or being overly friendly to tourists was my duty these next few days.

Mother walked beside me. She slipped her arm through mine, pinching the sensitive skin of my underarm. I groaned, giving her a fierce look, but she leaned in close.

"You are much too quiet. Walk beside her. Speak with her. Encourage her, if you want to secure this deal," she whispered.

"Miss Lane is not her father. She will not like my interference." Especially not after all I'd revealed that morning. Besides, we'd made a new agreement. She'd promised to form a fair opinion of Brighton, and I wanted to make that task as easy as possible for her.

"She is a woman. She may not want to talk numbers and calculations, but she'd rather have you as a companion than Tabitha."

"I highly doubt that," I muttered. Things were shifting between Anna and me, but not quite *that* much.

Mother, unfortunately, was set.

"Tabitha, come," she said, releasing me and reaching out for Tabs. Then her eyes widened, and she nodded purposefully toward Anna.

Without Tabs, she was left with Ginny, whose morose attitude could send even the cheeriest of tourists running. I braced my shoulders, took a few calming breaths, then stepped forward to Anna's side.

Chapter Fifteen

ANNA

Laughter carried on the salty wind. Through every door, around every corner, it mingled with the pattering sounds of horses' hooves on the dirt footpaths bordering what Graham called the Steine. Sunshine fell upon us from an open blue sky, and I felt as though my every breath reached deeper than the last.

The Steine pulled everything together, like a force of gravity. Shops, inns, houses, a library, the Royal Circus with a stone horse leaping at its top, and more were all situated on the borderline of the Steine's open green lawn. Rows of entertainment and commercialism growing outward, he'd said, and I believed him.

"That, just there," Graham said softly at my side, startling me, for I'd thought he'd been walking with his mother, "is the Marine Pavilion, where the Prince Regent takes residence."

Following his outstretched finger, I saw a white, long palace-like structure farther down on the northern edge of the green lawn with many windows and a dome-shaped entrance in the center. Graham had mentioned it at dinner with Papa, and several times a day since.

"It looks smaller than I imagined," I said.

Graham's brows furrowed.

"The library!" Tabs squealed. "You promised, Graham!"

Mrs. Everett shushed her, but Graham waved her forward. "Go on. Though they may not have anything you'll like," he said.

"Then I shall find something *you'll* like so you can read it to me!" She grinned at him, then tugged on her mother's hand, hurrying down the dirt path opposite the Pavilion.

Graham matched my slow pace, soaking in the views despite his family strolling ahead.

"You are never this quiet. It is disconcerting," I said.

He pursed his lips and gave me a look. "I am quiet because you seem to prefer me that way."

"That's not—" I started to protest, but he was right. I'd said things to him I shouldn't have. I'd been cross and cruel. It was just, after this morning, Graham seemed like a different person almost. Like I'd put on my own form of spectacles and the man I'd been hating so fiercely, had named my eternal enemy, finally came into view, his fuzzy edges layered on top of one another to form a clearer picture. "Perhaps I have been harsh in the past."

His steps slowed. He squinted at me, frowning. "Don't do this," he said, shaking his head. "Don't pity me because of what you saw this morning."

Was that what I felt? Did I pity him?

"I like my life as it is," he added sternly.

I bristled. Was it so wrong that my view of him had changed? That I wanted to be kinder to him? "Forgive my attempt at civility. It seems your preferences are so inconstant that I shouldn't have wasted the effort."

He winced, and we stared at each other, testing the limits of who'd break first. Or maybe trying to figure out how to talk to each other like normal people. How to have a conversation without reopening old wounds we'd been poking at for years.

"What do you want me to say?" he asked.

I threw my hands up. Intolerable man. I was *trying*, truly trying to understand him and treat him better. Could he not help me at all?

"I do not know, Graham," I sputtered. Perhaps he did not wish for things between us to change, but they had. And like it or not, we'd be civil.

We only needed to practice. I searched the view encircling us and asked the first question that came to my mind. "Are there gardens at the Pavilion?"

"Yes," he answered flatly, the slightest note of question in his voice.

"One day soon I would love to see them."

He narrowed his eyes. "Why?"

"Because that is what people do in gardens. They promenade." Mine was the well-worn voice of a patient teacher.

"The Pavilion does not seem to meet your expectations. Perhaps our time will be better spent elsewhere."

He loved the Pavilion, and I'd offended him. For so big a man, he was easily wounded. I thought of all I'd learned about him. I did not necessarily want him around when Papa returned, but that did not mean I had to reject him fully. We could be acquaintances who saw each other on the streets of London and waved a passing "Good day" now and again.

I sighed, then spoke with a gentler tone. "Sometimes the view is different when you look a little closer. I'd like to give the Pavilion a second chance."

A crease formed between his brows. He looked back at the Pavilion, raising a hand over his eyes to see it clearly. Then he glanced back, clear confusion written on his face. "You are never this kind," he said in as gentle a fashion as I had a moment ago. "It is *very* disconcerting."

I should've been offended or defensive, snapping back at him with some clever retort. Instead, I lifted my hands, palms up, and said, "Perhaps you should take a closer look, Graham."

He looked down at me, watching, waiting. The tips of his ears turned pink. How had I never noticed how sensitive he was? He'd endured difficult circumstances and often portrayed such a rough and confident exterior; I had never considered that it all was a façade. Until now.

"Very well," he said in a soft voice.

He offered me his arm with a question in his eyes as he swallowed hard. Like I might reject him. Like my refusal would hurt him. In truth, I'd stuck my nose up at his offerings a hundred times before. My cheeks pinked as I remembered how he'd once asked me to dance the last set at a dinner party, likely to impress my father, and I'd said no, claiming a headache and ending my night early just to spite him. I'd been laughing seconds before with two ladies my age. He'd straightened, then turned to the girl beside me, who'd accepted.

I hadn't hurt him then, had I?

I laced my arm through his. His arm flexed as though by instinct. Was this as strange for him as it was for me? Strange, but different enough to send sparks of warmth through my chest. Graham held his arm firm, supporting my hand and leading me toward an unconnected building just down the way. Tall pillars lined the front, and the closer we walked, the more distinct the music became.

"It's much more than a library," Graham explained as he led me inside. "There's music, a billiards table, a reading room. We've a family subscription, so if you find something of interest you'd like to borrow while you're here, I am happy to oblige."

"Thank you," I said, but I was distracted. The room was enormous. People were everywhere. *Books* were everywhere. There must have been thousands. Signs with things for sale were at every turn, and walls full of bookshelves welcomed the ladies and gentlemen gathered together, perusing the titles. Tables sat sporadically throughout the open space, perfect for flipping through pages or setting down one's things. A clerk worked at a larger desk at the back, loaning out books to patrons.

"I do not know where to start," I admitted.

Graham nodded at a man surrounded by a throng of ladies; he smiled amiably back. "Well, what sort of books do you enjoy?"

"Guess," I teased him.

He cocked his head to the side, smiled openly, then looked around the room. "Horticulture. But only the really long, excruciatingly boring books."

I sucked in an exaggerated breath. "How did you know?"

He squinted. "Novels, then?"

I lifted three fingers in turn. "The hero must be titled, wealthy, and extremely handsome."

"I'm sorry to report that I am unaware of any hero who meets all three of those qualifications. Shall I direct you to a clerk? I could ask for the catalog. Ah, here is one."

He directed me to a nearby table with a large, thick book placed atop it. There were lines of titles sorted by topics or genres, all alphabetized. Graham held up the book, turning pages until he found the listing for novels, then squinted and brought it closer to his sight.

The man was blind without his spectacles.

"*The Duke and His Forbidden Love*," he read, then cleared his throat and tempered his smirk. "It takes three whole volumes for the poor fop to secure his fate."

I took the catalog from his grasp, placing it down on the table in front of us. "I've already read that one, and I can tell you in no uncertain terms that he does indeed secure her."

Graham leaned his hip against the table, one hand resting on its top as he faced me. "What else, then? You can tell a lot about a person by what they borrow from the library, you know."

I started at the top of the page, tracing my finger down the rows of titles. My right side grew comfortable and warm, until I realized Graham was leaning close to read alongside me. My breath hitched, and my finger froze on a title.

"*Cecilia*. Isn't that an Ann Radcliffe?" Graham asked, squinting. "Quite controversial."

"Frances Burney," I muttered, shifting my hip to the left, decidedly away from his warmth. "Put on your spectacles so you can actually read."

Not responding, he folded his arms. "You could always try Shakespeare. I hear *Romeo and Juliet* is full of intrigue," he said.

"I refused to leave my bed for days after finishing that play." I flipped a page, finding nothing to interest me. When Papa was away, I lived at the library. I'd read so many novels, I was entirely tainted. I'd already read many of these, but there were many more I'd never heard of. I closed the book. "Perhaps, the music room?"

Graham straightened, nodded, then led me toward an archway that opened into another room. Ginny sat alone in a corner, listening to the small orchestra play a cheery tune. We stayed for a time, then left her to find the others. Tabs and Mrs. Everett were in the reading room; Mrs. Everett had removed her gloves and was reading some sort of mystery book aloud quietly. After a time, Graham slipped out of the room, but I sat beside them, captivated by Mrs. Everett's soothing voice and by how Tabs sat so close that the upper half of her body sprawled across her mother's lap. Mrs. Everett lightly brushed through her daughter's curls with her fingers.

Portraits and mementos from my own mother's life were all I had of her. Growing up without her, I'd wondered what her voice sounded like, if she ever grew angry and why, and what it might feel like to be held in her arms. I'd never missed her, but this past Season, I'd felt her absence as I watched other girls' mamas fuss over them, push them toward eligible gentlemen, or pull them out of conversation with reckless ones. How different life must be with a mother's guiding hand.

And watching Tabs, seeing the love that so clearly existed between a mother and daughter, I felt the hole expand in my chest. That desperate ache, that loneliness I felt when Papa traveled too much or spent long days out of the house, seemed to multiply.

Tabs didn't have a father, but she had a mother. And that was a glorious thing.

I excused myself, turning from the reading room back to the main library. Perhaps I'd rejoin Ginny in the music room for a time. As I started walking through the open space, I saw Graham with his back to me standing at our table and leaning over the open catalog.

What was he looking for? I realized I had never asked him for *his* favorite books to read. I paced over to where he read, a stupid smile curling my lips, and slowly approached the table until his profile came into view. I panicked at the sight of the man, spectacles on his nose and a serious look on his face, for I thought I'd been mistaken. But a step closer and there was Graham, in his round, thin spectacles, looking sharp and sleek and intelligent all in one perfectly packaged form. My pace slowed, shoulders relaxed, and I found myself *sauntering* toward him like a sodden fool, but I could not help myself. He'd put on his spectacles, and I had to get a closer look.

Slowly, I leaned against the table as he had done with me earlier. His finger was set over a line on the open page, but I caught his peripheral attention, and he looked up.

He jerked back, eyes wide. His hand flew up to his face, but on instinct, I reached up to stop him.

"Don't. You look so handsome."

The words were out of my mouth before I could filter them, and we stood there, his hand on the arm of his spectacles, mine on his wrist, frozen.

He let go, blinking and looking away, and I cringed so hard my face became a prune. *Handsome!* I'd just called Graham—my host and nemesis-turned-friend—*handsome*. Even worse, I'd said it *to his face*. I rubbed the heat from my cheeks, too proud to walk away and let him see how mortified I was. In truth, I wanted to hide under a rock like one of Tabs's dead sea things and never be unearthed.

Graham cleared his throat. "Thank you," he muttered, looking down at the catalog. He gripped the table, knuckles white.

My skin felt ten sizes too tight, my lungs laughing at my attempts to calm my nerves with a few deep breaths.

"I—" I started, swallowing hard. "I meant, handsome, as in—"

Graham bit his lower lip, perhaps to keep from laughing at my failing attempt to recover myself. He *knew* I was mortified, but he wouldn't save me.

"Everett," a man's familiar voice called from behind. Deep. Raspy, like he'd just finished a cigar.

I drew in a sharp breath. I knew that voice.

My shoulders tensed, lips parted, breath stilled inside my lungs. His gait was familiar, too, for we'd walked alongside each other often over the past few months. The thud of his fashionable cane came to a stop nearby.

Graham, instantly alert, tore off his spectacles as he swung around. He straightened, frowning, as Mr. Lennox took another few steps closer. "Lennox," Graham said, shoving his spectacles into his jacket pocket.

Mr. Lennox's round blue eyes found mine. I'd once searched for those eyes in a crowded room; now I wished to hide from them at any cost. His attention sent my mind into a panicked state. I should run. I should hide. And yet, I remained frozen in my spot. "And Miss Lane. What a delightful surprise. I had no idea you'd removed to Brighton." His tall form bowed low as he held fast to his sleek, lion-headed cane, then rose again.

He grinned down at me, his face so perfectly symmetrical, his jaw so manly and square. I'd half expected deep-set scars or black eyes as cold as his heart, and yet, despite the shocking revelation now between us, he remained unchanged.

Only now upon close examination did I realize that his cunning smile did not quite reach his eyes.

He had lied to me for months. Deceived me into affection, and when the truth of his engagement came to light, he'd claimed *he* was the one who'd been deceived.

I might be a poor judge of character, but I was not that daft.

What the devil was he doing here? From Bath, he should've traveled straight back to London. Were the unanswered notes not enough of a clue? He had somehow found and followed me.

Graham bowed in return, but I did not trust myself to speak.

"You vanished halfway through the Season," Mr. Lennox said to Graham, spinning his cane to reveal encrusted diamonds as the lion's eyes. Jewels he absolutely could not afford. "I hear you've been busy here in Brighton."

"I have indeed." Graham looked between us expectantly, like he waited for one of us to explode.

"Yes, well, some fortunes must be built, I suppose. Good for you." Mr. Lennox gave a solemn nod.

The arrogance! The whole of Society must know by now how he had wasted away his fortune near to nothing.

Then, "Miss Lane, may I have a moment of your time?"

He'd softened his voice, gaze pleading. Desperate, undoubtedly. But I had nothing left to give him.

"Mr. Lennox, as you can see, I'm quite entertained at present."

He raised a brow and glanced at Graham with a look of distaste—had I once looked at Graham that way?—that only served to anger me. How dare he look down upon anyone, let alone Graham, who was his opposite in every way. "I see that. Did you—well, I hope you enjoyed the roses I've sent."

Graham started to rub the back of his neck, and I realized there were eyes all around, watching us. I would not give them more to whisper about.

I tilted my head with a tense smile and said, "They've wilted."

"Mr. Everett! How nice to see you," a slender woman said as she strode to Mr. Lennox's side. Young, small, with a round, cheery face framed with blonde curls and a well-trimmed hat.

My face turned instantly cold, and I could not help but study her. Was she the woman? *The* woman Mr. Lennox had kept secret from me, all the while begging for an opportunity to court me? And I'd almost allowed it. The entirety of London had watched with bated breath until one brave soul stepped forward to speak the truth. A stranger, but a godsend, had saved me.

Graham straightened. "Miss Ryan, how do you do?" He bowed low, and she giggled.

"Very well, thank you, Mr. Everett. I see you are acquainted with my cousin. He is visiting for the week," she said, looking at Graham like a hopeful child in front of a sweet shop. She might as well have offered herself on a platter by the way she salivated over him.

Not her, then, for Mr. Lennox's intended had not been a relation at all. My shoulders dropped an inch, but I'd grown weary. I could not stand as tall as I had, for I felt like I'd run from London to Brighton and back again.

"Indeed," Graham said to the woman. "How is your family?"

"How kind of you to inquire. My mother is quite re-covered," she said in a quiet voice, and something secret passed between her and Graham. The feeling brewing in my chest turned colder. Uglier. Graham had a life here. People knew him, admired him, begged for his company. Judging by the way her eyes wandered over Graham's face, the two of them were well-acquainted.

Mr. Lennox reached for my arm, his eyes pleading as he stepped sideways and boxed me out of the circle the four of us had created. "Please, Anna," he whispered.

"Don't you dare," I snapped back, seething. The library had suddenly gone still. Hushed. "There is nothing you can say. No amount of roses will change my opinion of you."

"I understand why you're upset." He spoke low enough for only the two of us, but he still glanced over his shoulder to where Graham and that woman were conversing all too happily. "But please understand the engagement would never have hap-pened regardless of whether we'd met. It was a sham—a ploy to help a family friend have more opportunities. *She* cried off!"

"At your behest," I said, raising a trembling finger. My breath shook as I spoke. "I know your uncle paid her off. I know your funds are dwindling. And I am not interested in becoming your purse."

His jaw clenched as he spun his cane in hand. "That is not the whole of it. I truly care for you."

I scoffed. "If you cared for me, you would never have lied."

He threw up a hand as though *I* was the one being un-reasonable. "You are a woman. You have no idea the trials of men in our society. What secrets we must keep. What we cannot tell you for fear of ruining your polite sensibilities."

"I could've borne it, I assure you." I hated the thickness in my throat, how weak and shaky my limbs felt despite the rising anger in my chest. I felt like a rope pulled tight enough to snap.

"Let me prove myself—"

"No, for heaven's sake," I cried. I could not bear his attempts to reconcile for one more moment.

"*Anna*," he said, reaching for me.

"My answer is and will always be, no."

Graham cleared his throat. He'd been watching. Several pairs of eyes had been. If the whispers hadn't yet come, they undoubtedly would now.

I licked my lips and touched my hair, forcing a smile. "So pleasant to see you, Mr. Lennox. If you'll excuse me. My host and I have quite a full schedule this afternoon."

He bowed, frowning, shoulders tensed. "Of course. I do hope to see you again before my departure."

"What a pleasure," Graham said to Mr. Lennox, but he was frowning. Then he bowed to Miss Ryan.

Blindly, I let my feet carry me around a table, then another, trailing whispers with every step.

"Did you see how distraught he is?" one woman asked.

Then, another, "The way she spoke to him—how impolite!"

"I heard her father paid for his silence." That lie stopped me in my tracks. It was entirely unfounded! I'd yet to tell Papa a thing! "Apparently poor Mr. Lennox proposed, then cried off when he learned of her true character."

I looked up, eyes blurry, in a desperate search to match that ugly voice with a face, but a hand rested on my arm and tugged me backward.

"Come, Anna," Graham said gently. "Come away from here."

Chapter Sixteen

ANNA

Graham directed me around tables, then veered right to a quiet, secluded corner. He discreetly handed me his handkerchief, and I faced the wall, wrapping my arms around my middle and desperately trying to compose myself.

"Pay them no mind," Graham said. "Their tongues are constantly wagging, yet they know nothing of what they speak."

I buried my face in my hands. I'd thought everything would be well if only I'd removed myself from London, and yet Mr. Lennox and all his lies had followed me here.

I needed Papa. I had no idea how to navigate gossip when my name was at the center. They'd said such terrible things. Was I simply to grin and bear it?

"Maybe they do know." I dropped my hands. "Perhaps I am as awful as they say."

"Well, then, I feel much better about having thrown you into the sea."

I scowled at his attempt at humor. He likely thought me an arrogant, emotional woman too caught in her feelings to see reason. "Think of me what you will, Graham, but you cannot possibly understand."

He took a few steps near, until we were less than an arm's

length apart. "Believe it or not, I have endured my fair share from the gossipmongers over the years. Tell me."

His eyes bored into mine, searching for answers, like he truly wanted them. All I wanted was a friend, someone to understand how I felt, to tell me when I was wrong about a person or a circumstance, even if I did not wish to hear it. Someone I could trust.

And Graham had trusted me.

He'd sat at every table in our house at one point or another. I'd given him my very worst in every way—the sharpest words, cruelest looks, most hateful snubs. And, yet, he'd told me everything about his past. If Society found interest in this ridiculous upheaval between Mr. Lennox and me, they must have been relentless over Graham starting his life anew. I'd been so newly out in Society, I must have missed it all.

Indeed, he could have offered to take me home, put me in my bed, tell his mother and sisters what a dramatic, over-indulged thing I was. But he'd given me privacy. He'd stayed.

His gaze did not wander from my face.

I trusted him. I did.

Warmth splotched my cheeks, and I looked away. "Half of what they say is true. But they do not have the whole of it. Mr. Lennox and I . . . We were on the cusp of a courtship until I learned he was secretly engaged to another."

Graham's jaw flexed, and his nostrils flared. "The scoundrel. Does your father know?"

"No. I've yet to tell him, and I'd appreciate being the first to do so. Mr. Lennox's uncle paid the woman off, but I refuse to make amends."

He nodded once. "I am sorry to hear how terribly he has abused you."

"Fortunate timing, though. Can you imagine if I'd

discovered his true nature later? After I'd given him my heart? I'd have surely lost my wits and marred him with . . ." I let my imagination wander, then chose the most fitting of weapons. "His lion-headed cane."

Graham's eyes widened. He shook his head, a blend of terror and humor on his face. "Not the lion-headed cane. You ruthless woman."

I smirked. "Do not cross me, Graham."

He held a hand to his chest. "You have my word. And allow me to apologize again for every time I've wronged you."

I rolled my eyes, and he feigned terror for another dramatic moment. We listened to the gentle hum of voices and distant melodies carrying from the music room.

I huffed out a breath, less shaky than before, but I still buzzed with the shock of Mr. Lennox and the cruel wave of gossip that had followed. "I think it best to forget about all this. To pretend no one knows that anything is amiss," I said. "We should finish the day you've planned."

Graham nodded, watching me like I might shatter. I did not want him to look at me like that, though perhaps I deserved it after such a humiliating display.

"For what it's worth, Anna . . ." Graham seemed to hesitate, then shrugged. "Fear and hairpins aside, no matter what lies they spread about you, I'm a friend for as long as you'll have me. You know the truth, and that is all that really matters." Then he offered his arm.

It was such a simple offering. So honest and good of him. I laced my arm through his, then teased, "Ah, the promise every man of my acquaintance has offered . . . until my father walks in the room."

Graham groaned and tugged me toward the music room.

"What?" I asked sharply.

He gave me a sideways glance. "You truly believe the only reason a man shows interest in you is because of who your father is?"

I pondered his question. "Seventy-five percent of the time, at least."

"Seventy-five—?" He scoffed, then half laughed. "Where does that belief come from?"

"Men pretending to be my friend, and then abandoning me for my father's attention. Jesting about my dowry with their friends when they think I am not listening. When they smile more broadly and talk more enthusiastically with him than with me." Alexander Lennox had done every single thing. "I wish I could stop the spread of it. I am such a fool."

"You were trying to follow your heart. There is nothing foolish in that."

"Well. I am quite ready to follow it elsewhere."

"Come," Graham said. "Let us see where it leads you."

We maneuvered through the growing crowd, around tables and booths, and nods of "Good day." Then Graham said, offhandedly, "There is an assembly at week's end, if your heart should lead you there. Plenty of locals and tourists alike will be in attendance. The music is always prime, as are the refreshments."

He was buttering me for Papa, like I'd asked Cook to butter Papa's French beans. I frowned at him. "Is that so?"

He shrugged innocently. "I've seen you dance. I know you enjoy it."

"Oh?" My voice pinched. "And does your Miss Ryan enjoy dancing?"

Graham jerked his attention to me, eyes squinted. "*My* Miss Ryan?"

I scoffed at his attempt to deny it. "Good heavens, Graham, the way that woman looks at you is indecent."

Graham snorted, utter shock evident in the way his jaw hung open in a grin. "*Indecent?* I daresay not one vulgar thought has ever passed through Arabella Ryan's mind. She is innocent in every way of the world."

"I highly doubt that," I muttered, pinching the bridge of my nose to ward off an impending headache.

"If you'd rather, we can rest today."

"We do not have time." I felt a gentle squeeze on my arm, and I looked up at him.

"Perhaps we should make time," he said.

I huffed out a breath and pointed a glare aimed just for Graham. But he wasn't sneering, wasn't taunting or teasing me. He looked rather serious, and for a moment, I thought the crease in his brow might be concern. Care?

What would it be like to be cared for by Graham? To be the one he came home to with a hundred stories and ideas on his lips. Sharing a dinner that lasted twice as long merely because we had so much to say to each other.

Graham was studying me, his head tilted, eyes curious. "Whatever you wish," he said. But this time it wasn't to please me. This time, his voice was sincere, his smile encouraging.

"Do you concede so soon?" I teased—*teased?*—Graham. The hurt I'd been gripping so tightly seemed to ease with the growing grin on his face.

"Not a chance." He narrowed his eyes. "I am, as I said, following your heart's lead."

My skin prickled with heat. Goodness, how his gaze burned into me. "Perhaps you should follow your own for a time."

"Perhaps," Graham whispered to himself, "I should."

Our hearts were led by our hungry stomachs, and we walked down the Steine, Tabs skipping whenever her mother and Graham weren't looking.

We picnicked on the beach, which was more spacious than at our hidden spot from the other day. People came and went in droves, running, chasing, walking, riding, some dipping their feet in the water, others sitting on blankets beneath parasols, delighted by simply observing the chaos.

Graham stayed quiet, his spectacles safely tucked away, eyes wandering the crowds. Occasionally, he lifted a hand of acknowledgment or nodded hello to passersby. Eventually, Tabs went off to explore the shoreline, and Ginny offered to accompany her. The remaining three of us sat in companionable silence, enjoying the sun and watching as the gulls flew up, around, and between the beachgoers.

A while later, I noticed Ginny nearby in a circle of young women and gentlemen. They were laughing, and she was saying something to a cheerful man beside her. Even from a distance I could tell from the set of her shoulders and the way she held her neck perfectly still that she was impressed with him and did not want to misstep. I poked Graham's arm and pointed to Ginny. He looked over and huffed out a laugh. "That's Mr. Anderson. Younger chap, heir to a nice estate. She's had her cap set at him for months."

"Have you encouraged a match?" I asked.

He lifted a shoulder. "In some ways. She does not like my involvement."

Mrs. Everett added, "She is reticent. I do not think she is ready."

"She looks ready to me," I muttered to Graham, who finally smiled halfway.

Courtship. Such a ridiculous endeavor. Where two people present the best sides of themselves and try to impress one another. I grew tired of the game, tired of hiding my true thoughts. Why did we hide our excitement, our interest, even the first flutterings of feeling for another person? Shouldn't we celebrate connection? Prioritize friendship and be enthusiastic over every potential?

Indeed, I could think of others who'd inspired me, others who'd made me feel those first inklings of wonder, and yet I'd disregarded them for the possibility of feeling something with Mr. Lennox.

Mr. Lennox who I'd carefully picked based on his handsome face, his popularity in Society, and his ability to turn a phrase. How coy I'd played.

Lud, I could be daft.

But I had learned from my mistake. I would not choose another man based on what I wanted him to be or what I hoped he might be. I no longer had time for pretenses or best smiles. I wanted a partner. Someone who prioritized me without fail. Someone who understood me and loved me despite the lashing of my tongue on occasion, whose very days and hours were spent building a life that reflected the love we felt for each other.

Never mind Papa's secrets. Never mind Graham's investment. I could endure Society's gossip because eventually it would fade. But to find someone to laugh with—to enjoy life with—*that* I realized as I stared out at the rolling sea, was everything I wanted. And if no one would aid me, then I, like Ginny, would pursue this endeavor alone.

I would leave no stone unturned. I would welcome any

and all attention unless instinct told me otherwise. And I would start this very day.

After we had taken in enough sun, Graham walked us a half mile or so to the land he meant to buy. A little stone house sat on the far right, looking over the sea; it was scheduled to be demolished, Graham said. The land would be divided into parcels, each to become an apartment that would be rented out over a lifetime. Though he didn't say, it meant a lot of money for Graham, and in turn, his family.

Graham's proposal sounded smart. As much as I hated to admit it, Brighton seemed to have a little of everything for tourists. What, then, would I write in my notebook tonight?

Perhaps instead of writing, I'd find a different distraction worthy of my time.

"Shall we, Miss Lane?" Graham stood a few paces to the side and swiped a hand through his hair. Good heavens, he looked like Adonis standing cliffside above the sea.

Graham?

I laughed, and instead of shoving the idea aside, scoffing, and turning away, I reminded myself of my new goal and relaxed into my true feelings. I *wanted* to watch Graham. A smile lifted my lips as the gentle breeze brushed his hair over his eyes once more, and he struggled to pile it all back atop his head. He glanced over his shoulder at something Ginny said and grinned so widely, his cheeks creased. I almost bowled over at the sight of him.

Good heavens.

No stone unturned, indeed.

Chapter Seventeen

GRAHAM

I'd encouraged Mr. Lane to leave. To visit Ms. Peale. And I hadn't for one second considered Anna's feelings.

As I watched her ascend the staircase to dress for dinner, regret fell like an anvil upon my chest. How many times had I dismissed her desires, her needs, in favor of what I wanted or what her father wanted? The shame of it burned like bile in my throat. Never again.

No matter how she treated me or the barbs she threw in defense of herself, I was resolved. Anna deserved better than what she'd been given these past years. She deserved to be heard, considered, cared for.

A week ago, I'd have rolled my eyes at her tears and dismissed her as attention-seeking. But seeing her now—how different she was away from London—made me wonder if perhaps I'd been looking at her all wrong.

There was something about this Anna. She wasn't new by any means, but she was real. She was vulnerable. Spending time with her inspired a new fierceness inside of me, a need to protect her at any cost. When she'd fallen apart after our encounter with Lennox—that soulless slab of muck—it had taken all my strength to keep from wrapping her in my arms, shielding her, as she tried to hide her tears in the lending library.

And that frightened me.

She wasn't someone soft like Arabella Ryan, childlike, and as interesting as a little sister. Anna Lane was untouchable. Unattainable. So beautiful I couldn't stop thinking about her even as she walked away. The soft sweep of her hair. The little dip in her upper lip. How her fingers felt curled around my arm.

I shouldn't be thinking about her like this.

Not Anna. For the sake of my investment, and my relationship with her father, I had drawn significant and very resolute lines between family and business. Unspoken, but firm.

But she and I had made progress today. She'd seemed to enjoy the Steine, the sea, even the food. Nothing forced, nothing strained, just a simple outing. I'd even venture to say comfortable were it not for Lennox's abrupt arrival. Even then, we'd recovered the day somewhat. She didn't seem overly affected for long. I'd tried desperately to encourage her. To make her laugh again.

I could still *feel* her smiling back at me.

I shook my head to focus. *Business, Graham.*

A stack of letters on my desk had demanded my immediate attention upon arriving home, so I took a light dinner tray in my study and got to work, answering questions, calculating payments, then writing a long letter asking Tom to double-check my figures and triple-check my accounts.

Ink jar closed, pen in place, I stretched out my cramped legs and pushed back my chair. My candle, lit long ago to dispel the night, drooped under warm, dripping wax. Rubbing my eyes, I stood, pulled out my fob watch and read the time. Nine fifty-two. Had everyone gone to bed?

No. I could hear music trilling down the hall. I followed the sound—Ginny's harp mingled with bursts of laughter— to the drawing room. What were they thinking? Anna would be trying to sleep at this hour, all the while my wild family was—

I froze under the doorframe at the sight before me: Ginny, plucking strings on the harp, and Anna counting out, "One, two, three. One, two, three," as she and Tabs, whose hair had been arranged in curls and new ribbons, spun circles in the middle of the room.

"Put your feet on mine!" Anna called through a laugh. "No, left. *My* left!"

"I hate waltzing!" Tabs wailed, curls bouncing.

Ginny could hardly pluck the strings for her laughing fit.

I found Mother in the corner by a low-lit fire, a book open in her hands, though her eyes were trained on the sight before her. "You're too far apart, move closer together."

"Good heavens, Mrs. Everett, how scandalous." Anna snorted, laughing so hard her steps faltered, and she and Tabs broke apart, stumbling.

I stepped into the room, torn between righting Anna and aiding Tabs, when the music stopped suddenly, the fits of laughter silenced.

"Oh, dear, were we too loud?" Mother asked, closing her book. A stern look crossed her countenance. "Girls—"

"No, not at all." I stood in the middle of the room like a fool.

Anna cleared her throat and exchanged a look with Tabs, who glanced back at Ginny.

"I've just finished my correspondence, actually. Heard something," I said.

Blithering idiot.

"Anna taught me how to properly bat my lashes!" Tabs exclaimed, as though the fact were bursting from her. "And! Anna says if you wish for an introduction to a certain handsome gentleman, you need only drop your handkerchief ahead of him, and the gentleman will bring it to you and—"

I promptly fell into the nearest chair.

"Tabitha!" Ginny chided. "That was a *secret*."

"All secrets come out eventually," Anna said, finding a spot on the sofa adjacent my chair. She turned to me. "And before you lecture me, I also taught her how to hide in the event she is hunted by a persistent suitor, and that one should only dance the waltz with a gentleman she wishes to encourage in courtship."

"I'm to hide behind a fern. Or a marble statue," Tabs said proudly.

"Very well," Mother said with a laugh. "Off to bed with you, darling. Shall we?"

Tabs did not put up a fuss. She hugged Anna, then kissed Ginny on the cheek.

"I can take her, Mama," Ginny offered, and to my astonishment, the conversation ended there. Mother settled back in her seat across the room. Anna watched them go, and the room fell silent.

I should take my leave. I should get a full night of rest to be at my prime tomorrow. A full day with Anna. A full day of work.

"Are you always this busy at home?" Anna was watching

me, measuring something in my face. "I imagine you in your little room in London always working. But here? At home?"

"I—" I cleared my throat.

"My father never used to miss dinner. In truth, our dinners turned into business discussions, with the two of you prattling on, and me, with a plate and a drink."

I could picture it. Not-so-distant dinners where the most she'd say was a cutting remark to me or a general comment on some happening in Town.

"How are you feeling?" I asked, though the question sounded ridiculous as soon as I'd released it. Of course she was still upset.

"Your family is a welcome distraction." She gave a half-hearted laugh. "Your sisters and mother are lucky to have each other when you are away from their table."

In a flash, I pictured her in her own home, alone. One setting at the Lane's long, elegant table.

"I fulfill many roles in my family," I said as a way of excusing my frequent absences. I didn't say how I hoped that might change soon because she would certainly take that as a manipulation. "Busy, yes, but I try to be present when I am home."

"They love you very much," she replied. "You are, by all accounts, a very fortunate man."

A *fortunate* man. Me?

After all I'd lost. How far I'd fallen. I'd never considered myself fortunate.

"Is this all you do in Brighton, then?" She gestured around the quiet room. Mother had settled back into her book. "No tea, no port? Just sitting around, looking at each other?"

I straightened, defensive, until I saw the tease in her smile. "Well, typically it's the cotillion instead of the waltz."

She snorted, relaxing on the sofa.

"Or we often play cards."

She tilted her head. "Oh? Where are these cards you speak of? Or better yet, do you have a box of letters?"

She wanted to play? With me? "You want to play the alphabet game? Like we are children?"

She raised a brow, then nodded.

The hour was late, and I knew I should excuse myself and rest. But Anna's eyes found mine, bright and hopeful.

All I could see was that tempting smile of hers. Those full, alluring lips.

I, a man starved, and she, everything good.

She'd been so upset after encountering Lennox in the library. Perhaps she was scared to retire with nothing but her own thoughts.

If she wanted, I could be a friend. I could help calm her mind.

I rose from my spot, a challenge she quickly met, and while I retrieved the box of ivory letters from the side table, she moved the tea cart next to the sofa and flopped back in her spot.

I sat across from her, the tea cart between us. A far cry from the elegant furniture in her own drawing room. And yet, she settled in, her shoulders relaxed. A little smile on her face. I dumped the smooth letters, each carefully carved in ivory, out on the flat surface and mixed them all with a hand.

"First to five," Anna said. Then, "You're peeking!"

I jerked my gaze to hers. "I am not!"

"Yes, you are," she said, aghast, but humored. "You're

looking at the letters while you mix them. You'll know where the *A* is, and that is *cheating*, Graham."

"I am *not*." I laughed. "And besides, we have three sets mixed together, so there are three *A*'s. Calm yourself, woman. What're the categories, then? Color, animal, profession . . . ?"

"Color first, then animal, then profession. What else? Size?"

I snapped my fingers. "Four-letter word."

"No, no! The last is always the longest word you can spell."

Without thinking, I glanced down.

Anna's hands flew up, covering the letters. "You. Are. A. Cheat!"

I bit my lip to keep from laughing. "That was an accident."

Anna leveled me with a stern gaze that was more endearing than she could ever know. "Keep your eyes on me," she commanded, stirring the letters a few times more.

I swallowed hard as I watched her. Brown, honey-colored eyes. Skin as smooth as butter. Why hadn't she accepted any of the many offers of marriage that had come her way? She'd had more than her fair share. More than she needed to find *someone* worthy. Though who could ever be worthy of that smirk? Those clever eyes. Worthy enough to be chosen by *her* for a lifetime.

"Very well." Her hands stilled over the letters. "The first one to spell a color wins the first round. Are you ready?"

I nodded, eyes still set upon hers.

"On your mark." She dipped her chin. "Begin."

She lifted her hands and immediately picked out an *A*. "You felt it," came my ignited accusation as I stole a *B*, *U*, and searched for an *L*.

She giggled—giggled!—and dug around the pile, plucking out letters quick as lightning.

I grabbed an *E*, but I still could not spot the *L*. I risked a quick glance.

Anna had *B*, *A*, *C*, and *K*.

Blast, blast, *blast!* There should be three *L*'s. I pushed the letters around, mind scrambling. I found an *O* and an *R*, and briefly considered abandoning ship for *orange*. But then, at last, the—

"Finished!" Anna called, triumphant. She'd found a wayward *L*, just as I'd plucked out mine.

"It was a tie," I argued weakly, settling the *L* into place. Blue. Four letters to her five, and still I'd lost.

"Hardly." She tossed her letters back in, then stole mine, mixing them all up and grinning at my frown. "One to zero, my favor."

"Next category is animal," I muttered. *Dog, cat, lion.* A handful came to mind, but the choice would be determined by which letters caught my eye first.

"And, go," she said, lifting her hands but letting them hover above the letters, just enough to cloud my view.

"Cheater," I harumphed, reaching under and sliding a handful closer to me.

"You louse!" She collected her letters, while I finished *cat*.

"Done!" she called, a breath before I did.

"Bee?" I pointed at her crooked letters. "That's an insect. The category was animal."

"Well, I wanted *bear*, but you stole my *A*, so—"

"So, *I* win. *Cat*. One to one."

She groaned but conceded.

Next, she spelled *vicar* for profession, but I beat her by a half second with *cook*. I'd forgotten how much I loved to see her cheeks so rosy, eyes aflame and aimed toward me.

For our last round—the longest word we could spell—we did not race. One minute, timed by my mother from her spot in the corner.

We worked silently. At one point, I gave up on *pneumonia* to try for a longer word and pushed all my letters back into the pile. Then brilliance struck.

"Ten seconds," Mother called.

"Drat, where is the *U*," Anna muttered. Luckily, I was almost done.

"Time."

"Aha!" I called, triumphant. "Hands up, Anna."

"Happily," she smirked, and my good humor vanished at the length of her word.

"*Unequivocally*." She crossed her arms and leaned back, capturing my eyes. "Thirteen letters. You?"

"*Philosophize*." Our stare held. "Twelve."

"It would appear we are at a stalemate," she said with a smirk. "We must create a final category to determine the champion."

Mother stood, closed her book, and took a seat in a nearby chair between us. Her features were tired, and I felt a surge of guilt. She stayed awake for propriety's sake, not for lack of exhaustion. "Might I suggest a worthy finale?"

Anna's smile faded, and I wondered if she, too, could see my mother's weariness. "Please do," she said.

Mother looked between us, hands clasped in her lap like a doctor diagnosing his patient. "Your next word shall be an adjective. Chosen to describe your opponent."

What? Describe one another with one word? Things

between Anna and me were just turning civil again. We could not afford to swim in such dangerous waters. I gave my mother a look—one that told her that she had not, in her clear exhaustion, thought this through—but she continued, "You will have one minute, and I will choose the winner based on originality and thoughtfulness."

Anna swallowed, looking down at the letters between us. "An adjective," she repeated.

"I promise to be fair," Mother assured her. "You may choose any adjective, as long as you have good, even humorous, reasoning."

Anna seemed to relax, and I wondered which word had initially come to her mind to describe me.

Scrawny? Sightless?

What would I say about her?

I stirred the letters once more, hoping for another stroke of brilliance, something humorous, perhaps, to make her laugh. Would she laugh if I spelled out *romantic* after her admission at the lending library? Such a word felt too easy, too ingenuine.

Anna straightened her skirts, then brushed back her hair. The lights in the room seemed to dim, and I opened my eyes just a touch wider to see. Anna craved sincerity. She thrived on genuine, not easy. What, then, could I say about her in one word?

"One minute, and . . . begin," Mother said.

Neither of us moved. Looking down at the letters, a few adjectives for Anna over the years immediately came to mind: *hateful, brash, presumptuous.*

But also *generous, empathetic.*

Beautiful.

I could think of more than one word to describe myself, beginning with *coward*. For when had I ever, in our acquaintance, truly admitted to Anna Lane a single quality in her that I found admirable? Never. Not once in three years.

"Thirty seconds," my mother announced. Her presence loomed over me. What was *her* motive here?

What a childish game. Still, neither of us moved. I could feel Anna's breathing, see her still and thoughtful in the corners of my vision. What was she considering?

I lifted a hand. My fingers hovered over the letters. *A, P, G, H.* One word to describe Anna Lane.

I took two, then three letters. Anna followed suit, her gaze sure and serious. A few more letters, then I leaned forward like a schoolboy guarding my answer as I arranged them just so.

"Ten seconds."

Anna sat up, clearing her throat. And when I finally straightened, I found her eyes on mine. I couldn't say why, but I did not wish to read her word. I did not want to know which adjective she'd chosen for me, and yet I was impatient to hear it.

"Graham?" Mother prompted. "Your adjective for Miss Lane?"

She meant for me to read it? Devil take it.

"Don't look so contrite," Anna said, her voice low and smooth. "You've said worse, I am sure."

My brows knit together. She thought I'd contrived the worst possible adjective of her. What sort of man did she think me to be?

The one I'd been these past few years.

I wanted to be different.

"*Brave,*" I read, and she straightened. "I chose *brave* to describe Miss Lane."

"Do explain," Mother prompted.

"Well, staying in the home of her enemy is no simple feat." Anna raised a playful brow.

"I think Tabs proved that upon her first morning here. And yet, here she is, living as we live, opening her heart to a new place and new people. I find that very brave."

She locked eyes with me, then looked away, chin raised, with a face determined to maintain disassociation. Would that I could read behind those eyes.

"That is very thoughtful, Graham." My mother turned to Anna. "Miss Lane?"

She cleared her throat. "I chose *surprising*," she said, but instead of facing me, she looked to my mother. "Your son has surprised me this visit. How he behaves, his motives and priorities. In truth, I believe my assumptions of his character these past few years were . . . wrong."

My chest constricted, skin prickling from the sensation. She . . . *what?*

Mother smiled gently. The only sound was the ticking of the clock on the mantel.

"And I wonder," Anna continued, when the room stayed quiet, "how a man juggles so many things without going mad."

A hint of a smile quirked her lips, but the thoughts behind her eyes kept her from showing it fully. She seemed almost remorseful. But, why? I could not bear it. I wanted the fire back in her eyes. I wanted to make her laugh.

"Perhaps *mad* would be a better adjective, hmm?" I studied her even countenance, desperately searching for a way in, to no avail.

"*Surprising* is a very fitting word for my Graham," Mother said, and Anna looked up. "And while I agree that Miss Lane is exceptionally *brave*, it's a rather obvious description, isn't it? So, on the basis of thoughtfulness, I shall award champion to Miss Lane. Well done, my dear."

Anna nodded once, then smoothed her skirts. "Thank you both for the diverting game," she said in a quiet voice. Then, carefully, she pushed her letters forward, and stood. "I think I shall retire. Prepare for an early start tomorrow."

I stood so abruptly in response, my chair nearly toppled over. "I look forward to it," I said, clasping my hands behind my back.

Fool. Utter, utter fool.

With a gentle smile, and a nod of her head, Anna left.

"*Surprising?*" Mother muttered as I fell back into my seat. "How exactly do you behave in London?"

I hadn't considered the differences in my behavior before. More serious, perhaps? "Focused."

But it was more than that, wasn't it? I'd been so focused I'd nearly missed her. The most incredible woman. I'd lost myself, and somehow, she'd found me.

I watched the empty doorway, straining my ear for the sounds of Anna's departure.

The line between us was blurring.

"I'll admit that young woman is not an easy one to sway," Mother said. "But neither does she seem as biting a beast as you've portrayed in the past. She can be rather warm and inquisitive."

I leaned back in my chair, balancing my elbow on the arm, my jaw resting on my fist. Things between Anna and me were complicated. "She's said awful things to me. Made me feel so foolish and small."

"And you've been perfectly honorable back?" Mother smirked.

I raised a brow. She could not understand. Dislike had grown into distrust over the years. We'd both been cruel. We'd both defended ourselves and our homes. Still, Mother waited, as though she dared me to respond to her probing. I hadn't acted honorably, but Anna had kindled her fair share of arguments.

"The woman irks me to no end."

"She did not seem to irk you tonight. Nor earlier this morning at the lending library."

I rubbed my hands on my thighs, shaking my head. "What is it, Mother? Would you like me to admit that she's tolerable? *She's tolerable.* There."

Mother tilted her head in amusement, eyes glinting with secrets. "I am simply trying to say that in regards to your future, you should consider the fact that marriage to the right person—"

"Oh, dash it all—" I raked both hands through my hair, then over my weary eyelids.

"—could greatly increase your happiness."

"Thank you, yes. That's quite enough."

"She's lovely, Graham. She matches your wit and your humor. She looks at you like an equal."

"She is *Anna Lane*, the daughter of my best and most lucrative investment partner. She is only just beginning to tolerate *me*, and . . . Why in the world am I even discussing this? Anna and I would never suit."

"Wealthy, lovely in all respects, and, by your own

admission, brave. Which of all those qualities, pray tell, would not suit?"

I stood, grunting in frustration, and paced toward the fire.

What was wrong with Anna? Everything. Nothing. For even when she'd hated and rebuked me, I'd still admired her. Still loved to affect her any way I could. Perhaps, somewhere deep within me, I'd wondered . . .

But I'd never admit to having such a weakness aloud. An affection, let alone an attraction to her? Impossible. Especially when she made it so easy to resent her. And resent her I had, however unfairly.

"Her father cares for you. He would not be opposed to the union. Indeed, the thought must already have crossed his mind."

I doubted it. He knew about my past, and the shame that followed me from my father. My mother often tried to forget it, and this conversation proved it. I softened my tone. "I already have three women in my life, Mother. I do not need another. Not yet."

"If you worry for our financial—"

"It's not just the finances."

"What, then?" Mother asked, exasperated.

Pursuing Anna would mean extreme awkwardness if I failed. Her father would be less likely to maintain a friendship with me, and I valued that man like family. Rejection in any form resulted in pain, but rejection from *her*? The first time she'd snubbed me had sent me spiraling for a fortnight. Besides, we were finally becoming friends, and I could not bear things going back to the way they were.

"There are too many risks."

Mother leaned forward, as though she'd been waiting for

me to say those very words. "There might be risks. You might not be certain of success. But you and I both have proved that the greatest risk can yield the greatest reward."

I shook my head. She made it all sound too good. "You speak of marriage like it is an investment."

She grinned. "Is it not?"

My brow arched.

She stood and reached up to stroke my cheek. "Courting might feel uncertain at first. Terrifying, even. But if your heart pulls you in one sure direction, I hope you'll take the risk, Graham."

Then she kissed my cheek and left.

Chapter Eighteen

GRAHAM

I woke to her laughter.

Anna had risen early, and for the first time in a long time, I'd slept late. I rolled over to face the door. Just outside my room, her and Ginny's laughter carried as they reached the top of the staircase.

"What're you supposed to *do* with all those?" Tabs whispered-yelled.

I levered myself up on an elbow, ears perked to their conversation.

"I've never seen such a lovely bouquet. He is *sooo* romantic!" Ginny squealed.

He, who? *What?*

"Hush." Anna laughed, and I froze as a door opened. I could hear my own heart beating in my ears, waiting for her to say something more.

More squealing.

"Does this mean you're in love, Anna?" Tabs sounded annoyed. "Will you marry him?"

I jumped out of bed, tugged on a shirt, stockings, and

yanked up my breeches, throwing a banyan on over my clothes. Who on earth were they talking about?

"Not quite," Anna replied, but I could not match her tone to an expression.

A door closed.

I tugged on my boots. Something had transpired, and as their brother, and as Anna's host, I ought to know! Daresay, I *needed* to know! But by the time I opened my door, they were already downstairs, and the doors—notably, Anna's—were all shut.

Dash it all.

Fully dressed, I found Roland and an otherwise empty house.

I rubbed a hand over my forehead.

"A headache, sir?"

"Not yet," I replied, though I could feel one brewing.

I headed toward my study. A freshly drawn note waited on my desk, from Mother, saying they'd left for a walk before breakfast.

I drew in a long breath as I raked a hand over my face. Anna's business was not my concern. *A slow, deliberate exhale.* Her *heart* was not my concern. *Another long, deep breath in.* As long as she was safe, my duty toward her was fulfilled. My priority was the Brighton investment.

Time to work.

A stack of letters waited under Mother's note. The topmost held a familiar scrawl—Mr. Lane. I drew out my spectacles, and a quick tear of the seal revealed a short missive:

> *E—*
>
> *I plan to leave Bath tomorrow and shall arrive*

the day following for Anna. I hope all is well. More
soon.

L

Excellent. We would have time to speak of the investment and arrange the purchasing of land. No need to respond
to that one. I set aside Mr. Lane's note and moved to the next.

I answered each missive in turn, then penned a letter to
Tom about a few minor changes to my accounts, then wrote
myself a few notes to keep my thoughts and priorities organized. Finished, I set my pen down and stretched my arms
above my head.

My door swung wide. "Graham, come for breakfast!"
Ginny said.

Finally.

"Who were you talking about this morning?" I asked,
rounding my desk and pacing toward her. "Outside my door
with Miss Lane and Tabs?"

Ginny's eyes grew round, and a slight pink colored her
cheeks. Then she wiggled her brows and turned on a heel.

"Ginny!" I called, impatient and annoyed, but she'd raced
to the dining room, casting me a sly grin over her shoulder.

I took long steps that felt too eager, bounding into the
room.

Anna had a plate she'd filled with fruit and eggs and toast,
sitting next to my mother.

Tabs watched her every move, kicking her legs back and
forth while she chewed on toast.

I picked out a slice of ham and filled my plate before
taking a seat opposite Anna. "Your father wrote. He should
arrive the day after next, as he'd hoped."

She took a bite of egg and nodded.

"How was your walk?" I asked.

"Lovely," Anna said brightly. Curiously brightly.

Ginny grinned.

I narrowed my gaze. "Not too cold this morning?"

Anna looked like she was trying desperately not to laugh, her eyes bouncing from Ginny to her plate and back. "The sun warmed us adequately."

"*More* than adequately," added Ginny.

I huffed out a breath, already exhausted by their mystery. "Dare I ask?" I looked to my mother.

She smiled as she forked a square of egg. "Miss Lane received a lovely bouquet this morning."

"From Mr. *Cross*!" Ginny declared happily, wiggling in her seat.

"Ah," was all I could think to say, despite the sudden boiling of my insides. Anthony Cross was every woman's dream with enough generational wealth to rival the Lanes. He must've seen Anna's name in the papers declaring her arrival. I focused on spearing a bite of plum cake.

Ginny sat back in her chair. "His card said he hopes to see us tonight at the assembly."

I sniffed, then on instinct, looked to Anna for her reaction. She watched me, waiting.

Ginny could not temper her extraordinary enthusiasm. And for what? She didn't even know the man! "He offered his carriage should Miss Lane wish to attend the assembly alone."

My spine stiffened, fork poised midair. That cod-brained, loose in the haft—

"What do you say, Graham?" Mother prompted.

What did I say? A resounding *no* to Cross. How dare he

direct his intentions to Anna and not write to *me*, her host. A cut, if ever I'd seen one. To me, and to my family. He wanted Anna without having to go through me, without the association of my family.

Anna took small bites, decidedly avoiding my gaze. Did she see it? Or did she simply not care?

I clenched my teeth and inhaled a solemn breath to relax my jaw. "Should we all wish to go, there would be no need for Miss Lane to travel alone."

Ginny scoffed. "Of course we want to go. All of us, together. Don't we, Anna?"

"Perhaps Miss Lane would like the chance to go alone?" Mother asked innocently.

Anna looked up and smiled. A frustrating smile I could not decipher. Did she fancy Mr. Cross?

She seemed to feel our stares and startled. "Oh. No. We can attend, all of us, together."

Did she wish to? I did not want to force her hand for my sake. "We don't have to," I said, as nonchalantly as I could. I even shrugged a shoulder for the full effect. "If you'd rather take Cross's offer."

Mother cleared her throat, and I could've sworn she hid her own grin.

"We could dress together!" Ginny added generously. She had not touched her food as though her appetite depended on Anna's answer.

"I hate him," Tabs said from her end of the table. "Mr. Cross."

"Tabitha," Mother scolded.

Every muscle in my jaw worked against a smile. *Me too, Tabs.*

Anna speared a bite of fruit. "Miss Ryan would be happy to see you, I am sure, Mr. Everett. She wanted you to attend, remember?"

I raised a brow at her, our stares holding as we both took our respective bites. Why should I care about Miss Ryan? Why should *she*? "I shall have to ask her to dance."

Mother's foot stepped lightly on mine under the table. "What fun!" she said.

But, after a few bites, when I looked up, Anna was frowning.

Chapter Nineteen

ANNA

"Our shades are so complementary," I said to Ginny, who twirled in her apricot-colored gown just outside my door. Mine was blue with white embroidery.

"This one makes me feel like a queen," Ginny sighed, watching her skirt fly out. How she'd changed these past few days. No longer the defensive, huffy thing from our first acquaintance. She'd softened, sharing secrets instead of keeping them.

Mariah adjusted my shawl, a soft, sheer gold that matched the flowers on the hem of my dress. "A rose for your hair?" she asked, motioning to the bouquet Mr. Cross had sent. He'd been one of the few gentlemen Papa had approved at the beginning of the Season. He'd escorted me to the opera once early on, and out for a ride in his gig. It had been some time ago, but I could not for my life think of why I'd ultimately chosen *Mr. Lennox* over him.

"No. Thank you, Mariah." Though I bent over for a last sweet inhale of the blossoms.

Ginny and I had spent the day preparing. We cleared our faces of any imperfections and moisturized thrice over, during which I'd given her tips on how to engage when conversation stalled. Then, since we were nearly the same size, we'd tried on every dress in my armoire.

"Are you certain you do not want to wear the pearls?" I called to her. We'd pilfered through my jewelry as well.

"Yes, but thank you. I'd rather like my neck plain. Mama said its long and lovely and that men take notice of such things."

I tried not to laugh at her seriousness. "Oh, indeed."

I dabbed perfume on my neck, chest, and wrists, and just as I set down the vial, the door to Graham's room opened.

"So handsome!" Ginny crooned, and I looked up.

I'd seen Graham dressed well before. But this time, instead of blinking away, my gaze washed over his slicked-back hair, his smooth, muscled jaw, then lingered over his broad shoulders in a finely cut coat. Graham tugged at his sleeves, straightening them, and I imagined those arms, firm and strong, inviting me in, pulling me close enough to where I could breathe in the spice of his shave.

I touched my hair. Heavens, how much perfume had I inhaled?

Regardless, I could not deny the swift uptick of my pulse. Something within me fancied Graham Everett. I chewed on my lower lip. Was that so terrible?

He smiled at his sister while she spun a final time, his entire countenance brightening. Then his gaze met mine.

His smile faded; the light in his eyes softened.

"Handsome, indeed," I said, stepping forward. I offered him a smile and a little curtsey, like we were already in a ballroom and not the cramped hall of his second floor.

He grinned and bowed in return. His eyes grazed over my hair, my face, my gown. "Miss Lane. You are . . ."

"Isn't she lovely?" Ginny grabbed my arm, hugging it to her side, beaming up at me.

Her features were so similar to Graham's, so happy and excited. I wanted good things for her. I wanted her to dance with her favorite gentleman and to be admired all night long. I wanted her to shine.

"Extraordinary," Graham said, and I blushed, realizing he was still watching me. He cleared his throat, a faraway look on his face. "Shall we?"

"Mama is already downstairs," Ginny said, releasing me and running ahead.

Graham waited at the top of the stairs for me. He hesitated, then offered me his arm. "I am aware that you can safely descend the stairs alone, but—"

I laced my arm through his. "Thank you, Graham."

He smiled to himself, carefully taking each step as he led me down to his waiting mother and sisters.

Tabs's cheeks were still puffy from the fit she'd thrown at being left behind, but her eyes were alight with the excitement of it all.

We kissed her goodbye, promising to tell her all in the morning, then settled in the carriage for the short drive to the assembly hall in the center of Brighton.

The setting sun cast a shadowy glow on the pathway leading up to the Assembly Rooms. It was a tall building made of light-colored stone and ensconced with lamplight. A servant awaited us at the door, and we were greeted by a boisterous sound and music carrying from inside.

"Mr. Everett!" An older man strode over.

"Mr. Ryan," Mrs. Everett whispered to me. "And his wife."

The woman beside him, whose brown hair had started to gray, held out her hand to Graham before waving over—

Miss Ryan.

Introductions were made, and thankfully excuses offered for Mr. Lennox, who'd taken off on some errand out of town. Good riddance.

I watched Graham, how he bowed to the Ryans, smiling broadly and sincerely. But, despite their clear familiarity, my host never left my side. He took his responsibility seriously. Honorable in every way. I felt immense pride toward Graham and for all he'd done for his family. He could have abandoned them too. He could have declared the burden too heavy.

Look at them now.

"Miss Lane!" a man called from behind us. Mr. Cross. My heart stuttered a beat—from nerves or anticipation? I nodded my appreciation to the Ryans before I turned.

"Good evening, Mr. Cross," I said, and heavens, the man had made an effort. He smelled musky and sweet, his wavy hair sleek and shiny, and he wore an olive coat that complemented the fair color of his skin.

His brows lifted in appreciation as his eyes traveled every inch of me. "You are a vision."

I swallowed. This was what I'd wanted, wasn't it? A man who needed nothing from my father. Who made my heart stir with the possibility of more. Had I any reason to deny Mr. Cross my sincere attention? At present, no one else had sent me flowers or declared their intentions or affections.

His words were kind, his attention so flattering. Yet . . .

I glanced to Graham, who stood alone with Miss Ryan. Her small hand reached out, touching his forearm, and I felt fire fume in my lungs. Consuming me with . . . anger? Well, that would be silly. Whatever it was, though, it felt right. Deserved. I did not like her, not at all.

"I am so pleased you could come," Mr. Cross said, drawing my attention back to him.

"As am I. Thank you for the beautiful bouquet you sent. The roses are lovely."

"I am glad." He smiled, pleased. There was quiet between us for a beat. A few flickering gazes. Strange, not knowing what to say.

"What brings you to Brighton?" I asked, then flinched. Would he perceive the question as too intimate?

"Visiting my younger brother, actually," he answered quickly. Like he aimed to please me. But that wasn't necessarily a terrible thing. Of course a man would want to please the lady he wished to spend time with. I should let him try. "He and his wife recently welcomed their first son, and I did not want to miss an opportunity to see him. It's been years."

"Oh?" I heard the trill of Miss Ryan's laughter, and my muscles seized. I fought the desire to move far away. And to take Graham with me.

"He's a vicar—well respected. We are quite proud. And the baby is so still and quiet, often sleeping."

"As newborns are," I said, and he grinned. *Focus on him, Anna. Full attention.* "Congratulations," I added. I tried to think of something more to say, another question perhaps, or a compliment. But some corner of my mind warred for control of my eyes, flicking them every so often toward Graham.

What did I care if he relished in Miss Ryan's attentions? She was wealthy, obviously, and more than interested in him. He'd do well with a wife like her, already established in Society, pleasant . . . *scratch that last.*

"Are you hungry?" Mr. Cross smiled at me, offering his arm. "There are refreshments in the room across the way."

I nodded, determined to be amiable, going through potential topics of discussion in my mind. The Season, sea-bathing, his hobbies, if he liked goat cheese . . .

Indeed, as we walked together to the refreshment table, and as he poured me a glass of lemonade, I learned that Mr. Cross was not a Shakespearean but a hunting man. Hunting foxes and elk, to be specific, and his one great pride was his hunting dogs, the four of which he missed greatly when away.

I listened intently, reprimanding my gaze when it wandered down the line to Graham, who kept Miss Ryan in raptures with stories told with bright eyes and moving hands.

Mr. Cross filled a plate with cheese and bread, fruit, and a little cheesecake, all the while asking after my time in Brighton, politely nodding as I described my time with the Everetts. In between bites, I told him about my love for the sea, my hopes for traveling more in the future. He spoke of his own adventures and his family, but all too soon, conversation slowed. No questions about my hobbies or reading. No probing for personal details. And, unfortunately, I remembered why I'd forgotten our brief time together.

No, this would not do. I'd rather sit alone at dinner than have to work so hard for conversation. Besides, I did not care much for hunting and hounds. As handsome as the man was, the interest I felt stalled there, and I wanted more. I wanted easy. Perhaps finding a husband would take more effort on my part, but if I'd learned one thing from my pursuits, it should absolutely feel easy.

I could tell him about my favorite flowers or recite my favorite lines from *Romeo and Juliet*. I could ask if he enjoyed playing cards or the alphabet game.

Mr. Cross straightened, hands on his thighs, then with a tilt of his head and a small smile, he said, "Miss Lane, might I have the cotillion?"

"I'd like that," I said, and I let him lead me toward the music.

Neither of us said much as we found our place in the line. He offered a kind smile and a nod to those gathering around us. Graham stood down the line with Miss Ryan as his companion, but before I could react, the music started, and Mr. Cross took my hands.

Around and around we danced, and I forgot everything but the steps. Mr. Cross moved effortlessly, his motions graceful and practiced, thoughtful and sure. Until the dance separated us, and our eyes met only with every few spins.

Halfway through, I caught sight of Graham moving closer up the line. He danced with focus, giving attention to each partner he joined. I thought I saw him miss a step, and I laughed to myself as he recovered.

Closer, closer, and my belly knotted with anticipation to meet with him; each step, each turn brought us closer. But as nervous as I felt to dance with him, there was something else that stirred my heart. A feeling of being reunited with an old friend whose face you'd forgotten you'd memorized. The snug fit of a perfectly tailored coat. Climbing into bed with fresh sheets and a bed warmer at your feet after dancing all night.

Moments passed, then, finally, Graham stood adjacent to me. I hardly registered his partner at my side.

Graham's brown eyes, flecked with green and gold, were

so familiar they took my breath away. And I realized as he grasped my hands—it felt so obvious, I almost wanted to cry—that I hadn't needed to pretend with Graham since that day on the beach with Tabs. Even when Mr. Lennox had surprised me and those women had spoken so harshly, he'd let me fall apart. He'd listened and he'd stayed by my side until I'd settled. He asked after me without judgment. Then he'd distracted me in exactly the way I needed. I'd never felt more myself, more understood and cared for, with anyone.

"Have we ever danced together?" he breathed.

I turned, suddenly shy to meet him again in the middle. "I cannot remember if we have. Though," I turned again, my heart stuttering wildly, "this is hardly dancing *together*, Mr. Everett, as you did not ask me." Formality, of course, in mixed company.

"Shall we remedy that with the next set?" Graham asked.

I bit my lip to keep from grinning. A strange sensation paired with my already breathless lungs and heated my neck and into my cheeks.

He came back round. "I hear the next is Wilson's waltz." He winked, and we laughed. The same dance I'd taught Tabs in the drawing room.

"A waltz, then," I agreed before grabbing the hands of my next waiting partner.

I danced down the line, around Ginny and Mr. Anderson, with Mr. Ryan, and over again, until the music ended. The second song in the set went by in a blur and a hundred stammering heartbeats. I thanked Mr. Cross and curtseyed.

I did not have to look for Graham. He was already there, beside me, hand outstretched and waiting.

Chapter Twenty

GRAHAM

Finally. I'd about gone mad watching Anna in conversation with Cross. I'd tried with painful determination to find an interesting spot around the room while she'd danced with him. To train my ear to whatever Miss Ryan was on about. But all evening I'd wanted only Anna. Anna's attention, Anna's smile, Anna's hand in mine.

Lud, that dress. Her neck, and the swoop of her collarbone. My mouth went dry merely at the sight of her, and I pinched the back of my hand hard to refocus.

"The waltz, Miss Lane?" I reached out my hand.

She looked up with an instant grin that sent teeming waves of astonishment all through me. Her delicate, silk-gloved hand fit perfectly in mine.

"Have you danced the waltz in public before?" she asked with the faintest blush blooming upon her cheeks.

Something in me came alive at the sight; I wanted her to blush like that every time she looked at me.

I took a few unhurried steps backward, my thoughts hardly coherent as I led her away from the crush, and she followed, eyes still laughing into mine.

"Yes," I answered, lowering my chin, which only served to ignite her humor further. "We've been in the same ballrooms together on more than one occasion."

There were more than a dozen couples spread out, waiting, and I positioned us in the far corner. Private, intimate. Perhaps people would talk, and for once, some part of me hoped they would. To have my name linked with Anna's even once.

"I suppose I did not pay close enough attention," she said.

We'd stilled as the musicians shifted their papers. Anna held fast to my hand, and I studied the dusting of freckles over her small, perfectly rounded nose. "You were always surrounded by suitors and friends."

She tilted her head, a string of ringlets bouncing along the frame of her smooth cheek. I wanted to touch one, spiral it around my finger. Bring it to my lips.

"There are a few girls I would consider my friends, though not close enough to tell them *everything*, you understand," Anna said. She curled her fingers into mine, and my stomach clenched. "And as far as gentlemen . . . At present, you are the only man I'd consider a true friend."

Me? I was in a trance, enveloped by scents of jasmine and cherry blossoms, warm with wine and the feel of Anna's fingers in mine. She was looking at me intently, searching my face with an increasingly furrowed brow.

"You're my . . . friend, Graham," she said again, like pieces in a puzzle were falling into place. "You know everything about me."

"Well, not . . . *ev-everything*," I stammered out. There were decidedly a few things at present I would like to know that required more action than words, but perhaps not in the middle of a ballroom.

"I cannot recall the face of the person I last danced the waltz with," she said, "but I can easily remember how you used to fluff your hair before you knocked on our door."

I sobered instantly. Drew back. "You watched me?"

She squinted her eyes. "I may not have appreciated your many untimely visits to my home, Graham, but there are certainly aspects about you I do appreciate."

Oh? Her lips twitched, and so did mine, and we laughed so loudly, couples around us turned their heads. My pulse seemed to find a new beat, a waltz of its own, and I did not want this night to end.

"Perhaps I should step on your foot to make our waltz more memorable than your last," I teased.

She covered her mouth to stifle her laugh. "Don't you dare."

A violin played a few notes to signal the dance, but I was frozen. Captivated. Enraptured to have Anna Lane's full attention when every other man in the room would die for it.

Anna smiled softly as she guided my hand to her side, her eyes never leaving mine.

I felt the curve of her waist, letting my thumb drag against the silk pleats of her dress as she clasped my other hand and raised the pairing above our heads.

She smiled up at me. "You look terrified, Graham."

I swallowed hard. Nothing but bare truth on my lips. "You look beautiful, Anna."

Her brows raised in surprise. *Happy* surprise, that made me feel like I was suddenly ten feet tall.

Soft notes filled the air as the violinist drew his bow along the strings. I knew this music; I'd danced it several times before, practicing it with my mother and Ginny in the drawing room. But with Anna, each step we took seemed effortless, like we were floating in air. Her hand pressed gently on my back, and I felt the heat of it keenly like fire traveling up and down my spine. Our linked hands brought us close, so close I understood why many debated the morality of this dance. I could feel her breath, taste it in the air between us.

We watched each other for longer than either of us had allowed before. Then the music quickened, and our steps moved faster. My hands dropped to her sides, and Anna held my shoulders as we spun, faster and faster, focused only on each other. So fast, I feared I'd drop her or she'd slip out of my arms, so I tightened my hold on her waist just as Anna's foot knocked into mine, and she tripped.

She fell into my chest. I pulled her upright. "Dash it all. Forgive me, Anna, for my misstep."

Another couple had also failed to keep the pace and were moving away from the dancers.

But Anna only swayed as she laughed breathlessly. "Good heavens. I think he's playing too fast," she said, completely unconcerned that anyone had seen her falter. "Shall we finish?"

"Are you certain? I could get you a glass of lemonade . . ."

Her gaze trailed over my face. "I'd rather dance with you, actually. If you don't mind."

My heart fluttered against my chest like a caged bird, and I did not hesitate. I took her hands in mine, and she grinned.

The dancers were back in their original positions, the music slowing, and I raised our hands above our heads, one hand at her waist, her hand on my shoulder. We started slow. Her skirts brushed against my knees as we spun, entrancing my every thought. I would never forget this waltz or how it felt to move in tandem with her. To gaze, uninhibited, into her honey-brown eyes, so clear and beautiful I could fall right into them.

We spun round, and I couldn't think of anything worth saying that would elevate this moment in my memory. I could not take my eyes off her as our feet slowed with the music. Her chest rose and fell with breaths that equaled mine in measure, and as the last notes of the waltz echoed in the hall, she watched me like I was the only other person in the room.

"Thank you," she said on a breath. Her grip loosened on my shoulder, but she did not quite let go of me.

"The pleasure is entirely mine, I assure you." I released her waist, then turned her hand in mine, mindlessly thumbing her palm.

Anna's lips parted, and then—

A cough. And a man waiting nearby.

A gent Anna recognized from London asked her for the next set, and after ensuring she was comfortable, I trailed off, not quite walking a straight line.

Lud, she was unlike any other woman. A category all her own.

As her host, I'd stay nearby, watching, keeping guard. I noted Mr. Anderson, who was standing a little too close to Ginny on the other side of the room.

"Graham?" Mother's hand touched my arm. "May I introduce Mrs. Hughes and her daughter Miss Harriet Hughes. They are staying in Brighton for the month."

A slender woman with a pretty face and three, large blue feathers in her light hair curtseyed with a practiced smile.

I bowed. "Pleased to make your acquaintance, Miss Hughes. From where do you hail?"

"Hampshire. A far cry from a place as magical as Brighton." Again, she smiled. Her voice was soft and breathy.

I nodded. All too well, I knew the motions. I held out my hand. "Would you care to dance?"

My mother grinned. Mrs. Hughes practically purred like a cat spotting a dish of cream.

"I'd love to," Miss Hughes said.

And so the night went. Dance after dance. Anna being offered another drink from Cross, then taking the hand of a man he'd introduced her to. I'd found Ginny just outside the door with a group watching a man stuff a handful of olives into his mouth. I promptly extricated her from the scene.

Until finally, at just after two in the morning, we all moaned with relief as the carriage creaked to a stop outside Highcliffe House.

I'd never felt happier to be home, safe and away from prying eyes and unknown intentions. This was why mothers were in charge of marrying off their daughters. Were it up to me, the women in my household would remain young and unattached forever.

"Perhaps next time Mr. Anderson will kiss my hand," Ginny sighed, leaning into Anna's side as they walked into the house.

"There will be no kissing of hands," I muttered.

At that, they laughed.

Chapter Twenty-One

ANNA

A piercing wail jolted me awake.

Slowly, I found my bearings, tangled as I was in my covers with feet still half numb from dancing. I fumbled to light the candle on my bedside table. Another wail sounded, quieter this time, but loud. It sounded like a nightmare. Tabs?

A door opened from down the hall, followed by quiet whisperings, then another door closed.

"I'm frightened," called her little voice. "*Please*, help me!"

Without thought, I ripped off my covers, my bare feet aching and sore, and hurried to don my dressing gown. With candle in hand, I swung open my door. "Tabs?" I called, my foggy mind still trying to fully wake up. Her room was two down from mine. I took a few steps through the dimly lit space in front of me.

"Anna?"

Tabs was sitting up in her bed, a candle burning beside her on the little table by her bed. Her hair was a mess, like she'd tossed and turned all night while we were away, and her little pout and tear-stained cheeks nearly tore my heart to shreds. I stepped through her doorway, stopping suddenly when I noticed a figure kneeling by her bedside.

Graham. In a banyan and breeches and bare feet.

"Forgive me," I said, stepping back. I did not wish to intrude where I had no right to be. "I thought—"

"Don't go," Tabs whimpered. "Please, Anna."

"It's the middle of the night, Tabs." Graham's voice was hoarse from sleep, and my heart leaped forward, wanting to be near him. His hair was still ruffled, cheeks creased and eyes puffy.

Beautiful, he'd called me during our waltz. And he'd said it with such conviction. Not to please, but to admire. My skin prickled, remembering his hand at my waist. Such tenderness in his eyes like I'd never seen from a man before. Those same eyes that had arrogantly teased and frustrated me over and over again were now warm and full of care.

"He came for me again." Tabs sniffed. "The dark monster of the sea."

"There is no dark monster of the sea," Graham said as he rubbed her leg. "You've nothing to fear."

Tabs turned my way, and the fear on her face beckoned me closer. "He has horrible claws and scales for skin. He's as tall as a house, Anna. I cannot outrun him." She choked on the last word.

I deposited my candle near Graham's and sat beside her on her bed, just in time to catch her little body as she crumbled into a fresh sob. Graham shifted near my feet, and my eyes caught on the thin, loose nightshirt beneath his open banyan, the line of his neck, and each shadow along his bare chest, which rose and fell with one—two—breaths.

I cleared my throat before saying into Tabs's hair, "If such a thing as a sea monster existed, your brother would take care of him, I am sure. There is no need to fear."

"Graham?" Tabs cried. "He cannot even hold a sword properly."

"I beg your pardon?" Graham's tired voice came out affronted. His brows knit together at the assumption of his weakness against Tabs's imaginary foe. "I could fight off any sea monster ten times the size of Highcliffe House."

"*Ten* times?" I blurted in disbelief, and Graham's eyes flicked up to mine. I clapped my hand to my mouth to cover the humor, but he'd seen it. His face split into a grin.

"A hundred times," he exaggerated. "Indeed, the next time the dark monster of the sea comes, send him straight to my room. Five minutes against my sword should send him diving back into the depths."

Tabs's lips twitched as she wiped tears from her cheeks. "His eyes are so dark, and his teeth are so scary," she whined. "Once you see him, I know you'll be too afraid."

"Graham Everett?" I countered. "He has the fiercest glare on this side of the sea. Show her, Graham."

"Show her?"

"Your fierce glare," I enunciated, nodding my head to Tabs.

"Right. Of course," he said, straightening. He ruffled his already fluffy hair—a nervous habit, perhaps? Then he formed his fists into claws, scrunched up his face, and bared his teeth. He growled, low and menacing.

A thrill shot up my spine, and Tabs shrunk into my side. She smelled like strawberries and cream, her favorite after-dinner dessert. "Graham!" she laughed. "I do not like you doing that."

"See?" I squeezed her tight, grinning at Graham over her head. "Ferocious."

Tabs yawned and gave me more of her weight. I rubbed her arm, while Graham reached up and tucked a lock of hair behind her ear.

"Your brother is right," I said. "It is very late, and you will be tired tomorrow if you do not sleep tonight."

"I want to come sleep in your bed," Tabs whined to Graham, reaching out for his arms. Her nightdress was trimmed with ruffles and lace. Clearly, the baby of the family.

Graham reached forward to wipe her wet cheeks dry with his sleeve, his arm brushing mine. I felt sparks of warmth all through me. "You are brave enough to sleep in your own bed."

"Pleeease, Graham. Only one night more. I swear it."

"She's had quite the day," I reminded him. Urged, more like. And for once, we felt like partners. A united front.

"Very well." He sighed, and Tabs threw her arms around his neck. His shoulders relaxed under her weight, and together, we stood.

Tabs's already tiny room seemed to shrink, especially with the three of us crowded between her bed and the doorway. I retrieved my candle and started to turn but could not fit around Graham holding Tabs.

"Ah, sorry," he muttered, trying to retreat but bumping into a chair behind him, stumbling sideways.

I reached out to steady him as Tabs slid down from his hold to land on her feet.

She led out of the door first, stumbling down the hall toward her brother's room, and I handed Graham her candle.

Slowly, he sidestepped out the door, then turned and

leaned against the doorframe, boxing me inside. Our two candles flickered between us, casting him in gold and shadow, and the depths of his eyes searched mine. "Thank you," he said, lingering. "For coming. She settled much faster than usual."

"All she needed was a less ferocious face," I teased.

Surprise and another sleepy grin brightened his features. "Well, then, lucky for us, your face is the opposite of ferocious."

"Oh?" I smirked, then poked his chest.

I poked his chest. My bare finger. On his bare, rather firm, chest.

He raised his arm against the doorframe and leaned in, as though my mortification pulled him to me. His shirt fell open with another breath, revealing lines of definition and strength, and my gaze clung to the spot I'd touched like a fly to honey. His voice came out husky as he said, "Thank you for tonight, and for earlier this evening. Yesterday evening as well."

"Hmm?" My eyes found his lips. Graham Everett's full, inviting lips.

He rubbed his jaw, and I slowly dragged my gaze up to meet his. They were uncertain, hesitant, but I could swear they bore a similar wanting.

"I enjoyed your company," he said. "Dancing. Playing together instead of tempting each other's wrath."

Sleep beguiled me, my fuzzy mind blurring the lines of propriety. I pulled my own dressing gown tight, crossing my arms for some semblance of modesty, then lazily leaned toward him. My shoulder hit the inner doorframe. We were much, much too close. So close I heard the hitch in his breath.

"That sounds dangerously like kindness, Graham," I whispered on a breath.

He shrugged, giving me a half grin. Then his gaze dropped to *my* lips. "That's how I meant it, Anna."

I smiled, laughing softly under my breath. I felt like a girl in a dream, all fluttery and floating, like a queen in her night-dress.

"I want to take you to the Marine Pavilion tomorrow. For that second look." Graham swallowed hard. "In the morning, perhaps?"

"I daresay everyone will want to sleep well into the afternoon."

He lifted his other shoulder, unperturbed. "Just us, then."

My heart danced wildly in my chest, sending sparks throughout my stomach. How simply he'd said it. Just us.

I bit my lip, and his eyes watched the motion. I nodded once.

"Hurry, Graham," Tabs whisper-shouted from down the hall. "Anna, won't you come and tuck us in?"

Graham's lips quirked, his eyes laughing into mine as he straightened. "Yes, won't you, Anna?"

I dropped my jaw dramatically. "You scoundrel," I seethed, laughing as I pushed him out of my way. "Good night, my darling," I said to Tabs as I stepped toward my room.

Graham lingered, walking backward a few steps as if in a trance. Then he turned, and, like a dream, vanished into the night.

Chapter Twenty-Two

GRAHAM

I want her.

As a friend, a confidant, a wife. I wanted to dine with her, dance with her.

I wanted to spend my nights with her in my drawing room, my study, in my bed.

I wanted all of her.

And I was finally unafraid to admit it.

I somehow managed to fall asleep with Tabs burrowed into my back, pushing me to the edge of my mattress, and I awoke with greater purpose than ever before.

I wanted to court Anna Lane.

An impossible feat, really, but I'd tackled the impossible before. And after our dance, after last night, I knew things between us had shifted. I could have sworn last night, she'd leaned in almost like she'd wanted *me*.

And that changed everything.

Anna wanted her relationships separate from her father's wealth and connections. I could do that. If she'd take me as I was, knowing how we lived and what we lacked, I'd abandon the whole Brighton investment proposal. I could find another way to create a future, keep our earnings on an upward climb. One that did not involve her father's interference.

We were secure. We had enough to live on, though the living I could provide would be nothing compared to Anna's father's. Perhaps I'd gone mad, but Anna hadn't seemed to mind our lacking this past week. Slowly, carefully, over time I could create a more solid future. Things would only grow brighter from here.

Indeed, I did not need the investment. Not like I needed Anna.

Anna was air to my lungs. Being with her was like walking along the beach just as the sun crested the earth. Captivating, enlivening, and so unbelievably beautiful.

Together, if I could convince her, we'd find a comfortable balance. I'd sacrifice whatever she asked. If she'd take me.

For the first time in my life, I held the world in my hands.

I had nothing, yet everything, all at once.

Courting Anna would be a risk. The odds were, at best, sixty percent in my favor. But I wanted this life. I wanted her.

And when I wanted something, I'd do almost anything to get it.

Chapter Twenty-Three

ANNA

"Good morning, Miss Lane."

Finally.

"Out here, Mariah," I called over my shoulder. I'd been waiting for her since my eyes opened. Mariah's presence meant I could ready myself for Graham's attention. And I wanted Graham's attention.

I'd awoken late, but the house still slept, so I'd dragged a cushioned chair—patterned with violet flowers and green vines—and a little writing table from my room onto the balcony. After freshening up, I'd spent my morning hours facing the sea, writing in my notebook and waiting as the crisp morning air dried each page.

Mariah brought out a tea tray with fruit, a slice of ham, cheese, and bread, which, after moving my notebook and ink jar, she laid upon my writing table. Then she scurried around my room as I chose a slice of cheese.

This morning felt different. New. For the first time in a long time, I sat and simply watched rays of sunshine beaming through leaves on the trees. A warm, cozy spot, and several deep breaths rejuvenated me, and I felt so content to simply be.

Despite my father abandoning me, despite my empty home, despite all the answers I lacked, for the first time in a very long time, I had not a worry nor care in the world.

"The brown dress today?" Mariah called from half inside the armoire.

"Something with color," I shot over my shoulder. I curled my legs together in my chair, then lifted my teacup to warm my hands. It would do no good to pine for Graham, but out of dozens of suitors, I hadn't felt this eager for anyone.

Not that Graham counted as a suitor. He wasn't *courting* me. But the admiration in his eyes last evening, the way his cheeks creased when he smiled so fully at our exchanges . . . it was *different*.

We were different.

But was his attention genuine? Could I trust Graham, despite his clear interest in investing with Papa?

I wouldn't let his flattery sway my opinion on the Brighton investment. He could grin and flirt and play his best hand, and I might relish in his attempts, but I would hold fast to my own opinions.

I'd agreed to this arrangement, and so I had a decision to make. Tomorrow, my father would return. If I agreed that Brighton was worth investing in, would Graham shift all his attention to Papa and abandon me?

Just us, he'd said.

"Gold embroidered dress over the light-green petticoat?"

I turned around. Mariah held up a thin muslin that practically shimmered over the colored petticoat. "Perfect."

After I sated my appetite, Mariah helped me dress, fixed

my hair in curls atop my head, and dabbed the lightest touch of color to my lips and cheeks.

I felt confident, but also a flicker of nerves and a restlessness I could not vanquish. Would he like this dress? My perfume?

Rising above it all, there flamed a hope for something more. Something real and lasting.

"He's waiting in the drawing room for you, Miss Lane," Mariah said as she closed the bedroom door behind us.

I took the stairs with grace, noting the oddity of being awake in a house that was still fast asleep. No sounds of Ginny's harp or Tabs's stomping foot and frustrated groaning.

I found Graham on the sofa, one arm loosely stretched along the back, his other hand grasping the armrest. His ankles crossed, legs hanging open comfortably as he sat in thought and waited for me. He'd brushed back his hair and wore a pressed brown jacket with tan breeches.

I'd stopped in the doorway. "Good morning."

He startled, straightening. "There you are." He rubbed his face with a hand, then smiled. "You look lovely."

My heart flew into my throat. "Thank you," I said, lifting a hand to brace myself against the doorframe.

We watched each other for a moment, then he stood, and stretched. "Are we ready?"

I nodded. "No chaperone?"

He took a few steps closer to me, clasping his hands behind his back. "If you're agreeable. I am your host until your father returns, so a chaperone is not necessary. But if you are unsure, we could bring your maid . . ."

"No, no. I am comfortable."

He smiled, then motioned for me to lead the way.

The carriage awaited us, steps set at the ready for me to climb. He gave me his hand, and I squeezed his fingers as I ascended. He followed, sitting opposite me.

A moment passed. Me, situating my skirts, while he tried out several different positions for his hands.

"The weather is fine," he said at last, and I readily agreed.

"Hardly a cloud in the sky," I added.

"Did you sleep well? . . . After." He squinted one eye, and I grinned at the silly look on his face.

"I did," I said. "And you?"

"Well, I awoke with Tabitha's arm choking my neck and the rest of her splayed out like a starfish in my bed, but there were no more visits from the dark monster of the sea, so . . ." He shrugged.

"Thank heavens for that." I leaned back and crossed my arms as the carriage swayed to and fro.

"You did not break your fast this morning."

It was a statement, but I still heard the question beneath the words. "Mariah brought me a tray. I had some writing to do this morning." I looked up at him through my lashes. Innocent, but provoking him nonetheless.

He squinted. "What sort of writing?"

I shrugged. "Just a few pages in my notebook."

"Ah." He looked out his window, his lips quirked in a near smile.

"What?"

He shook his head. "Nothing."

I raised a curious brow. "*What*, Graham?"

His eyes flicked to mine, testing. "I would not ask about that notebook if you begged me. Not if you offered me a hundred pounds or the body of the dark monster of the sea."

I looked heavenward, and he laughed. "No business, Anna. Not today."

Did he think me daft? "Today is entirely about business. We have but one day left to—"

He cut in. "On the contrary. Today is about promenading and falling in love—"

I flushed, hand to my chest. "I beg your pardon?"

"—with Brighton."

I touched my cheeks, willing them to cool. "With Brighton, yes. Which is *not at all* business-related," I said with deep sarcasm.

He peeked out his window as the carriage started to slow. "I can ask my driver to get us closer to the Pavilion. Or if you don't mind a walk . . ."

"I don't mind," I said, and he drew back, studying me as though I were a new creature. I blushed under his scrutiny.

"Is she in there?" Graham asked. "The Anna who tried to make me ride in the saddle all the way down the Brighton Road from London?"

"Oh, she's still in here," I teased, lifting my chin. "Always lurking. *Waiting.*"

He visibly shuddered, and I laughed.

The carriage door opened, and he hopped out to receive me. Strange, to be out alone with him. But Brighton stayed busy. People walked everywhere in all directions, some with purpose, some meandering at a snail's pace. And it seemed, as I stepped down from the carriage, as though we'd been dropped precisely in the middle of the chaos.

"Mr. Everett," an older man called, tipping his hat. The younger woman on his arm watched Graham with interest, her gaze only briefly flicking to meet mine.

Graham tipped his hat back. "Mr. Lewis."

"You're quite popular here," I muttered as the driver closed the carriage door behind me.

Graham faced me and smirked. "Oh? Thank you for the compliment."

I snorted, narrowing my gaze at him. "More like a commentary on your lack of—"

"Mmm," Graham said, and I stopped short. He tugged at the ribbons hanging from my hat, and I drew in a breath of surprise as the motion pulled me a step toward him. His eyes were soft, lips lifted into a half smile. "Save that hit for later, would you?" he whispered. "Only the good today, Miss Lane."

My eyes traced the gentle slopes of his brows, the curve of his upper lip, and his smooth skin warmed by the sun. "Only the good," I found myself promising.

Miss Lane, he'd said as though he'd decided today was a fresh start, and he'd have to earn that familiarity.

"Will you take my arm?" he asked, that serious gaze still set upon mine.

I nodded, reaching out for his left elbow, which he tucked at an angle to receive me. Our steps crunched atop rolled gravel as he led me along the Steine. Shops burst to the brim with tourists. Salivating scents wafted out of certain doors; strong perfumes out of others. Ahead, the Marine Pavilion waited, stalwart and looming, a long rectangle across the level field.

As we walked, a group of boys chased a large, rolling wooden hoop across the lawn, calling to each other, and sometimes daring to hop through the opening. Fishermen's nets, some still dripping with seawater, were strewn long over low fences.

Brighton was a town that lived and breathed.

"Will you live here forever?" I asked, taking in every sight, every sound, every scent.

Graham tilted his head in thought. "I imagine I'll keep a house. Admittedly, I have not thought much on forever."

"Why not? You've always been a man with his life ordered and set."

"In some respects, I suppose I am. My life since university has been so focused. On money, on my family and our basic needs. I have not thought much beyond merely living day-to-day in years."

"How dreary." I squeezed his arm.

"Thus is my life, Miss Lane. Thus is my life."

A throng of ladies walked toward us, hiding whispers and giggles behind their gloved hands.

I glanced heavenward. "Tabs says *the ladies* are always following you around," I said pointedly.

He became suddenly less dreary, smiling as they passed. "I've been cursed with good looks and a mysterious past," he said to me.

I leaned into him and laughed.

We moved west down the Steine toward the Pavilion's expansive front lawn, where various guards stood at attention as we approached. Blue shutters framed the windows on either side of the Pavilion's dome-roofed centerpiece, rounded with pillars at the entrance. Another, newer, building stood just beside it.

"Now that you've found such success, perhaps there are many people who would not mind your focus shifting," I mused. "Less of the day-to-day toward more of . . . forever."

"Oh?" Graham stared straight ahead, his features betraying nothing. He led me down a footpath lined with flowers, and we rounded a tall hedgerow. "People such as . . . ?"

"Look at that." I breathed in the sight as our steps hit the grassy lawn and the scene changed. Bushes of brightly colored flowers marched along dirt footpaths leading around the house. Where Brighton itself fell into disarray, the Pavilion's lawns were primly manicured. Trees stood in stately rows, and I wanted to linger under their shade and rest.

I spotted some unusual orange flowers to our right, and I tugged Graham along the footpath. He slowed our pace, and though I did not want to release his arm, I crouched low, bringing a bloom to my nose. So sweet and smooth and absolutely beautiful.

"Look at this!" I called to Graham. "Is it not the most interesting flower you've ever seen?"

"We've only just started," he said. "There is much more to see. Huge bushes of roses are just down the path."

"Posh, roses. Look at *these*. I've never seen anything like them."

"Are roses not your favorite flower? Your house is always littered with them."

"A testament, I should think, to the lack of originality among your sex." I inhaled another sweet bloom.

"No one knows your favorite flower?" The idea seemed to befuddle him beyond reason.

"No one has ever asked."

I shouldn't have said it, because Graham spent the entirety of the Marine Pavilion's west lawns trying to unriddle me.

"Is it a daisy?"

"No. Heavens no." I tried losing him down a trail of rounded bushes, but he followed me.

"A lily?"

I laughed at his persistence, then reached a hand inside a cluster of tall grass to uncover a hidden blossom, blue with yellow stripes. "No."

He waited until I popped back up to say, "Tulip, then?"

"*Graham.*" We were rounding the house, eyed by guards standing at the ready, and I tried to look like I belonged. I could spend all day wandering the footpaths and admiring the flowers.

Graham stole around me, stopping me in place. "Put me out of my misery. Please."

I cast him a weary glance. "Red as roses, black at the heart."

His brow knitted together. "Carnations?"

"Poppies," I said with exasperation.

He scrunched his nose. "Aren't those a weed?"

"They are not!" I tried, despite my humor, to be appalled. "And I thought you'd promised to be nice!"

He laughed, hands raised in defense. "I am nice. But poppies are so easy to grow. They are . . . common."

"They are perfect. They make a simple field beautiful. They can paint a whole scene red."

He considered my words. Then, as though to be certain, he said, "Field poppies?"

I nodded once. "Poppies."

We continued our tour, and Graham trailed close behind as I wandered endlessly amidst flowers, manicured bushes, and statues. I caught him in conversation now and again with a stranger, but he was never more than a few steps away.

We must've walked a mile when we came upon a large square pond, facing what Graham told me was Prinny's new stable house.

"But it's almost more elegant than the Pavilion."

"Do not tell him that," Graham warned. "There's talk he means to remodel the whole thing to match it."

"Why change something already so beautiful?"

"Because he can." Graham led me to the water's glassy edge and around a tall rosebush to a little stone bench.

My feet sighed with relief as we sat. Three gentlemen and an older woman peered at the water on the opposite end.

"What do you think?" Graham asked, gesturing to our surroundings. "From a non-business perspective."

I narrowed my gaze, and he smiled innocently. "I love it," I admitted. "A hidden castle tucked away by the sea."

"Would you return, then? Add Brighton to your list of sea resorts for the summer?"

"Business," I chided him.

"I meant to visit me, not to invest." He acted as though I'd offended him.

I pretended to ponder the thought. "There is a sixty per-cent chance I'd return to visit you, Graham. As long as we visited the Pavilion."

"Sixty, hmm?" He folded his arms. A fish flopped in the pond, causing ripples to cascade toward us. "I might be able to persuade another ten percent increase. Are you hungry?"

"Starved."

We lunched late at an inn. Graham ordered us both prawns, which were heavenly. Buttery goodness, the flavors were an explosion of garlic and salt and witchcraft. With only one left, I nearly wept, so distraught I licked my fingers like a heathen.

"Anna Lane, I am embarrassed to be seen with you." Graham leaned back in the seat across from me, watching me with that splitting grin that claimed victory.

I moaned. "Mmm. Seventy-five percent."

He bit his lip and chuckled. "Shall I call for another plate?"

I swatted him with my napkin.

From the inn, we walked to the rocky shore and sat on a boulder in the sun, watching the tourists walk up and down the shoreline.

Graham, leaning on one elbow, told me about his child-hood. Around thirteen years of age, he realized his family did not meet typical criteria. His father either laid in bed all day or left for a month at a time. And around that time, his maternal grandfather came to visit and sent him to school.

"I regret that most of all," he said, tucking one leg under the other. "Leaving my mother and Ginny. Ginny won't talk about it, but I know things were dire. I wish, more than anything, that I could have protected them from my father's abandonment."

"But how could you have?" I shook my head. "You cannot look back. You have come so far."

He sniffed, thumbing loose pebbles on the boulder. "And you? Do you ever wonder about your mother?"

"Sometimes I study her portrait and wonder what her voice would have sounded like. Papa says she had a razor-sharp wit and unparalleled humor. I would have loved knowing her, but I never felt her absence as keenly as Papa did. I always had him."

"You'll see him tomorrow. Are you eager to return home?"

I considered. "To London? No. But, home? Yes, of course."

He held up his hands. "I mean no offense. I just wonder, given all your options, why you have not yet chosen a home of your own. With Mr. Cross, perhaps?"

I narrowed my eyes. Sly fox. "If I wanted Mr. Cross, I'd already have him."

His lips twitched.

"What?"

"I rather thought you fancied him after that bouquet."

"Flattered, after the bouquet. But after the assembly . . ."

He waited, silent.

"After the assembly, I have realized even a friendship might be difficult to create with Mr. Cross."

Graham grinned, then sat up and slid down the boulder. He lifted his hand for me to join him. "Is it odd that hearing that brings me great joy?"

I took his hand and slid until my feet touched the rocky ground. "You hate him so much?"

Graham tucked my hand safely in the crook of his arm. "Surprisingly, no. Not that."

But instead of elaborating, he waved to an older gentleman and his wife, then led me up a small path to the land overlooking the shore.

Chapter Twenty-Four

GRAHAM

A thousand apologies, Cross, I thought smugly to myself as Anna clung to my arm for support. As happy as that revelation made me, another realization crept in—if Anna did not want a man as wealthy and secure as Cross, how could she possibly return *my* feelings?

Mr. Lane would return tomorrow. I wanted to speak with Anna openly, but not before she had another man's protection to escape to, and certainly not before I had a moment to explain, to ingratiate myself with Mr. Lane.

I led Anna back up to the Steine, too afraid to say something that might spoil this otherwise perfect afternoon. Instead, I snuck glances as she marveled at birds dipping low, then flying off into the bright cerulean sky. I noted the softness in her eyes, mesmerized by the sway of the grass in the cool breeze. I walked her farther out to a shore between East and West Streets, where the locals to Brighton often met. No business today, so I couldn't tell her about the economy nor the history of our fishing town. But I could show her.

Down to the base of the hill, where a slope of earth met the rocky shore, makeshift tents, carts, and various tables displayed an array of goods and local foods. At odd hours, smaller fishing boats brought back their modest catch, displaying it at reasonable prices in the market. Fishermen would set off for their living closer to sunset, which was still a few hours away.

Anna took her time, seeming to take everything in stride. She pointed out a little booth, and I followed.

"This is lovely," she said, lifting up a little bracelet made of shells. "Did you find these shells here?"

A slender woman with a hopeful expression stood to meet Anna. "Yes, miss. All here."

Anna grinned at me. "Wouldn't Tabs just love this?"

My sister had already made several shell bracelets of her own, but I wouldn't tell Anna that. "I do believe she would."

"Allow me," a raspy voice said.

Anna startled and dropped the bracelet onto the little booth's table.

I knew that voice. I found the man's outstretched hand first, filled with coin to purchase the bracelet, then his lion-head cane.

Mr. Lennox.

Chapter Twenty-Five

ANNA

"Forgive me," I said to the woman, who'd taken Mr. Lennox's coin and was placing the bracelet in a paper bag. Then I turned to face him.

"What are you doing here?" I demanded in a low voice, seething and stalking away from the other shoppers. Luckily, I saw no one else I knew, but that did not mean others did not know me. "I have told you—"

Mr. Lennox kept my pace, followed closely by Graham, until we were well on our own down the shoreline. "There is an urgent matter we must discuss." His attention flicked to Graham. "In private."

"Absolutely not," I said, crossing my arms. Being alone with him was the last thing I wanted. "You have already inconvenienced me and my host enough. Say what you must, and make it your last, for my patience is running thin, Mr. Lennox. I cannot be seen with you."

"You do not mean that. This, between us, is merely a lover's spat."

"Is that what you are telling everyone? Is that why everyone in Brighton is already speculating over what happened?"

"I said I would prove myself to you—prove that I have your best interests at heart. That I think only of you, only of your happiness. And I have."

I scoffed and shook my head. "You cannot possibly—"

"There are others who have deceived you," he spoke over me in an almost desperate rush of emotion. He stepped closer, his words spilling out in an unfiltered flood. "Others who have kept secrets from you. I swear to you, Anna, now and forevermore, that my engagement to Miss Clarence was purely transactional and mutually broken. Accept me now, and you and I shall start on even footing. Both knowing where the other stands, with no more secrets between us. I swear it."

"That is quite enough," Graham said with a dangerous edge to his voice. He'd gone entirely rigid, and I realized I'd never seen him truly angry before this moment. "Miss Lane has asked you to leave, and if you do not do so at once, we shall have a problem, you and I."

"Sheath your sword, Everett. I need only a moment more."

The man spoke in riddles, and I had no patience left. "Tell me at once, Mr. Lennox. Plainly. What are you saying? What secrets?"

He focused on me, one hand outstretched between us. "I crossed paths with your father in Bath."

The silence that followed prickled against my skin. My father had been in Bath, yes. Mr. Lennox seeing him there would not be unusual. What, then, caused him to stare so solemnly at me?

"Very well." I said, curt. "And soon he'll be in Brighton, come to claim me. What of it?"

Mr. Lennox leaned in, watching me with a fervent interest

that sent a cold chill down my spine. "He took tea with Ms. Peale in the Pump Room the very morning I left for Brighton."

I took a step back, gaze trailing to the rocky brown shore beneath my feet as my mind raced in circles. Bath, yes, that was where my father had returned for business. *Business*. With Ms. Peale? I did not know a Ms. Peale.

Furthermore, why would Papa engage in business matters with a woman?

"Ms. Peale," I tried the name, but still, nothing. Who the devil was she?

Mr. Lennox shook his head, then scoffed in evident disgust. "He has not even mentioned her to you?"

"Lennox, this is not your story to tell. Leave." Graham stepped between us, gritting his teeth. "Now."

But Mr. Lennox sidestepped him. "They were inseparable all morning."

My entire body went cold, save for a burning in my neck and cheeks. My father . . . and a woman?

Graham started to move between us, but I lifted a hand to stop him. He waited a step away, watching.

Mr. Lennox nodded, his eyes never leaving mine. "Indeed, I have never seen your father so encouraged. Makes a man quite jealous, to be honest."

Graham was watching me, frowning at Mr. Lennox, denying nothing. He'd known where my father was going. And clearly, he'd known why.

My heart dropped to my toes.

I rounded on Mr. Lennox. "Are you quite certain this was *my* father?"

Mr. Lennox leaned in, his musky cologne overtaking my senses. "I should not be the only one willing to tell you the truth, and yet here I am. I may not be a perfect man, but I am loyal to a fault. And I always will be.

"I did not want to say anything until I knew for certain, so I immediately sought out anyone who could support my theory. I now have it on good authority from someone close to your father that this past week was not his first rendezvous with Ms. Peale. I came for you as soon as I could."

My throat tightened, and I coughed to combat the pain filling my chest. The idea was preposterous. Ridiculous. Papa would never keep such an enormous secret from me.

My knees turned wobbly, my eyes pricking with emotion I did not know how to control. I needed to get away. I needed to think, to make sense of what Mr. Lennox had just said. But the more I thought, the fuzzier my mind became. Papa had a . . . a Ms. Peale.

I stepped past Mr. Lennox, toward the emptiness of the shoreline as my breaths came in shallow wisps. Where could I go? Where could I run?

I had no one.

Not even Graham, whom I'd been foolish enough to trust. To love. He'd been playing our old games this whole time. He would do anything to win my father's approval, even keep a secret he'd known would break me.

"Anna—" Mr. Lennox followed me, but he stopped short of reaching my side. The most decent thing he'd ever done was lend me privacy after such a blow. "You must feel incredibly betrayed. I certainly would." The rocks shifted under his feet as he took a single step closer. Please consider my offer. Should you not wish to return with your father, you are most welcome to stay with me at my cousin's home for the next few days. We can prepare further details together. Anything you need—anything at all—you need only send word. I am at your service."

I said nothing, only wrapped my arms around my middle and begged the tears not to fall. Not in so public a place. Not when I had no choice but to face Graham. I would not let him see me so affected.

I felt the air change as Mr. Lennox turned to go. His offer was a double-edged sword. To choose him would be the biggest mistake of my life. It would be a life of loneliness, for he'd never be faithful. He'd never truly love me.

The rocks crunched beneath boots behind me once more. Different steps this time. Hesitant, slow. I did not turn my head, but I could feel Graham an arm's length away, silent and tense.

I thought he might stand there forever. Or perhaps until the tide rose and swept us both away.

"Does he speak the truth?" I asked, proud of how strong my voice sounded.

Graham moved to my side, and I shifted away.

The tide crashed against the rocks once, twice, then he said, "Her name is Ms. Abigail Peale." His words were quiet, calm, even. "She's a widow, no children, very lovely, and very taken with your father." Details lined up like they were statistics, figures in a business proposal. "We'd traveled to Bath to consider an investment, and they met. And, yes, we've visited several times since to see the investment through. There were dinner parties, dancing. Though this past week, she *invited* him. He didn't tell you because—"

"Why did *you* not say something?" I looked up then, exasperated and surprised by the tremor in my voice, the way my heart ached and echoed sadness like an empty hall in a tall, abandoned house.

Graham's shoulders sank; he lowered his voice. "We haven't exactly been sharing secrets of late, Anna. This one was not mine to tell."

He should have told me. If he had any regard for me at all, he should have told me. "How long have they been acquainted?"

Graham looked down at his boots, then kicked at the rocks between us. "Since last year. But only seriously the past few months."

My heart fell to the ground. "A year?" I breathed.

My throat ached with emotion I could not release, and I tried to swallow it down, but tears threatened instead. Papa had promised me he would not entertain the idea of marriage before I wed. Promised that we'd always have each other. And after Mr. Lennox I'd been relying on that fact. That I wouldn't be left to navigate Society alone.

Graham reached out again, this time handing me his handkerchief.

I took it and turned away from him to compose myself.

"Anna, I'm so sorry," Graham started. "He should have told you. I assured him you would understand. That you'd be happy for him."

"*You* assured him?" My voice cracked as I rounded on Graham. "Why are you and my father conversing privately about matters in *my* life that have no bearing whatsoever on yours?"

He stepped back on instinct. "You're upset with me."

I wiped my nose on his handkerchief, scoffing. "Brilliant, Graham. I can see you've used your education well."

He raised his hands in a show of surrender. He was an island all his own, declaring no alliance, friend to all. But I didn't want neutrality. I wanted his allegiance. I wanted the truth, or I wanted to be rid of him. I'd rather be alone than lied to.

"Try to see things from your father's perspective. He promised you he would not marry until you did—"

"How do you even know about—"

"—but then he met someone." Graham raked an impassioned hand through his hair. "Someone . . . unexpected. What was he to do? Let her slip through his fingers? He tried to temper his feelings, I assure you, but he simply could not."

I leaned my head back to keep the tears from falling and pinched the top of my nose. This was all too unreal. Too unbelievable. And too soon after Mr. Lennox. I'd thought everything would be well if only I'd removed myself from London, and yet, lies and deceit had followed me, even from the one man I trusted fully. I was in a terrible nightmare, and I could not wake up. I clutched my neck.

"I do not know what to do. I cannot breathe."

"I am certain he means to tell you when he returns. In truth, in his study before we left, he nearly gave her up because he feared your reaction. He loves you." Graham nearly pleaded.

I looked at him. I could feel the sincerity behind Graham's words, but the frustration in my chest made me want to scream. "Why do you defend him? The only man I have ever fully trusted has hidden a whole second life from me. If you care for me at all—" I stopped myself, too hurt to be embarrassed, and lowered my voice. "You of all people should understand what that feels like."

"I do indeed." Graham's features sharpened. "The difference being, my father abandoned me without a single thought. He never loved me. Never cared about my happiness, whether I was scared at night, or if I went hungry. Your father, however, loves you so fiercely he would have forfeited his only chance at real love again because of a promise he made to you when you were a child."

My eyes welled with tears. His words felt like a reprimand, though he'd said nothing harsh or unkind. I let them sink in, tried to reason with the truth clawing free despite the pain. But my feelings were so wounded, hurt from all the gossip that continued to follow me, from my father's choices, and even from Graham, who'd known so much and said so little. A girl could only bear so much before breaking.

"Anna," Graham spoke gently, as though he could read the thoughts behind my eyes. "I do not defend his choice to hide this from you. I simply want you to see that everything he has done has been with you in mind."

I shook my head. "He's done a wretched job."

Graham reached out, and this time I let him lightly cradle my arms in his hands. "He has indeed. And I should have told you. As soon as things changed between us, I should have told you straightaway. I've hurt you, and I cannot bear it. Please. Forgive me."

I sniffed and drew up the handkerchief, hiding my wobbling chin. "I am so angry with him."

"You should be." He crouched down and retrieved two fist-sized rocks. He handed one to me; the other he kept for himself. "Honestly, I am starting to feel angry myself. He should not have put me in this position at all. It is not my responsibility to keep his secrets." He scrunched his face and threw the rock far out into the sea.

We watched it fly to a satisfying plummet.

"No, it is not." I agreed.

"I won't," he said, eyes serious and focused on mine. "I promise, I will never keep a secret from you again, no matter who asks it of me. And I will have some choice words for your father when he returns."

I nodded once, heart brimming over with Graham's sincerity.

I believed him.

I believed that he cared for my father and had subsequently, as a friend, kept his secrets. I believed that he'd also not considered how it might affect me should things come out before Papa had a chance to tell me himself. But most of all, I believed him when he said he was sorry, and when he promised to never repeat that same mistake again.

There was no false flattery. No impossible promises. Just care and devoted friendship.

And that made all the difference.

I reared back my arm, rock in hand, and threw. My shoulders fell as it landed halfway to the ripples Graham's had made.

He stared out to the sea with a hand over his brow and winced. "We shall have to work on your arm, Anna. Or your anger."

He looked over with a stupid grin on his face and winked at me, and somehow, that was enough.

I started to laugh, and he knocked my arm with his shoulder.

Papa had broken my heart, but somehow Graham had

loosely stitched it back together. I still felt betrayed. I still could not forgive Papa. But I could smile, albeit marginally.

"Mr. Everett!" a rough voice called from the distance.

We turned, and a portly man strode toward us.

"Oh, good grief," Graham muttered. "Brace yourself, Anna. You're about to meet a wild man."

Chapter Twenty-Six

GRAHAM

"Mr. Everett!"

I returned Morton's waving hand. He was usually among those who fished late, so I hadn't expected to see him here so early. I stole a sideways glance at Anna, whose eyes were still puffy and red.

Devil take that man Lennox. I had half a mind to call him out for exposing such a delicate situation and hurting everyone involved. I hated myself for my part in Mr. Lane's secret, but most of all I hated how brave Anna had to be to face this mess, and so soon.

"Morton." I tipped my hat as he approached, bringing with him a strong scent of fish and the sea. His dirty hands were stained, scarred, and weatherworn, my own paling in comparison, and his shirt had been torn in several places. "Heading out early for the catch?" I asked.

He grinned. "Soon, yes." He took off his cap and scratched his greasy head, then wiped the sweat from his tanned, crinkled forehead. "I've a celebration for my eldest daughter this evening, and I'm in need of a dozen or so fresh fish before I set out with the big boats."

The man knew fish, I had no doubt he'd find success despite the hour. "I hope good fortune finds you, then."

"What brings *you* down to the markets? In want of fish? Or perhaps something pretty to win over your lady here."

Anna smiled and took him in with grace, though I wondered—admittedly with a little humor—what a man like Morton did to her sensibilities.

"Mr. Everett would need a heap of good fortune in that case." She grinned, clearly pleased with her own teasing.

I pursed my lips and raised both brows. Something so very like Anna to say, and yet, knowing her better, the barb did not sting at all. "Miss Lane, this is Nathaniel Morton. He's a local fisherman."

"Best fish in all Brighton." He grinned widely.

"Lovely to meet you," Anna said with a nod, and I felt a rush of pride, of near possessiveness, to have her at my side. A high-bred lady who was perfectly comfortable conversing with a common fisherman.

"She is Mr. Lane's daughter, of London."

Morton widened his stance, arms folded across his chest. "I see. Is this your first trip to Brighton?"

"It is. We've just come from the shore. We saw the Marine Pavilion and walked the Steine."

"Well, then. You've been around, haven't you? Taken her to the baths yet?" he asked me.

"She's not keen," I responded, and Anna pinched my arm.

Morton watched with a gleam in his eye. "Been on the water?"

"We have limited time to see all that Brighton offers, unfortunately. And Miss Lane prefers a tame experience."

"I beg your pardon?" Anna placed her delicate hands on her hips. I shouldn't have said it with a challenge in my voice, but there it was. Her flame, ignited. I grinned.

"Which part, exactly, of our trip so far has been *tame?*" she asked. The gravelly sound of sorrow in her voice was dissipating. She was distracted, and I longed to keep her so.

"Well, in that case, why not an excursion?" Morton asked. "The sea is what brought people here in the first place. She's a fishing town at her heart, Brighton."

"What sort of excursion?" Anna asked.

"A boat ride, out on the sea. Some get lucky and see a dolphin. Others pull in a fish or rest their worries for a time and bask in the sunset. Very popular among you tourists, the sunsets."

Anna raised her brows at me expectantly.

"You wouldn't like it." I shook my head. "The waters look steady from here, but out there"—I pointed farther out, knowingly—"a small boat will rock and rage, and you'll feel like the whole world is spinning."

Anna looked out at the sea, which, admittedly did not seem all that rowdy at present.

She turned back. "It cannot be worse than a carriage ride down the Brighton Road."

"Brave girl," Morton declared, winking at her.

And she thought *I* tried to sway her on matters of business.

"Do you take tourists?" Anna asked him.

Morton situated his cap back atop his head. "Occasionally. I prefer the fish as company. I only offer rides to select visitors such as yourselves. I'd take you, but tonight I have fish to catch."

Morton looked sideways at me, then down at his hands, flexing his fist as if examining the dirt under his nails. I took his look for what it was—could I make it worth his while? He knew me to be a frugal man. Taking us on a boat ride would mean both fish for his celebration and a sure purse, so I had little doubt he'd oblige us. But Anna had already endured enough hardship this evening.

"I do not think Miss Lane would fare well on the sea."

Morton crossed his arms and turned to Anna for her reaction.

Anna did not miss a beat. "I should like to go and watch you fish."

I lowered my voice. "You realize he's talking about taking you out on a boat, in the middle of the sea."

She narrowed her eyes. Yes, apparently, she did.

I continued, "As entertaining as Morton is, it's a rough start and a new feeling for some. I can't promise you'll enjoy it. I'm not even certain your father would allow it."

Oof. The look she gave me at the mention of her father could have killed an army.

"Do you have a weak stomach, Mr. Everett?" she asked. "Perhaps I should fetch your sisters instead."

"I—" A patient breath escaped me. We stared at each other for a long, tenuous moment. She wouldn't like it, but she needed a distraction, and if she wanted to try . . .

"Are you in the hogboat tonight?" I asked Morton. A nice fishing boat, large enough, but flat and uncomfortable. It wouldn't do for a seaside excursion.

"Just the jolly. But she's got room enough for three. And she cuts smooth through the waters." Then he muttered, "An hour or so for a shilling." He sniffed, then looked about, having made his offer.

"You have yourself a deal," Anna declared, reaching into her reticule. "You can come with us, Mr. Everett, or you can stay on the beach and watch."

"Oh, he'll come," Morton said with another show of his teeth. "I happen to know Mr. Everett loves to fish. We've had an excursion or two of our own, haven't we?"

I silenced him with a look. We had fished together before, but that was because I was of different upbringing than Anna. This would not end well. I stopped Anna's searching, reaching in my jacket for my coin pouch to pay him. I'd hadn't spent so much money in one week since we'd remodeled Highcliffe House. But this was business: encouraging, obliging, gifting, showering prospects with everything to suit the lifestyle of the *ton*. Or, as was my current goal, attempting to court a woman as fine as Anna Lane.

A worthy investment.

Morton led us closer to shore where his jolly boat awaited us. The craft was of a smaller size, with forward, middle, and back thwarts. He'd already stocked the boat with fishing supplies for his catch but asked us to wait a moment while he ran into a nearby bathing house. A few moments later, he returned with blankets in hand and a brown paper sack. He'd done this before, I had no doubt, and he knew as well as I how to exceed someone's expectations. How to leave them wanting more.

Morton laid the blanket out on the front thwart of the jolly boat, where Anna would sit, then he called us over.

Anna's face was unreadable, her shoulders stiff, determined.

"Are you nervous?" I asked her.

"No." Her voice sounded unusually tight, small.

Had I ever seen her nervous before? Uncomfortable, sure. But Anna always had *something* to say. She seemed to have recovered some after Lennox, but I wasn't entirely sure she was thinking with a sound mind.

Morton stood with one leg in the water and the other inside the boat as he offered her his hand and hoisted her up, then over the side. The boat rocked, and Anna sucked in a breath, swaying on her feet, eyes as wide as saucers. Morton's strong hold kept her steady.

"Take a seat there at the front, Miss Lane," he said, holding fast to her hand while she settled.

Once seated, Anna's knuckles were white, holding fast to one side of the boat and the bench as though she'd instantly regretted her decision. The muscles in her neck were taut, jaw set, eyes still round with worry she refused to voice.

"Should I take the back thwart, or—" I started.

"No." She did not budge an inch, frozen as she was. "I'd like you here, please."

The bench was so small, I'd barely fit in the narrow space beside her, but those simple words, and the weakness in her otherwise steady voice and demeanor, did something to me. A compulsion to simply be near her. Unexplainable. Unavoidable. Urgent. The very fact that she'd forgiven me, trusted me still, set my feet in motion. I braced myself on the other side of the boat, threw a leg over and hopped in, but the subsequent rocking motion seemed to turn Anna's worry into terror.

I sat down beside her, my leg brushing hers, and I placed my arm along the trim of the boat. Her shoulders relaxed a touch, and I realized how tight my own chest had become.

With every breath she took, my muscles relaxed. My senses softened. Like we were connected.

"Are you sure about this?" I whispered. Then, more teasingly, "We could abandon ship."

Anna would not meet my gaze. Staying was so obviously *not* what she wanted to do. "You've already paid Morton."

That she even considered my money meant more to me than a wasted excursion. "Don't worry about that. We paid for an experience, and however long that lasts, it is well worth it to me."

She looked up then, a worried crease between her brows, as though she measured my sincerity.

I gave her an encouraging smile. Whatever she wanted, I'd give her. Whatever made her happy.

She considered for a moment while Morton heaved a wooden bucket over the back end of the jolly, whistling some seaman's tune. When her eyes met mine again, they'd eased, as did her hold on the side. "I'd like to see this side of Brighton."

Morton hopped out of the boat with the nimbleness of a man half his age, and said, "Best be on our way, then. Fish to be caught before the crowds rush in."

With that, he shoved hard on the boat's stern. Rocks groaned beneath our weight until the water's edge pulled us into the sea. Just as the boat started to sway, Morton splashed in the water, heaving himself back in and over the center thwart. His weight tipped the boat to the right, and Anna went rigid. Her arms flailed out, and I caught her with a laugh, pulling her closer on instinct.

"I have you," I said through my humor. "I won't let you fall in."

"But we might *both* fall in, and I shall drown."

Morton cast me a humored glance. He practically lived on these waters. "If we both fall in," I said, loosening my hold on her as the boat evened out, "Morton here can swim us both on his back."

"I've wrestled sharks in these waters, miss," he called over his shoulder, and I rolled my eyes. "Three at a time, and I only lost the tip of my right little finger." He held it up, wiggling it for effect. Likely a tale he told his children. He uncovered two long, heavy oars at the center, secured them on the boat, then, his back to us, dipped them into the water.

The jolly boat rocked as Morton paddled one side, then another, humming a new, hoarse tune that carried on the wind.

"There are sharks in these waters?" Anna breathed.

"None that you will see." I gripped the boat along her back, leaning halfway into the corner of my side of the bench, my knees angled slightly toward her. "Though perhaps we'll watch Morton reel in something substantial."

"That would be exciting," Anna admitted, looking up at me through her lashes.

A gush of wind blew past us, followed by unsteady waters. The boat rocked hard, and Anna gasped. She leaned into her corner, gripping the side, the bench, anything, like a cat bracing over a bucket of water.

She paled, muttering something about "Still alive" and perhaps a few choice words she shouldn't've. The waters would not relent. In truth, she needed a distraction until Morton found a good place to fish.

Her face scrunched, gaze aimed at her feet. I tried to think of a witty remark, but nothing came. I should've insisted we stayed on land. Should've bought her one of those ridiculous shell trinkets from a tent shop and gone home. The boat hit an even rougher current, rolling from one side to the other, and Anna struggled to stay upright. I shifted in my corner, an attempt to keep an appropriate distance, but accidently knocked her shoe with mine.

I started to draw back, but she followed, moving a mere measure on the bench. The toe of her shoe met my heel as though that little contact could ease her suffering.

I stopped breathing, focused entirely as I was on Anna. What should a man in my position do? I was her guardian, but I was also a man who very much wanted more than a host should. My mind reached for something to say. Conversation was the safest option.

A tremor jolted through her.

"Are you cold?" I asked.

"N-no, not exactly," she said on a breath. "This ride is rougher than I imagined."

Another high wave knocked her sideways, nearer to me, but this time, neither of us tried to avoid the shifting of the boat. I let it pull me right, then felt her thigh align with mine.

My breath hitched, but I tried not to move. I sat still, my hand gripping the frame of the boat, afraid to move. Afraid to scare her off. My heart pounded like a drum against my chest, sounding wildly in my ears, as the boat rocked once more. Anna must've lost all strength, for her side brushed mine, and she stayed.

"Anna?"

"Forgive me." She forced a self-conscious laugh. "You must think me some fragile thing."

I shouldn't allow her nearness. Not when it made my mind so hazy. But she needed me. And she felt so soft, so enticing. Like a warm cup of chocolate after a snowstorm, pooling low in my belly.

I let my fingers gently graze her arm. "I think you are delicate. There's a difference."

She pinched my side and made me jerk upright. "I think *you* are *delicate.*"

"A weak retort," I teased, settling back. "You must be very ill."

"I'm afraid I am very much that." The waters roiled, and she braced herself, leaning her weight into my side. Jasmine filled my senses.

"It's all right," I whispered into her hair as I rubbed her arm. "We are almost far enough out. Things will settle."

"My stomach feels odd."

I hated the pain in her voice so much that I wanted to slice it into quarters and wring it out with my bare hands. "Lay your head on my shoulder."

She pulled back, pale as porcelain, almost more afraid than before. "That would be so improper, Graham, and I'm already—"

"Anna. I do not mind," I assured her. "We've known each other for years."

"But there are others out, and Morton—"

"—knows I am your host at present. You'll feel better. Lay your head on me and let yourself acclimate to the sea."

With a little huff, she swallowed hard, then settled back at my side. The waters were unforgiving, but at last she relented, nestling into my neck with a sigh.

The sound unwound something in me. Holding Anna compelled me to be a stronger, more capable man. A man she'd turn to in times of uncertainty. A man she could trust with her safety, her thoughts, her dreams. I wanted to be all that and more, but only for her.

I held her close.

No one would ever hurt her again. Not even her father.

"Ho! Did you see that jumper, Everett?" Morton called from the center. He glanced over his shoulder and caught sight of us together, then smirked so wide his missing teeth showed. "Don't s'pose you did, eh? Almost there, Miss Lane, love. The winds are heavy this evening."

She sighed again into my neck, her warm breath tickling my skin, and holding her felt so natural, so right, I leaned in and brushed my lips to her hair.

Lud! *I brushed my lips to her hair.* I froze, my mind reeling.

But Anna laced her arm through mine, drawing me even closer. Lands, she smelled good. So, so good. Her warmth at my side was a siren calling to me. Reeling me in. Squeezing my heart to bursting.

Chapter Twenty-Seven

ANNA

Do it again, I thought. *Heavens above, please, do it again.*

My heart expanded, bursting and flaming and burning me through. What was this feeling? I'd never known I could ache for a simple touch. And for Graham.

Did he feel this too? Could he tell how he affected me?

My cheeks were burning, surely as red as a sunned strawberry. I held fast to his arm, distracted by his strength and warmth, bracing myself against the sick feeling in my stomach that roiled with every lurch of the sea.

Not as bad. The waters were settling. I took another deep breath through my nose. Yes, definitely settling. And my stomach followed suit. I could manage. But the problem at hand: I did not want to.

Graham felt so unbelievably good.

Nothing had ever felt so right. So comfortable and warm and whole.

And suddenly nothing else mattered. Not Papa, not his secret, not this wide-open sea.

I wanted to stay beside Graham, like this, forever.

The jolly had slowed, and I was feeling better. But how

could I sit up now? How could I look Graham in the eye with my feelings so obviously displayed? Especially after I'd completely fallen apart earlier.

Perhaps he hadn't kissed me. Perhaps his jaw had simply brushed my hair. But it had felt like a kiss. Like comfort and care. I'd never felt anything like it before in my whole life.

"This'll do," Morton said, and I peeked open an eye. He stashed his dripping oars alongside the bottom boards on the right, then braced himself as he stood. "You still with us, Miss Lane?"

I watched him step over the center thwart toward the stern, still letting Graham bear my weight. "How can you stand like that with the floor moving?" I said through a painfully hoarse voice.

Morton laughed his rough, scratchy laugh. "Give it a try. T'easier than you think."

The jolly drifted slowly, smoother than when Morton was rowing. I squared my knees, balancing my feet on the bottom planks. Then I sat up, scooting a small width away from Graham, and held fast to the bench. Chilly air blew through the space between us like the smart eyes of a chaperone, and we both seemed to sober.

"Come, see what I have in my bucket," Morton said. He held a spool of thick thread that he was unraveling.

"What sort of fish are you after?" I asked, decidedly not looking in Graham's direction.

"I'll tell ya when you've made your way up to the center thwart."

I gave the man a scowl, and he cackled.

Graham shifted in his spot, and I felt suddenly, horribly shy. Hobbling up to Morton seemed more comfortable than staying on this bench under Graham's study. I held fast to the left side of the boat, then tested my weight on my feet. The jolly's motions were rhythmic, like a song. Rolling back and forth, up and down. I felt the motions move up my legs to my hips. A dip made me step back, and I fell hard upon the bench.

Surprised that Graham hadn't reached out to save me, I looked over. He wasn't even watching. His eyes were set on the horizon, cheeks rosy from the chill. Still right there, waiting, but giving me the privacy I needed. Morton was busy knotting a hook on the end of his line, so I tried again.

I was steadier this time, but still I hunched my back, ready to fall forward or backward to whichever thwart was closer. A few steps, and another dip, but I was close enough to the center thwart to throw a leg over and hold tight.

"There she is," Morton cheered. His bucket was roped to the back thwart. It sloshed with water. "You'll like this," he added, nodding his head toward the bucket.

"Here," Graham said from behind. He spread a little towel on the bottom boards in front of the bucket for me to crouch upon. "Are they still alive?" he asked Morton.

"Just enough," the man responded. "Don't go stickin' your hand in there, Miss Lane."

When the waters eased for a moment, I took my opportunity to move from the center thwart and kneel beside the bucket. The bottom boards smelled putrid and fishy, so I touched my nose. No wonder I was so queasy. Fish and the sea were an awful combination I did not remember from Lyme.

Graham had moved behind me at the center thwart. I peered inside the bucket. Many small bulbs bounced around inside. They looked squishy and soft like jelly, tinted pink, and had long twirly legs protruding out from every side, twisting around each other so that I could not tell which belonged where.

"Octopus?" I asked.

Morton tugged on a large leather glove, then reached inside the bucket. Water sloshed out, wetting the edges of the towel, but my attention was focused on the little arms that curled around Morton's glove.

"Bait," he answered. "The real prize is the cod we'll catch with 'em."

"Close your eyes," Graham said gently as Morton lifted up his line, with its hook and heavy lead sinker.

"Poor thing," I moaned, obliging.

"Not poor thing when I make a living off the cod and families fill their bellies. It's the way of nature, miss. Nothing less, nothing more."

A quiet plunk, and I opened my eyes to find Morton unwinding the line. His movements were quick, calculated. His rough hands worked with surety and precision. Satisfied with the length of it, which seemed to go on forever, he held fast to the line, then reached behind him for another spool.

I winced as he hooked another small octopus to that line, then cast it out close by and let the thread unwind a while.

"Hungry, already?" he called to the sea. Then he yanked fast on the first line, reeling it in, one handful at a time. I glanced to Graham, who was grinning, leaning over the side of the boat with boyish wonderment on his face. "A big one, too. C'mere, Everett. Give us a hand."

Graham did not need to be asked twice. He hopped over

the center thwart, his coat brushing my back, then took the first line from Morton and continued to reel it in.

"It's a good weight," Graham agreed.

Our eyes met, and I forgot to be shy. I couldn't help but grin back. Perched upon the center thwart, I leaned over the side of the jolly boat to watch the line come in.

An eternity of anticipation, then finally, the water broke, and the fish flapped free. Its body was as long as Graham's arm, tail flopping wildly as Graham reached down and gripped a space near its head.

Morton yipped, then took the fish from him, and Graham took hold of the other line.

"Want to try, Anna?" he asked. But I was still partly in shock that we were in a boat, surrounded by the sea and its inhabitants, and quite far from the shoreline.

Morton leaned over the other side of the boat with a knife, then flopped a bloody fish into a bucket. He looked at me and laughed. "She's gone green. I don't suppose your little lady is used to a seaman's life."

"Not in the least," Graham said, and I considered defending myself. But Morton had called me Graham's lady. And Graham had not denied it.

"What sort of fish is that?" I asked instead.

"Cod," both men answered.

So that was what my dinner looked like before I ate it. "They look so smooth and slimy."

Graham handed Morton the second line, then baited the other and threw it out.

"You're in luck today, Morton," Graham said.

And so it went. For nearly two hours, the sun lowered in the sky while Graham and Morton reeled in fish. At one point, we rowed a little further out, and I had to take another half hour to recover. In time, they filled an entire bucket to its brim with cod, and I sat back, laughing at the two of them jesting and poking at each other. In time, I forgot about my heartache and let the sea revive me.

The men reused their bait when they could, arguing over whether a cod could be caught on half an octopus. I'd never seen Graham so happy and carefree. I could tell he liked using his hands, seeing something tangible come from hard work. And I liked watching him laugh.

"You two shall sink our little boat if you continue on with such success," I teased them. My stomach had settled, and I'd become one with the sea. At least for now. I liked how the salty breeze brushed through my hair. Though I could do with less fish and guts and blood.

"Not until you've at least tried your hand," Morton said, but it was less a command and more a taunt. I could see why he and Graham got on so well. "One cast is all."

"*One* cast," Graham agreed with a look so hopeful, I wanted nothing more than to please him. "Try your luck, Anna."

Morton had already cut the hook off his line and was spinning it back around his spool. Graham held his empty hook at the ready.

"I am not baiting that hook," I said with finality. "But I suppose I will try one cast."

"There's my girl!" Morton laughed, reaching out a hand to help me over the center thwart.

I stood, a little wobbly, but took a few steps to the front thwart until I sat facing the water. Graham held up the octopus-baited line, which I took and threw as far as I could. It landed with a familiar *plonk*, and the line released, sinking, sinking, sinking.

"Let it out a little at a time," Graham directed.

Having retreated toward the back thwart, Morton stood with hands on hips, watching over us.

My fingers fumbled on the line as I tried to unwind it. It was tough on my hand. Graham noticed and took off a little woolen half glove and offered it to me. He held the line while I tugged the glove on, then he handed it back.

Still, I fumbled to unwind the line as quickly as they had. I looked to Morton, half embarrassed at my inabilities.

He winked, then nodded toward Graham.

Graham stepped forward. "There's a rhythm to it," he said, "like everything on the sea."

Then he rested a knee on the thwart and crouched behind me. "May I?" His deep voice rumbled at my back, and my skin prickled with anticipation. The thwart's length was barely enough to fit us both.

I glanced over my shoulder and nodded. The line in my hand drifted, pulled by the sea, while my other hand held fast to the wooden spool.

Graham placed one hand over mine, holding the spool with me, and my breath hitched. Graham Everett. He wasn't supposed to feel this way . . . this exciting. Then his other hand slid down my arm to the line. I felt his touch all the way down to my toes.

"Place your hand on mine," he said, and I could feel him swallow hard.

I released the line and stared down at his strong, capable hand. With every movement, however slight, my back brushed his chest. Was I alone in this feeling? I tilted my head to find his expression as though it would be some key to his thoughts, but he was *right there*, and my forehead met his cheek.

"S-sorry," I mumbled, turning back.

He laughed, a gentle sound. "Anna, take my hand. I'll show you the rhythm."

Hesitantly, awkwardly, I placed my hand over his. My fingers grazed his knuckles and the spaces in between, and held fast.

"Ready?" Graham anchored the spool at my hip so the line came out horizontally. He let the line sink into the sea, but every time it pulled, he flicked off the end of the spool with a *swip, swip*, keeping time like a measured song. I felt like a puppet, and I started to laugh, leaning back into his chest.

Graham's deep chuckle vibrated through me. "Hold the line, Anna. You're making me do all the work!"

"But you let the line out so much faster than I can," I whined, still laughing. I held tighter, aiming to please him.

Graham kept up the rhythm, and soon, let go altogether.

I unwound a few more times until Morton said, "That'll do. Now, we wait."

Graham took the spool from me and hung it on a little knob attached to the jolly. He positioned my hands, one above the other, on the line. "Feel the vibrations from the sea?" he asked. His breath tickled my neck.

"Yes," I said in a shaky voice. "I feel them."

"When you feel a tug, start reeling."

He pulled back his hands, but I turned. "Wait," I said, finally meeting his gaze. He looked like he'd just woken from a long dream. "Stay."

He rubbed his jaw. "It may take a while," he said, but he didn't retreat.

"I don't mind." My heart hammered inside my chest, but for the first time in a very long time, I knew exactly what it wanted.

I turned back around to face the sea, my skin acutely aware of every movement Graham made as he shifted, then slowly settled behind me. I froze as his long legs encircled the small space around me, brushing my thighs as he situated himself. Then he leaned in and felt the line. He was so close. He was everywhere.

"Now?" I breathed.

"Not yet," he answered. "You'll know."

My mind registered distant sounds from Morton rummaging in the back, but I could not be bothered. I wanted nothing more than to catch fish for the rest of my life.

Graham's arm flexed around mine, and he grunted. "Mmm. Maybe there. Did you feel that?"

"No," I admitted. Though the only thing my mind could comprehend at present was the feel of *him*. The smell of sweet leather and musk from his coat. His chest moving at my back with each breath. We sat there for an eternity, feeling each other's movements, each other's breaths.

"I'd wager you've caught ten fish for how long you've let that line out, Everett," Morton teased, chuckling.

"Hush, you," I teased back. "We are trying to catch a fish."

Morton snorted. "He's tryin' to catch *something* all right."

Graham bent over, then threw something that looked like a ball of rope at Morton's chest, which only made the man laugh more. The two of them were insufferable, but I couldn't help but smile.

Then my line tugged right. "Oh!" I shrieked, half standing. "Graham!"

He stood abruptly, yanking hard on the line. "Quickly, Anna! Reel it in!"

Panic struck me. "*You* reel it in! I do not know how!"

"One handful at a time," Graham directed, taking the first pull with his own hands.

I took the second, he the third, and I kept his pace until my arms ached.

"Almost there," he grunted, for he must've felt me tiring out. "Can you feel him resisting?"

"He's too strong." I grunted back. The line swerved in different directions as my fish fought for its freedom.

Morton looked on greedily. We'd definitely hooked a nice-sized cod. Perhaps the best of the day.

Graham nudged my shoe with his. "You cannot give up now. Look!"

Just then, the surface of the sea erupted around our line, and I gasped, staring hard at the spot. I'd done it! I'd caught my first fish!

Graham gave one more tug, and the fish broke free.

Only it wasn't a fish.

It was *a snake*! My shriek filled the air, and I twisted around. My legs tangled on the thwart as I heaved all my weight as far from the creature as I could. Graham caught my waist, but only after he'd released the line, and we fell to the bottom boards.

"That's not a fish!" I screeched again. I was tangled in a rope, splayed most indecently across Graham, so I pushed up on his broad, hard chest. His eyes were as wide as mine, mouth parted as he sat up. He must have not heard me, so I repeated, "That is not a *fish!*"

Morton had jumped the center thwart, then over us, and taken the line in his hands. Steadily, he reeled, completely unafraid. Excited, even. "Did you see the size of that beast, Everett?" he called over his shoulder.

"Cut the line!" I begged, twisting around Graham for protection. I never wanted to see that creature again as long as I lived. "Graham, make him cut the line!"

Graham hesitated, then, "Morton," he said in a deep voice.

But Morton heaved a final time, and there it was, flopping its long body—or tail?—around like a swimming snake. The sea beast of Tabs's nightmares. I held in a screech, backing over the center thwart, as far away as I could go.

"Well done, Miss Lane. Look at that eel. Twenty pounds at least." Morton looked positively giddy. He flung the twisting thing toward the front thwart and made quick work of slicing the head, then rinsing it out and flinging the eel into his ice bucket. "With a haul this full, I ought to pay *you two* for this trip."

"Row us home before Miss Lane faints," Graham ordered, then tossed a rag to Morton. He followed me over the center thwart. "And before the sun sets completely. Then you can pay us a cod or two for putting up with you." His voice sounded the slightest bit cross, but his amusement won out. Especially when he looked at me.

"All is well," he chuckled, grabbing a blanket from a basket under the center thwart. "The eel is dead, and Morton has caught more than enough to take home."

I stilled as Graham wrapped the blanket around my back, then sat down beside me. This time, far enough away to make me miss him.

The sun was setting, framing Brighton's hills in a fiery glow. Pinks and oranges and yellows lit the sky as Morton started to row us toward the shore, humming his happy tune.

In companionable silence, we watched the sun's last reflections on the sea as gentle waves careened us to shore. I glanced at Graham. So handsome, his wavy hair windswept, lips parted, and cheeks creased as he smiled softly toward the sea.

I'd been surrounded by his family all week, and it had been a dream. But, sitting beside him, I realized, even when we were silent, I never felt alone in his presence.

I felt like *me*.

I felt wanted. Cared for. Like I'd be missed. And Graham did that. He made me tingle all over, made me laugh so hard I ached, and when he spoke to me, he spoke *to me*, and he listened.

How had I been so foolish? How had I let my pride and jealousy fuel this fire against him? For thinking back, even when I'd wanted him gone, his presence had felt like home. He'd fit with us. Never out of place, even when I'd served him goat cheese and tortured him with the most awkward questions. He'd matched me flame to flame, and I'd loved it.

I'd loved him.

I love him.

Stupid, stupid girl. How had you not seen?

I watched his profile, the curve of his nose, round at the tip, and the soft dip in his upper lip. I wanted those lips. I wanted to kiss the crease of his mouth, the dimple in his cheek. I wanted . . . too much for one night. But I hoped he wanted the same.

I plastered on a smile, hoping for nonchalance instead of *"I have just realized my heart's desire,"* as Morton splashed into the sea and tugged the boat the rest of the way inland.

"Out you go." He raised a hand to steady Graham, who jumped out.

"You did well on the return," Graham said to me, extending his own a hand to help me over the side of the boat. "Did you enjoy the trip?"

Heavens, but his eyes were so sincere. How had I never paid attention? Graham wore his heart on his sleeve, and he *cared.* "Very much. Thank you, Graham."

I braced myself against the unsteady motion and took his hand as I lifted a leg over. He caught my waist to steady my one foot as my shoe found enough purchase on the rocky beach to swing my other leg over. Still, I stumbled into him. A second's worth of his hold seemed to brand me with something new. Something only he could give. Something I would not mind having forever.

"Steady?" His low chuckle rumbled between us.

Hands locked on his strong forearms, I swayed. How had I missed it? Why had I locked these feelings away until now? "Not quite."

His gaze swallowed me whole, and I shouldn't have let him look at me so openly. Like there weren't fifty other tourists scattered along the shore ahead. I also shouldn't have reached up to smooth the hair from his—

"Here you are," Morton called, and I dropped my hand, flushing.

Graham stepped away from me, rubbing the back of his neck.

Morton had two large fish wrapped up over one shoulder, and the packaged eel over the other. A young boy trailed beside him, waiting. "You're both of you welcome on the jolly anytime," he said.

"For Tabs's odd fascinations," Graham said, motioning to the eel. "If you're agreeable."

I nodded. Her own dark creature of the sea, defeated. She'd love inspecting that thing even more than the prettiest shell on the coast. As long as I did not have to see it ever again.

Morton gave the fish to the little boy, and Graham told him where to deliver them. Then he and I offered our thanks to Morton.

The sun had dipped low, darkening the earth. Only an orange, golden glow haloed the sky, and it was glorious, but signified the ending of a day. Tourists were gathering to go home; stragglers finding their shoes and collecting their last purchases from the markets.

I wanted that too. I wanted to go home.

I tugged on his arm. "Come, Guardian Graham. Light on your feet. I have a reputation to save before night falls."

He tugged me back, mischief alight in his eyes. His full attention sent shivers all over my skin. "Let's tarry a while," he said in a low, silky voice. "I am suddenly not in a rush."

His cheeks were pink, chin dipped with the most becoming adoration on his face. So I obliged him. Was it the sunset? Or did he feel as content as I?

He took my hand and secured it in the nook of his arm. Slowly, releasing all our pains and cares to the salty breeze, we walked in silence, admiring the sea, pocketing a shell for Tabs, laughing as a tourist dipped down to clean his hands in the water, then struggled to rise and splashed sideways into the sea. Graham led me up to the Steine as stars began to light the sky and lanterns glowed on every storefront.

He stayed by my side all the way to the carriage, where he handed me up, then sat opposite, humming Morton's sea tune, and watching out the windows with me.

I wanted to lean in, to feel his hum against my lips, feel the pressure of his hand at the back of my neck, and the warmth of his mouth on mine.

Goodness, Anna. Who have you become?

We only had a day left. Surely, I could control myself. Surely, I could wait to have a reasonable conversation with this man in the morning.

Surely, I could . . .

Chapter Twenty-Eight

GRAHAM

Anna climbed the stairs, and I followed behind her. She'd borne enough hardship tonight for ten people, so I tried to be a gentleman and not watch the sway of her hips by candlelight, nor the curve of her neck, but dash it all, I'd have to walk blind. Today had been unlike any other day of my life.

The Pavilion, the promenading, the prawns. Even Morton's excursion. It had all felt like a dream.

Anna made it so. Her sharp wit and audacity, how she pushed forward despite her heartache and fears, how she'd forgiven me my part with her father so quickly and so fully. And her laugh, that musical sound—it filled me up and shattered me all at once.

I'd made the biggest mistake of my life pretending not to love this woman.

I hadn't the slightest idea I'd been living a half-life. But now it was like a missing piece had returned and the part of me I'd locked away was now free. Alive.

Her father would come tomorrow. He and I had always kept business and family separate, and the mere thought of crossing that line sparked fear like lightning through me. But something had to be said. I'd stand beside Anna if she needed me to. I'd speak for her if she let me.

The Brighton investment could hang for all I cared. If Anna would take me as I was, we could live like this, by the sea, forever. If only she'd have me. If only she felt as I did.

Was I imagining things, or were her steps slowing the closer she got to the top of the stairs? Her hand glided along the banister, then—

She stopped on the top stair, slowly turning to face me, her silhouette lit by candles hung on either side of the wall. She was mesmerizing.

I froze a step below her; our heights made us nearly even. My heart hammered in my chest. I dared not move as I waited for her words.

She licked her lips, and a moment's hesitation flashed across her face. The candlelight glowed and crackled all around us.

My fingers itched to touch her, but I couldn't. Not yet. I could only watch as she lifted her hand and pressed it to my chest, her own rising and falling with measured breaths.

This had to be a dream. I'd drowned in the sea. Her attention, her focused touch was paradise.

Then her eyes fell to my mouth. She bit her bottom lip, and my stomach clenched, my entire body ignited.

"Graham," she whispered.

We needed a chaperone. Someone to keep her safe, to have her best interests in mind, because the more she looked at me with that longing in her eyes, the less I worried about *later* and the more I wanted *now.*

"Anna—" I started. My voice came out pained, with all the longing I felt but dared not speak.

She smoothed her fingertips over my lapels, then up and over my shoulders.

I couldn't breathe. My arms were frozen.

Do not move. Do not touch her. Don't do anything that might make her stop.

But how was a man to stay silent when the only woman who'd ever made him feel alive was showing him, clearly, that she was feeling it too?

I lifted my shaking hand to her hair and wrapped one of those silky brown curls around my finger.

She held my gaze as she lifted her hand to mine, pressing her cheek softly into my palm.

This cannot be real. And yet it was. Anna. Everything I wanted.

The greatest risk.

But was it a risk? I was good at calculations, at determining whether or not I'd lose, and there were always consequences, but she was leaning closer. Her free hand moved up my shoulder to my neck, her eyes measuring something in mine, and my frozen limbs were thawing, melting.

A risk, perhaps, but one with consequences I would willingly face.

"I want to kiss you, Graham," she whispered, and my breath hitched, my stomach flipping over itself.

"You're tired," I breathed. One last chance for her to change her mind and retreat.

Her fingers played with the hair at the nape of my neck. "On the contrary, you have me wide awake. I have never thought more clearly in my life."

My shaking fingers brushed the soft fabric of her bodice, and I was wholly encompassed by the feeling of her body in my hands. But I had to think this through. I had to be sure she knew what she was doing.

"Anna, you are not ignorant. You can see that my life is vastly different from yours. I will never have what your father has in money or connections or holdings."

"I do not care," she breathed. Her perfect little nose bumped mine. "I love—"

"I love you, Anna. I want nothing as badly as I want you."

She kissed me firmly then, so sure, so intently that I forgot to breathe. Her lips were soft—softer than I'd ever imagined— and so warm as they pressed against mine once, then again.

Anna.

A rush so strong jolted me to my senses, and I took her fully in my arms. Took her lips with mine and breathed her in. My thumb grazed her jaw as I tasted her lips—sweet like honey and salty from the sea—and she tasted mine. We were two candles burning, she and I, melting together, growing brighter with confidence by the second. She grasped my lapel, her other hand tightening around my neck, both of us untethering, unafraid to show our hands for once and beg.

I wanted more of her, all of her. Recklessly, eagerly, with a fiery urgency I'd never before felt. Her lips, her hands, her body pressed up against mine. I moved up a step, standing even with her, then angled her back and pressed her up against the wall, so I could—

"Graham?" A door squeaked as it opened.

In a breath, Anna pushed me back, eyes wide and set upon mine, like she couldn't believe what we'd just done. She was flushed, chest heaving, frozen.

It took a full ten seconds for me to come to my senses.

Tabs sniffed. "Graham?"

I cleared my throat, swallowing hard, and forced myself to take a half step back from the wall, my eyes never leaving Anna's.

"I'm coming," I called to the darkness. "Get back in your bed."

Somehow, by the grace and goodness of the Almighty, I heard the rustling of her blankets as she plopped back down on her bed.

Anna sidestepped. "Heavens, I forgot where we were. I should not have—I'm so sorry," she whispered.

"I'm not. Not at all." I needed to say something *right*, something perfect to get her to stay.

"I lost myself for a moment." She retreated a few steps, fingers touching her swollen lips.

I moved to follow her, palms raised in surrender, mind whirling. She'd kissed me. She'd *kissed* me, and nothing else in the world mattered. "We should have lost ourselves ages ago."

She placed a hand on the wall, retreated another step.

Wait, I silently begged her. *Don't run.*

Her eyes were full of the same fear I felt, like a cornered rabbit, its only options to run or be caught in a net. But hers was a net I desperately wanted to be caught in.

Cautiously, I took a half step nearer. Just close enough to reach out and graze my fingers along her jaw. "Don't leave me."

She lifted a hand to hold my wrist, neither pushing me away nor pulling me close, just holding me there. "You are just saying this to please me. My father, your investment—"

"I do not want the investment." I shook my head, struck with how freeing a string of words could feel, suddenly desperate. "You have the power to tell me no. Your father gave it to you. Anna, tell me not to invest in Brighton, and I'll prove it to you."

I moved closer, wrapping my other arm around her waist. "I love you," I whispered again. "I want nothing more than to be tied to you."

She raised her chin, looking up at me. "Just me?"

I took her lips with mine. "Only you."

She laughed against my kiss. "Very well, then. You cannot have your investment."

"Balderdash." I feigned a disappointed groan, nuzzling into her neck. "How about a trade? I'll have you, instead."

Tabs started to cry. "Graham!"

Slowly, Anna traced her hands down my chest. "Go. We'll speak more tomorrow," she whispered, then pressed her lips to mine.

"Tomorrow, then," I said as she turned in a flash, a flurry of skirts past Tabs's room, then closed the door to her own.

Chapter Twenty-Nine

GRAHAM

The next morning, Anna's door remained closed as I descended the stairs and stepped out into the dewy dawn. I'd slept all I could, anxious for Mr. Lane's return this afternoon and for Anna to wake so our conversation from last night could continue. I felt alive with hope and possibility, somehow wide awake despite the little sleep I'd managed.

I fed the cow and the cat, then delivered milk to Cook. I met Roland at the front of Highcliffe House with a ready horse and set off on my search.

I was well into the outskirts of Brighton before I found a patch of wild poppies. But she would love them. And how desperately, how completely I loved her.

I tied them with a ribbon I'd taken from Ginny's box of notions, wrapped the small bouquet loosely in paper, then secured them in my saddlebag. I'd arrange a tray with all her favorites—a plate of biscuits with jam and a cup of warm tea—alongside the flowers, and have Mariah bring it to her when she awoke.

I urged my horse homeward in a gallop, slowing only when Highcliffe House came into view. A carriage waited in my drive. Was Mr. Lane here early? I gripped the reins and kicked the horse's side. Drat it all. Anna deserved more warning than this. She would be as anxious to confront him as I.

I'd support Anna while she mended things with her father. Then I'd tell him that we could no longer invest as partners, that I was sorry I'd wasted his time but the Brighton investment I'd proposed was off the table. But, most terrifying, I would tell him that I loved his daughter and wanted to ask him for her hand.

A chill ran down my spine.

How could I ever say the words?

But the closer I rode, the easier it was to note the lack of details on the carriage. No black-and-gold crest of the Lane family. Not a polished shine, but a dull texture.

That was Tom Richards's carriage.

Thank heavens. He'd die from shock when he learned how things between Anna and I had changed.

I dismounted as Roland came to take the horse. I unbuckled the saddlebag to remove the poppies.

"Give these to Mariah, for Miss Lane this morning," I directed him, adding in the details for biscuits and tea.

"Graham?" Mother called, and I looked up to find Tom standing beside her in my doorway.

I raised a hand in greeting as I approached. "To what do we owe this nice surprise?"

"Everett." Tom nodded solemnly. "May I join you in your study?"

I knew that look. Whatever news he brought, I would not want to hear it. Either his bank had taken a hit or an investment wasn't paying out as quickly as we'd planned. "Shall we break our fasts first? It is still early yet."

"Afraid I'm short on time." He held his hands behind his back. Serious, then.

My stomach dropped. I nodded toward the back of the house as I entered. "Come."

Tom followed me down the hall, closing the door behind him as I moved around my desk. My muscles were too tense to sit and wait for him to settle.

"Out with it, then. What has happened?" I asked, hands gripping the back of my chair.

He did not sit. Neither did he waste a breath. "The Bradley account. Their company has gone bankrupt."

A beat of silence.

"Tom." I started to laugh, watching for him to join in. The Bradley account was half my current income. A loss that big would mean devastation. I'd have to find work, or else dip into my savings—but I had plans for my savings. "Do not jest over such matters."

He stared back hard, his entire body rigid. Silent.

I shook my head. This must be some grand misunderstanding. "Mr. Bradley has always been transparent with his numbers."

He stood firm, with a steely gaze. "I am afraid I am quite serious. He's been embezzling and gambling away the excess all year. I left straightaway to tell you in person, before you made any . . . significant financial decisions."

He meant purchasing the land. I rubbed my face, my throat suddenly dry. The room seemed to shift like the sea, and my stomach lurched.

Without the Bradley account, I'd have to pull money from my savings simply to live; we'd have a few years at most. And that was living very modestly.

That was without Anna.

"I need that income. I have dependents, Tom."

Tom leaned in, talking low. "It is unfortunate, and we will take legal action against him, but honestly, Graham, this could all be much worse. Your investment has already paid out and increased substantially. Regrettably, there will be no further payments, but as things stand with your savings, you are still able to support yourself, your mother, your sisters for some time. That is saying something."

But what about Anna? I finally sat down, legs weak and wobbly, taking steady breaths to calm the tightening in my throat. Without adequate income, I could not provide for her. I'd be inviting her into poverty. Worse, if I failed to secure more income. Not to mention the fact that her father would certainly oppose an engagement now. What could I do? How could I save this?

"It's not enough. Without Bradley, I need the Brighton investment."

Tom took the seat opposite me. "I strongly advise against it. Think smaller for now. Build up a bit more, then a big purchase won't feel like such a burden."

How long would that take? Another few years? I'd lose her. And I could not lose Anna. I stood and moved around my desk, determined to strengthen my legs, to pull out of this unsteady feeling.

"I am tired of living like my life could fall apart at any moment. I need security, Tom. Not mere stability."

Tom threw his hands in the air. "Then you should've taken a job as an accountant."

My heart raced up my throat. This couldn't be happening

to me. Not when I had everything planned. Not when, for once in my life, everything had all fallen perfectly in place.

What can I do? How can I fix this? What am I missing? My mind raced in one continuous, relentless circle. I needed money. No, I needed time. I needed the Brighton investment.

"Perhaps the seller will lease the land to me instead, then I can purchase in increments—"

"Graham." Tom's voice was steady, and I realized my own was shaking. "Think about this."

I had enough money to start. I'd have to rely on buyers as they came, but with time . . . "I could sell the plots before I've even bought in full."

He shook his head. "Sell the land before you even own it? Are you mad, Graham?"

"One hundred percent of the profits would be mine." It was mad, yes, but it could work. "And I wouldn't need Mr. Lane. We'd be fine. Better than fine."

How could he not see? I spun around to face him.

Tom looked at me like I'd truly lost my mind. "You are making plans for a future based on assumptions. And without a partner to make the financial sacrifice bearable."

"Perhaps, but if I took the risk, I would own Brighton land and control the income. This big of a hit would never happen again."

"If, if, *if.*" Tom hit the desk with his palm. "*If* you can sell the plots. *If* they sell quickly and not one at a time over years. Whether or not you pay at once, you tie up all your money in one fell swoop if you agree to this purchase. You risk too much."

But without it? How could I support my family, let alone

a wife who was accustomed to luxury, and later, a family of my own? I needed *more*. Lest I lose everything.

"I must consider it."

He stood abruptly, red crawling up his neck, his tone clipped and harsh. "You are not thinking with your head. I don't know when it happened to you—this pride, this greed—but stability used to be enough. Stability was what drove you to invest in the first place."

His words struck me like daggers, and I reared back.

Tom's face fell. He rubbed his forehead, then looked up. "Forgive me. As your banker, I've overstepped."

Heavy silence pulsed between us, pulling our frustrations taut.

"But as your friend . . ." Tom shifted his feet, his jaw set. "Your family is safe. They are happy. Don't risk that."

He let himself out of my study, and I sank back into my wooden chair. True, my family had survived on less. But I'd worked so blasted hard to give us more. To *be* more. And I had finally had everything I'd ever worked for—a house to be proud of, servants employed, and Anna. I had Anna.

What had I to offer her now beyond food and shelter? A tattered sofa, secondhand furniture, not even a pianoforte. Replacing them would mean taking from savings. Without the steady income from the Bradley account, we could not live as we'd been living the past two years.

I stood, my breaths so shallow my head felt light and full of wind. Tom was right. But how could I tell Anna? How would she look at me if she knew I'd just lost half my income and would have to substantially alter my budget in order to live?

My future as I'd seen it only hours ago slipped away,

like water through my fingers. No matter how hard I tried, I could not hold it.

I hated my father for abandoning us. Hated him for leaving me with a dying farm and no means by which I might save it. I hated how embarrassed I'd been, arriving on Mr. Lane's doorstep with nothing more than my late grandfather's name and hope for a connection. Yet, he had kindly received me, and oh, how desperately I had wanted to be like him.

Look at me now, I thought. Nothing has changed. I was still the same worthless boy barely managing to keep his family together.

No, some men weren't born to have it all. Some of us were destined to pretend.

Pretend such meager savings were large enough that I could walk side by side with men whose unfathomable wealth spanned generations. Pretend I hadn't restructured half my house and its holdings with my own two hands instead of hiring out. Pretend I deserved a woman so beautiful, so rare, despite the countless nights I'd lost sleep trying to keep the money coming in.

She deserved a better life. She deserved to want for nothing.

Heat engulfed me, my pride a welcome pool of relief. I could not tell her the whole of my misfortune. I would simply have to find an alternative before asking for her hand.

Tom had left the door ajar, and after a brief knock, it opened.

"Graham? There you are," Ginny said. Her gaze sharpened. "Are you unwell?"

I pulled a random book from a shelf and turned back to my desk. I swallowed hard and tried to sound nonchalant.

"Thinking over business matters with Mr. Richards. What do you need?"

She blew a piece of hair from her sight. "Ah, yes. Well. I'm half embarrassed to say, but my stays are growing tight."

Another expense. I nodded. "Very tight?"

"I'm a woman, Graham. When I eat, I gain weight in my—"

"Very well. Very well." I waved a hand to stop her.

"We've been eating so well with Anna here." She laughed. "It isn't dire, but yes."

The fact that she asked at all meant it was dire. But I appreciated her attempt to give me the leeway.

"If Ginny gets new stays, then I want new shoes!" Tabs called as she stomped into my study. "Mine have holes!"

"They do not," Mother said, rounding the corner after her.

"Well, my toes are pinched, and I'm certain holes will appear any day now!"

Mother chuckled, then sighed. "She is growing as well, I suppose."

Stays. Shoes.

I plastered a smile on my face. "I shall write it all down. We'll make a special trip in the coming weeks."

"Oh, can we take our list to London?" Ginny leaned against my desk and picked at her nails. "We could all squish in that little room you always rent. Things are so much better done there."

A trip to London would cost . . .

"It has been a time since we left Brighton," Mother agreed. "And having Anna here . . . She is so elegant and accomplished. Perhaps London would rub off on us."

I set aside the book in my hands. "Yes. Well, Anna comes from a very different lifestyle than we are accustomed to."

"She does," Mother agreed.

Ginny's eyes grew wide. "Perhaps she'd invite us!" she exclaimed. "Show us around. Introduce us to her friends."

"We could see Anna's house!" Tabs agreed.

My head started to pulse. I'd thought I'd designed the perfect life for us here, away from all that. "We cannot invite ourselves. And London is an unnecessary expense. We have everything we need right here in Brighton."

Ginny groaned. "Anna would invite us. It would cost us nothing."

I looked up at her, at the easy way she tossed around our finances as though they were fluid and simple to manage. My nostrils flared, and I raised a pointed finger. "Let me tell you something, sister." My words were clipped, jaw ticking. "*Nothing* in life comes without a cost. Even if you are not the one who pays it."

She jerked back, nose scrunched, and looked to Mother.

"Come, girls," Mother said, frowning at me. "Let us leave your brother to his thoughts."

Tabs bounded from the room while Ginny stood from my desk and turned. She held the doorframe and cast an ugly look over her shoulder.

"Never mind the stays. I can manage on my own. You've ruined the very idea of them."

"Genevieve." My voice was too rough, too deep. Too much like my father's. Still, I stood, hands fisted, with half a mind to follow and release every grievance upon her. If she only knew.

Mother raised her palms. "She's upset. Give her a moment to come to her senses. What you said was equally offensive."

Slowly, I sat, eyes fixed on every unanswered correspondence left scattered on my desk.

Mother stepped closer to me. "What did Mr. Richards come to say?"

I cleared my throat and sat back. I needed out of here. I needed room to think things through. "The usual ups and downs of investments."

"Downs, it would seem," Mother muttered.

"Is there anything more you need?" I could hear the whip in my voice, feel the guilt rising up in my chest. The skies outside my window had darkened, the shadows in the room growing longer in each corner.

Mother raised a brow and put my stray pen back in its jar. "Go have a walk. Breathe in the sea air. Before Mr. Lane arrives."

My throat tightened. *Anna.*

I palmed my eyes. "Has Anna come down yet?"

"Mariah just went up. With a beautiful bouquet of poppies." Another raised brow.

I looked past her to the door. "I'll return," I said.

Mother stepped back, out of the way of the door. "I know you will."

Chapter Thirty

ANNA

I'd never thought I'd visit Graham Everett's home, let alone feel comfortable there.

Indeed, I'd wanted to leave the moment I'd stepped foot in Brighton, and yet here I was, snuggled in bed, a healthy combination of fear and excitement and nervousness fluttering in my stomach.

Remembering how bold I'd been last night heightened every feeling. Oh, I wanted to hide under my covers and pillows. Facing Papa almost seemed easier than facing Graham after all I'd said and done.

But then my heart softened, remembering Graham's declarations, how adamantly he'd relinquished his plans, and likely a great deal of money, for me. No, for the mere *chance* of me. He'd done all that for the chance to court me. He'd kissed me back. A lot, actually. His intentions clearly laid out.

A gentle rap sounded on the door, and Mariah walked in. "For you," she said, handing me a tray. "From Mr. Everett."

A bouquet of poppies, tied with a yellow ribbon, and a plate of biscuits with tea.

He'd remembered. I lifted them to my nose. Soft and sweet and velvety. Where on earth had he found them? "No note?"

"I do not think he had time," she said as she shuffled around the room. "A visitor came just as he'd returned home."

Home. But who would be visiting him at this early hour? "Quickly, Mariah. I must dress." I laid the poppies on the desk beside my bed and paced to my washing table.

I chose a simple white day dress and had Mariah pin a few poppies in my hair. My shaky hands allowed for only a few sips of tea and a bite of a biscuit before insisting I find Graham. If he was entertaining, I would find him in the drawing room.

With no one in sight, I practically flew down the stairs, slowing only as I reached the bottom. Laughter carried out into the foyer, but inside the drawing room, I found only Ginny, covered in threads of all colors, and Tabs curled up at her mother's feet, reading a book aloud.

"Anna!" Tabs cried, jumping to her feet and racing to throw her arms around me. "Thank you! Thank you, a hundred times, for catching me an eel."

"Yes, Anna. Thank you for the many details we've involuntarily learned about an eel's size, smell, and innards," Ginny muttered with evident sarcasm.

"Graham says you caught him with your own hands." Tabs's eyes grew wide.

"Well, your brother did help, and Morton—"

"Cook let me watch while she split him open!"

"Oh, Tabitha," Mrs. Everett chided, disgusted. "Enough."

She leaned in close. "His insides were pink and blue, all slimy and soft."

I started to gag, but recovered. "You are welcome," I said,

patting her shoulder. "Where is your brother?" I looked around the room, rocking back and forth on my heels.

"On a walk," Ginny said, with a curious note of censure in her voice. "Clearing his head."

"His banker visited this morning," Mrs. Everett explained. "An old friend."

"Ah," I said, stepping farther into the room. "Is everything well?"

Mrs. Everett looked up with a measuring glance. "There is always something. Success from investments means constant motion. This is not the first time Mr. Richards has visited unannounced."

My shoulders relaxed. "Of course not. Forgive me. Perhaps I will try to catch Mr. Everett on his walk."

"No, you cannot leave!" Tabs held fast to me, her little arms encircling my waist. "Your father returns any moment."

Mrs. Everett added, "Indeed, he sent word just now, Miss Lane. Your father arrived in Brighton and is settling at a local inn before visiting Highcliffe House directly."

Goodness, he'd had an early start. It didn't seem real, having to face him now that I knew everything. He'd likely apologize. I'd listen to his excuses, but I knew I'd forgive him because Graham was right. Papa loved me. He'd wanted to protect my heart, and wasn't that what I'd been asking for all along? Through all that Mr. Lennox had done and all the gossip that had followed, I'd wanted Papa to keep me from the pain of a broken heart. But sometimes pain demanded to be embraced. I had to trust that there would be something worthwhile on the other side of whatever conversation Papa and I would soon have.

"This week has flown by with the gulls," Ginny said, peering up from her embroidery.

"Perhaps your father would like to stay at Highcliffe House," Tabs suggested as she released her hold on me to mosey back to her mother. "I wish to read to you my favorite story."

"In time," her mother said. She kissed Tabs's brow, then looked up at me. "Graham does not often walk farther than a quarter mile down the shoreline."

I took that as my cue.

I forewent my hat and skipped down the steps to the drive, then hurried around to the back of Highcliffe House to where a narrow, dusty path led down to the shore. A bit of a walk, but I needed to see Graham. I wanted to see his face, measure his gaze, take his hand in mine.

The breeze carried me around the house, down toward the little shed and its fenced plot where Graham's cow grazed. I remembered our time together that morning. How much of his past he'd revealed, and the sorrow in his eyes. The little path branched, and I took the route that led me down a steep decline, which I managed with careful steps, then hopped down to the rocky shore. I looked both ways down the shoreline and saw him not far away, sitting on a rock and facing the sea.

"Good morning," I called, carefully pacing toward him.

Startled, Graham looked up, then slowly rose to his feet. "Good morning," he returned. "You're awake."

He looked exhausted and serious—perhaps Tabs had kept him up all night again with nightmares?—and combed a hand through his hair as though that might fix it all.

I watched him paint a smile on his face as I stopped in

front of him. Our eyes met, and we smiled together remembering last evening. The delicious awkwardness of a new beginning. I studied every curve of his face, and he studied mine. Every freckle, every scar, every line of worry and age brought about too soon. I reached out and ruffled his hair back to the way it usually was, the way I preferred it, then asked, "Am I interrupting your thoughts?"

Slowly, he placed one hand on my waist, then the other. "You *are* my thoughts," he answered, pulling me nearer.

I bit back a shy smile. "Thank you for my poppies."

He nodded, eyes set upon mine. "I'd have bought you roses or lilies, but you did say they were your favorite."

"Rare to find, I'd wager, so close to the sea."

Graham said nothing, only studied my face as I slipped my hands up and over his shoulders. Slowly, so slightly, his features turned downcast. Something had him out here, sitting alone, staring at the sea.

"Graham," I said gently. "What is troubling you?"

He smiled halfway, looking over my shoulder and shaking his head. "It's nothing."

Hardly. "If you're worried about my father, I am resolved to forgive him. Indeed, I feel much more understanding this morning than I did yesterday."

He raised both brows in surprise. "I am happy to hear it."

He said the words, but his smile did not feel sincere. It worried me. "I can see something in your head spinning round. What is it?"

His arms fell from around my waist. One hand found mine and squeezed, then he released me and stepped back to sit upon the boulder where I'd found him. He rubbed his face in his hands as though to brace himself.

I watched, anxiety brewing like a storm in my chest, then spoke softly, "Please." Hesitantly, I took a few steps forward, stopping an arm's length away from where he sat. He looked so helpless, almost lost, like he was not sure exactly what to do. He reached out and tugged on my skirts, pulling me toward him until our knees brushed. Slowly, he wrapped his arms around my waist again and looked up at me with round, hopeful eyes.

"I do not want you to worry. I have everything in hand. I just need a little more time."

I took his face in my hands, smoothing out the creases in his brow. He closed his eyes, and I weaved my fingers through his hair. His banker had come this morning. And while I knew a little about money and what it took to run an estate, I imagined it was stressful. This, however, felt different. This was more than stress.

"Tell me. Perhaps I can help."

His eyes flew open. "No. Please, do not fret over this, Anna. I can manage. I will manage. It's actually not so bad, I just—" He laughed, but there was no joy in the sound. "I just need time. Nothing between us has changed."

But *something* had. "Do you love me?" I asked.

"Absolutely," he said without pause.

"Then please tell me what happened with your banker this morning."

Chapter Thirty-One

GRAHAM

She was adamant.

And was that not why I loved her? Her intelligence, her unfaltering desire to help and support and encourage?

It felt different when aimed toward me. I did not want *help*. I wanted to stand on my two feet, and I'd been so close. So blasted close to finally being independent. To having Anna and a life of my own where I did not need to rely on anyone for anything ever again.

Fate apparently had other plans.

I glanced up at Anna, who waited patiently for an answer she most definitely deserved. I'd offered her everything last night, and I'd meant it.

"I lost an account," I said, hating the meager sound in my voice. "But I'll find another. I always do."

She only said, "A significant loss." Simply spoken, without judgment.

"Yes."

Her brow creased. "My father can help."

I dropped my hold on her waist. "No, Anna—"

"He'll be here soon. I'll wait to confront him, and you can speak with him directly. Ask him for whatever you need."

I shook my head. "No. He is your father, not mine. You need to speak with him and reconcile. His focus should be you, and only you, from now on. I can manage on my own."

But she wasn't listening. Her mind was fitting every piece in its spot. "And, of course, you can have the Brighton investment. I would've allowed it anyway had you not asked me to say no."

If only I could afford it. I stood and paced a few steps around her. I tried again. "I will work everything out. Your father has done so much for me already; I will not ask for his aid when I am capable."

Anna did not want a life where her father was at the helm. She wanted a husband who lived independently, who did not rely on her father or aim to utilize his wealth. I knew this because she'd said so relentlessly. And after Lennox? I refused to become at all like the man she despised. Not to mention the fact that this very scenario—me, investing with her father—was exactly what she was against in the first place.

"He has already offered it. If this investment will solve your problems, why will you not take it? For us? For our family?"

Our family. Gads, I did not deserve this woman. I felt pain behind my eyes, a welling of emotion pooling behind them, and bit the inside of my cheek hard to keep it from spilling over. She did not understand how much I'd lost. How uncertain our life together would be if I used my savings on this investment partnership now. "I cannot. I am sorry."

Anna followed me, stopping at my side, and I felt her gaze on my face, perhaps measuring my sincerity, questioning. "It must be very bad, then."

I swallowed hard. I could not meet her gaze. "Yes."

"Will you return to London? Stay with us instead of

renting a room?" she asked. "If I'm to wait, at least give me that."

I looked down and rubbed the back of my neck. "I could never ask for an invitation."

"I am inviting you. My father will not bat an eye. Indeed, I should think he would be pleased at our getting on so well."

She smiled, but I could not return it. I did not feel it. What if I couldn't manage things? What if recovering my annual income took a year, or more? How could I make Anna wait? How could I avoid telling Mr. Lane everything for that long? Keep another secret? I wouldn't.

Anna grasped my arm. "I shall invite your mother too. And your sisters. I daresay Ginny will love the shops."

I grimaced, thinking of all the things she'd want. On top of all the things she actually needed.

"Or the gardens," Anna quickly corrected. I could not meet her eye. "Hyde Park. No one needs the shops when there is Hyde Park to explore."

"We should return," I said.

She stiffened beside me, only relaxing marginally when I offered her my arm.

We walked back up the shoreline, up the path, back home where everything came more clearly into view.

The chips of paint on my shutters.

The unpolished door handle and the creak as I pushed it open for Anna. Old carpets, and even older furniture because we had focused so much on having a home and less about what it looked like for company.

I hadn't cared before. But now . . .

I led Anna to the staircase, which I assumed she'd follow up to her room, then trudged toward my study.

Chapter Thirty-Two

ANNA

I was losing him.

It wasn't my place to ask after the account Graham had lost, but the loss inspired enough fear for him to retreat, and I couldn't shake the feeling that I was losing him in the process.

What could I do? I wanted to be his companion, the person he shared the heavy weight of trials with, not his burden. And yet, a burden was exactly how I felt.

And completely helpless. As soon as he left me at the foot of the staircase, as soon as he'd turned his back, reality had set it. The reality of a goodbye as soon as Papa arrived to claim me, paired with an uncertain future afterward.

My heart had swollen and twisted; its pain burned my throat and behind my eyes. I'd cried after hearing about what Mr. Lennox had done, but this was different. These tears seeped out straight from cracks in my heart, and I could not control them.

Graham loved me, but he would not ask for me. I wanted to believe that he'd find another account, but what did I know about accounts? I'd seen Graham worried before, heard his serious mumblings with my father in times past, but this was different. This loss had shattered things, and I could do nothing to fix it.

After Mr. Lennox, I'd cared so much about the opinions of others. I'd worried they might talk about how stupid I was to fall for a man already engaged. What they might think of me. What their judgments might do to my reputation.

How foolish I felt now for caring about such minuscule things. My feelings for Graham felt so big, so mountainous, everything else seemed so small.

Opinions? What were opinions and judgments against love? I'd choose love any day, with no thought to who might hate me for it or who would drag my name through mud and filth because of it. That's how big my love for Graham felt.

I'd thought he felt the same. Perhaps, as he'd said, he still did. But what happened when love wasn't enough? When circumstance forced two people apart no matter how enormously they loved?

I'd only just rinsed my face and dried it when Mariah peeked inside.

"Your father is arriving," she said, closing the door behind her.

Despite all he'd kept from me and how angry I still felt at him, I felt a sudden urge for his safe embrace. I swiped fresh wetness from my eyes, trying desperately to calm my wobbling chin.

Mariah watched me with apprehension. "Salts?" she asked, holding up a vial.

"No. Thank you, Mariah. I hate the way they make me feel." What I needed was to speak with Papa. Graham had said he did not want help, but he'd also said Papa was his close friend. And like it or not, friends should know about one another's struggles. They should help each other.

"Miss?" Mariah prompted.

I drew in a breath through my nose and swallowed it all down. "I'm finished here," I said, motioning to my things all packed and organized, ready to follow Papa to the inn when he came.

"I am to ride ahead," Mariah said, eyes frantically searching for any missing piece. "I shall see you at the inn."

Another dabbing of my cheeks, then I followed her toward the staircase, where happy voices carried up from the foyer.

I heard his deep, familiar laugh before I saw him—Papa. Descending the stairs unnoticed, I waited for him at the bottom. I caught sight of his peppered hair, his bright face wearing a wide grin. My aching heart leaped toward him. No matter what he'd kept from me, Graham had been right. He was my father. He loved me. He would never knowingly hurt me.

"Anna, you *cannot* leave." Tabs bounded toward me, falling into my arms in a fit of tears at the bottom step. It took every effort to wrap my arms around her, to comfort her, for I was frozen, watching Papa and Graham interact like this morning hadn't happened. Like Graham and I hadn't exchanged our hearts only last evening.

Tabs squeezed my middle, and I crouched low. "You shall come and visit me in London soon," I whispered. "You are my very favorite, and I shall write to you. I promise."

"There's my darling girl!" Papa's deep voice bounced around the hall.

Graham turned, and I caught the strain in his eyes as I

rose. The worry he could not shake. No matter how hard he tried, he could not pretend with me. Not anymore.

Papa held out his arms, and I drew near, but the air around us shifted, heavy and tense with secrets as he placed a kiss on my temple.

"Ginny, Tabitha, shall we see to tea?" Mrs. Everett motioned, and Ginny, despite her curiosity, nodded and followed, leaving the three of us in the foyer.

"Please, Mr. Lane. Make yourself comfortable," Graham said, motioning to the drawing room.

"What a stunning location, right above the sea," Papa said, stepping through the doorway.

Graham smiled at me as I passed through, but I could not hold his gaze. Our unspoken words grew louder by the second. "Thank you. Yes, I could not pass up the opportunity, despite the house's character."

"You have a good eye for it; that I have never doubted." Hands on his hips, Papa glanced out the back left window, which overlooked the sea.

"Thank you, sir." Perfectly polite. Compassionate. No declarations on his lips.

My smile became tight, and I realized, as I took a seat, my legs were shaking.

Papa sat on Graham's settee and turned to me. "Am I to assume Brighton is as lovely as Mr. Everett claims, Annie?"

I glanced sideways at Graham. His stare was like fire on my cheek.

"Surprisingly, yes. I have enjoyed my time here immensely." The polite thing to do would be to inquire after his time in Bath. Part of me did not wish to hear the truth, but

I was decidedly through with pretending. I raised my chin. "How did you find Bath?"

Papa chuckled uncomfortably, his gaze moving meaningfully to Graham's. "Very amenable."

Graham cleared his throat from the chair opposite me. To his credit, he did not smile, did not encourage Papa's secret. "Your daughter has made quite an impression on my household, Mr. Lane. I am quite reluctant to give her up."

"Is that so?" My father furrowed his brow, then straightened in his seat. "Then I am to assume our investment is in order?"

Graham lifted a hand to rub the back of his neck, then shifted in his seat. His brows scrunched as he said, "I am afraid things have become more complicated than—"

"Perhaps the two of you could renegotiate the terms." I gave Graham a meaningful look. "Brighton is indeed worth the investment, Papa. Perhaps . . . perhaps we should increase our share in the investment."

"*Anna*, please," Graham worried aloud, but he'd clearly spoken my name without thinking. He winced and rubbed his face with a hand.

Papa frowned, the crease deepening in his brow. "Everett? What is the meaning of this?"

Still, Graham watched me, a pained expression on his face that I instantly regretted causing. None of this was his fault. None of it was mine. We were simply the products of a very unfortunate circumstance that needed mending, and I was making a mess of it.

But if I didn't try, who would? Papa would take me home, and I had no idea when I would see Graham again.

"Forgive me," I said, swallowing back the rising emotion

in my throat. Dizzy, I stood and paced around the settee. "My head is aching, and I fear I am not well."

What could I do? I did not wish to leave, but neither could I intrude longer on Graham. Not without invitation.

Papa stood and quickly wrapped his arm around my back as though I might faint any second. "I have you, Annie. Let us go and rest at the inn."

"Where are you staying?" Graham asked, following us. "I'll send the doctor."

"No need," I said, even as the room spun. Papa muttered off an address.

Mrs. Everett and Ginny reentered, slowing their steps as they took notice of Papa with his arm around me and Graham, a frightened look upon his face.

"Ready the carriage at once," Papa barked out as he led me toward the door.

Roland flew through the foyer and out the door, and Graham stood helpless as we emptied the drawing room. Mrs. Everett grabbed his arm. They spoke with a single glance, and she pursed her lips.

I turned as we reached the front door. "I cannot thank you enough for welcoming me into your home. My room was perfect, our days well spent, and I shall miss you. All of you."

Mrs. Everett smiled, her eyes soft though unsure. "You brightened our home, Miss Lane. I hope you'll soon return."

Ginny reached out and drew me into a hug. "Please come again soon. It's been so lovely to have a constant friend."

I squeezed her back. "I promise I will."

"You are my very dearest friend, Anna," Tabs said, hugging my legs. I couldn't help it; tears started to well up, and I sniffed, wiping the wetness.

I couldn't do it. I couldn't look at Graham. Why would he not ask after me? Why wouldn't he beg me to stay? Why would he not *speak* to me?

"I will call upon you soon," I heard Graham's voice from behind. "And if you need anything—"

"Thank you," Papa muttered, and a servant closed the door behind us.

Neither of us spoke as we entered the carriage. Papa sat directly across from me.

I tilted my head back against the carriage wall and pinched the bridge of my nose. My head did not hurt as much as my heart did.

The carriage bolted forward with a creak.

"Odd, that. He's never spoken to you so directly," Papa said quietly. "Never so forcefully. Nor with such familiarity."

"Perhaps not in front of you," I breathed. My stomach lurched with every turn of the wheels, with every word Graham hadn't said. I did not want to stoke this fire between Papa and me, but we needed to have an honest conversation, and I feared the longer I waited to divulge my secrets, the worse I would feel.

"I do not understand."

I shook my head. There was so much to say, and I hardly knew where to start. "Mr. Lennox is engaged. Or was, before I encouraged his attention and his uncle paid the woman to cry off."

A long moment passed as my words found their place among Papa's befuddlement. He blinked, scoffed. "That cannot possibly be true."

"He has admitted as much. And just yesterday he told me more. About you and some woman in Bath."

I watched as the color drained from Papa's face and realization dawned. He grasped the edge of his seat. "What, exactly, did he say?"

"Ms. Peale, is it? He saw the two of you in Bath. And Graham told me the whole of it."

"I—well." Papa fell back against his seat, cheeks turning rosy, eyes wide with surprise. He started to laugh. "Forgive my ignorance, Anna, but this is all very unexpected. Ms. Peale is a friend, yes—"

"You should have told me."

He nodded slowly, the surprise in his eyes refocusing into seriousness. "I should have. Though in truth, there has been nothing to divulge save for the past few weeks. We met some time ago, but I've only just admitted my feelings to myself— once I realized she never quite left my thoughts. But by then, I did not know what to do, not with the promise I'd made to you."

His eyes met mine, focused and intent. "You are the most important person in the world to me. Since your mother passed, you've been my first priority. We've been a team, you and I. So I should have told you, and I am truly sorry that you discovered the truth before I could tell you myself. You must have thought—well, I can't quite imagine. And I am sorry. Can you forgive your old Papa for his poor judgment?"

Tears welled in my eyes, and I wiped them with the backs of my shaking hands. I did not need his promises; I just wanted his truth. He'd tried to protect me. And he loved me.

"I want you to be happy," I said thickly. "And I never want you to keep such secrets from me."

He moved to my bench and put his arm around me. "I shan't. I promise, I shan't ever again. Indeed, I spoke with her about our promise just now in Bath. And she understands. She supports me. I've told her my intentions, and now I feel bound to tell you the same. I love her, Anna. I would very much like to introduce the two of you, knowing that absolutely nothing will be made permanent until you are ready."

"I am happy for you, Papa. Truly, I am." I angled my knees toward his. "And I would very much like to meet her."

"You would?" Papa straightened. There was hope in his eyes, and my heart startled. I wondered how I'd missed it. The joy. The happiness that once hadn't been there.

"But there is something I must also admit," I said.

Papa covered my hands with his. "Tell me. What has happened?" His voice was serious and business-like.

I took a deep breath. Where to start? Where had it all begun—truly? "I told Mr. Everett—Graham—that I did not want him to invest with you ever again."

Papa reared back. "Anna. But, why? Why would you say that? Mr. Everett is a good man."

"I grievously disliked him, Papa. Every time he visited, he took you from me. Sometimes when I needed you the most. Like this past Season. I thought I had everything in hand, but I was wrong. I chose wrong. The whole of London has heard how stupid I've been."

"Not if the engagement was kept secret," Papa said quickly. "Lennox will wish to keep his own transgressions quiet, despite his failed attempt to win you. I will make sure that whatever story might reach the papers reflects favorably on you. Indeed, I will ensure that the Lennox name is never entwined with ours again."

I stifled a cry and fell into his side. "Thank you, Papa."

"I only wonder why you did not tell me in the first place. Why did you keep such a great burden to yourself?"

"I meant to tell you that night after dinner. But then Graham came, and you were so interested in his investment."

"I see."

"Besides, it's a bit humiliating to admit that I am so terrible a judge of character. I thought Mr. Lennox a saint, and Graham a loathsome snake. And I've botched everything."

Papa sat back, shoulders drooping. "Darling, you've not botched anything. We can put all this to right. You and I will start anew. No more secrets. If Everett's investment is not sound, then I shall tell him so, and he will understand."

"No. The investment is sound," I groaned, covering my face in my hands.

"Then why—"

"Perhaps I've gone mad. I *feel* mad trying to explain. In truth, yes, in the beginning, I had every intention of rejecting the investment and invalidating Graham's claims. I loathed him. I thought him arrogant and overconfident and brimming with greed.

"But then this week, I met his family. I sat at his table and listened to them bantering and laughing, watched how they play together and support each other. I see now why you care for him. Perhaps why you've taken him as a protégé of sorts. Graham *is* a good man. He is kind and honest and incredibly aware. He treats me like an equal, as someone with thoughts and intelligence, with feelings and dreams. Before this week, I did not understand what it felt like to be understood, and loved, by someone."

Papa fell silent. I'd shocked him, like he'd shocked me. But we both deserved to lay our cards openly on the table.

Slowly, I continued, "He and I—because of your rela-tionship—have spent quite a lot of time together over the years. Some memories are better than others. Some, hope-fully, more easily forgotten."

"Annie, what exactly are you saying?"

"I love him, Papa."

Like a wave crashing into my heart, memories flooded me, and I remembered the way Graham had looked at me when I tried on his spectacles, how he'd offered me a blanket after dropping me in the sea, how our laughter had entwined as we played the alphabet game, and how closely he'd held me dancing. The spicy smell of his shave.

I missed him already. I missed his home. Tabs, Ginny, their mother, even their shabby-armed settee. I wouldn't change it. I wouldn't change *them*.

Papa's eyes had grown round as saucers.

"So I kissed him. But then—"

"You *w-what*—" Papa stammered.

"—something happened this morning. His banker came, and he's lost an account. Now he says he needs time to man-age things, to recover, but I cannot bear to leave him like this. He won't ask you for help, but he desperately needs it."

Papa swallowed hard. He blinked several times, then seemed to collect the thoughts behind his eyes. He seemed uncannily calm for a father who'd just been dealt his daugh-ter's bleeding heart.

"Forgive me, are we speaking of the same person? Graham . . . Mr. Graham Everett?"

I nodded. "I cannot rise above this feeling that he fears he cannot provide for me. I do not need fancy things, Papa. I truly do not. But I think Graham believes I do. I think he is in trouble. And I . . . I feel so—" I sputtered, choking on the emotion rising in my throat. "So sad."

Papa sighed, and I felt his arms encircle me, his head lean down against mine.

"Anna, I am inadequate," Papa said, his own voice thick but determined. "It is times like this that I dearly wish I had your mother's ear, her words and wisdom. I do not know the proper thing to say to assure you that all will be well, but I do know that as your father I must speak with Mr. Everett straightaway. I will make this right."

Our carriage rolled to a stop, and I peeked out my window. We'd stopped in front of a building within the Steine. The very inn where Graham had taken me for prawns. A fresh sob escaped me.

Papa did not wait. He opened our door and jumped out. "I shall get a horse," he said, a shadow casting over his features. "I'll return before luncheon."

Before I could respond, Mariah appeared. She took the steps up and sat beside me in the carriage, offering me a handkerchief to dry my face. In time, she led me to my room, speaking in hushed tones about peppermint tea and a cool rag for my head. She didn't leave me. She brushed out my hair. Made me eat two crumpets. Then she tucked me into bed and curled up in a chair.

She hummed a gentle tune as she stitched, and somehow between thoughts of Papa riding off and Graham's worried eyes, I drifted into sleep.

Chapter Thirty-Three

GRAHAM

Mother waited until the Lane carriage had disappeared down the drive before rounding on me.

"Why did Anna leave in such a state?" she asked harshly. "Tell me at once before I die of humiliation."

I stood firm. I could not keep such an enormous secret from my family, not when I was bursting at the seams with problems that concerned us all. But that did not mean I had to tell all three of them at once. I'd start with the obvious.

"Miss Lane did not wish to stay. She was unwell."

"She was fine this morning, until the two of you returned from your walk." Ginny's words were an accusation.

"Whether Miss Lane is unwell or not is *none* of your concern, Graham," Mother chided. "She is old enough, she is of age, and by speaking out in front of her father with such force and familiarity as you did—"

"Embarrassing, even for you," Ginny added, with Tabs at her side.

"I am not a fool," I said sharply. I left them, moving into the drawing room, but they followed me. Mr. Lane's expression had said it all—I'd spoken out of turn; I'd spoken to

Anna like she was already mine to speak for. I'd attempted to keep some semblance of control over my life, but everything had completely fallen apart. He'd expect an explanation, one that I was not yet prepared to give.

Mother's frustration settled, and she took my arms in her hands. "She is not yours to speak for, Graham. Not unless you ask her, and she accepts."

"Wait a moment." Ginny touched our arms, then laughed in clear disbelief. "Graham, you're not in love with Anna?"

My shoulders fell in resignation. Why was I fighting against my own family? To save myself from their pity? We were a family. And I could no longer hold the weight of my burdens alone.

Besotted. Every worthless bit of me.

Tabs must've noticed the change in me, for she sucked in a breath. "I knew it! I knew it all along!"

"It does not signify," I said to Mother. "I need more time before I can offer for her. Tom brought unfortunate news this morning. The Bradley account . . . It's gone."

Mother raised a hand to her chest. "What?"

"What is the Bradley account?" Ginny looked between us, worry creasing her features. "Our savings?"

"No, but a good portion of our income," Mother answered shakily.

I hated that the women in my household knew so much about our finances, that they had to worry at all. "We'll be fine."

"Yes. Of course. We shall manage," Mother added.

"No, we won't," Tabs cried. "Not without Anna!"

Her little face scrunched, tears welling in her eyes, and I understood. I wanted nothing more than to cry and scream and shake my fists. What was money, what was this house, this view, without Anna? She'd brought life into our home, and I'd pushed her away.

"We can sell my harp," Ginny said, serious and resolved. "It's an antique. It will fetch a good price. Enough to pay for Anna's expenses for a year, maybe two. It will give you time to find something more."

A lump settled firmly in my throat. "Ginny, I would never sell your harp."

She turned to Mother. "What else do we have? Books?"

Mother snapped her fingers, her mind alive behind her eyes. "I have a lovely jeweled necklace your father gave me when we were young. I've been holding on to it in case of an emergency—"

"This *is* an emergency!" Tabs said with feeling. "You have to go and get her *now*, Graham, and bring her *back*!"

"If you love her," Ginny said.

I nodded, feeling more the grieving boy freshly home from Cambridge than the wiser man I'd been forced to become. And certainly more humbled.

"I do."

"Yes!" Tabs jumped up atop the settee.

"Absolutely not!" Mother scolded her. "Down!"

Ginny grinned. "Let us hope she hasn't already come to her senses."

Mother drew out a paper and pen and ink, handing everything to Ginny, who marked even lines from one side to another. "The harp, the necklace . . ."

"I could sell my shell collection!" Tabs chimed in.

"Girls," I said sternly. I could not allow this. "No one is selling anything."

"Oh, and I have a ring!" Mother chimed in, waving toward the paper.

I fell into a nearby chair, listening to the three of them plan and plot and scratch nibs on paper, too exhausted to argue. I missed Anna already. Hated myself for letting her go. Would she have understood if I had told her the whole of it? How poorly we'd been living so I could build my savings? I couldn't have borne the pity in her eyes. No, I needed to be the man she deserved. I'd give her everything first, then I'd tell her.

Minutes ticked by, when suddenly, a loud rap landed harshly upon the door.

Roland moved past the drawing room door, then announced, "Mr. Lane."

I instantly sobered. Anna's father? Here?

"Go," Mother commanded me, yanking Tabs's arm and moving toward the left front corner of the room with Ginny. She'd calculated just right, for Mr. Lane bounded into the room, puffed up and tense. Perhaps he'd heard about the Bradley account. Though the loss would hurt him much less than it had hurt me.

"Mr. Lane," Mother said, curtseying. "What a lovely surprise to see you again so soon. We were just leaving. Good day."

"Good day," he said gruffly. "Everett."

I waited until they'd left, Roland closing the doors behind them, before offering Mr. Lane a seat. "Allow me to apologize for my forwardness earlier."

"Very good. You were out of sorts. We all were."

I nodded. Why had he come? "Is Miss Lane well?"

"She is resting." Mr. Lane crossed his legs, then uncrossed

them. Then he sniffed and squared his knees. "We spoke in the carriage. I have been thoughtless on many accounts, Everett. I shall have to earn back her trust. But I will do anything for my daughter."

Brave girl. She'd already spoken to him. Pride swelled my heart, as did that familiar claim linking me to her. "Mr. Lane, I—"

"I have not had more than the ride over to think this through," he said, shifting again in his seat.

"Sir?"

"I had the passing thought," he started, then stifled a laugh, "how dreadfully funny it would be if she was jesting with me, just so I'd make a fool of myself, coming over here, demanding things. Because that would be like Anna, you understand. She has a sharp wit like her mother. Loves to play. She feels things very deeply and must have laughter, or she'll go mad."

The very sound of her name gave me a measure of confidence. Enough to face the discomfort of this conversation with her father, no matter his reaction. I drew in steady breaths. Listening. Waiting for whatever Mr. Lane wasn't saying.

He tilted his head, then crossed his legs again. "Did my daughter kiss you, Everett?"

By George, I hadn't expected *that*. A rush of blood warmed my face. How did he know? Had she told him? I shifted in my seat, parting my lips, then closing them. He did not seem angry at the possibility. Though neither did he seem particularly pleased. I steeled my resolve.

"She did."

"Dash it all, that girl." He shook his head, chuckling at some private thought. "Well? What did you do?"

I washed a hand over my face. Was it not obvious? "I, uh, I kissed her back, sir."

"No, you ignorant boy. What did you do to make her kiss you in the first place?"

Now *that* was a reasonable question. "I've no idea," I answered blankly.

"Well, then." Mr. Lane slapped his hands on his thighs, still amused, but as serious and formal as though we were discussing an investment proposal. "Shall we move to your study?"

Equal parts relief and terror split through me. Relief that he might actually consider an arrangement. Terror at the thought of him hearing just how unworthy I was. "Mr. Lane—"

"We will resolve this here and now, Everett, if you want anything more to do with me. Certainly, if you want the Brighton investment." He stood, starting to walk toward the foyer.

I shook my head. He had it all wrong. "My relationship with Anna is not connected to the work you and I engage in, sir. I told her I would forfeit the investment, even before—"

He spun around. "Before, what?"

I stood, wiping my sweaty hands on my breeches. "Before Tom Richards came."

Mr. Lane remained unsurprised. "Your banker."

"The Bradley account has gone under." I watched his face fall, then recover with understanding of the whole of it.

I continued, "As it stands, we still made a fine purse. But my family's lifestyle depended upon those earnings. I cannot spend my savings on land when I must now support my family with those funds. Let alone . . ."

"Anna," Mr. Lane supplied. "I see."

Did he?

"You love her, then?" He would not meet my eye.

"With everything I am, sir. I have always admired her, but sometimes it is easier to argue with a person than try to see them clearly. She fits with my family like I never imagined anyone could. She is talented, accomplished, intelligent, wise, and kind. I will never love another the way I love Anna."

He pointed an accusing finger. "You should have told me straightaway."

"I had every intention. The very moment I had my finances back in order."

"Do you think so little of me?" he asked, taking a step closer. "That I would not help you?"

"Please, Mr. Lane. Do not take offense by it. I have spent my whole life relying on other people to survive. I'd much prefer to do this on my own."

"Respectable. But foolish."

I held his stare. "I want to be the man she expects of me. I want to deserve her."

"You will never deserve her," he said blankly. "No matter how much money you make. You could shower her in jewels, buy her every convenience, and it will never be enough."

I blanched. The man was cutting my legs from under me. "I want to try."

He shook his head and rubbed his tense jaw with a hand. "I do not mean to be cross. I have traveled far this morning, and I fear I am not adequately prepared for this conversation. That is not to say that the idea of an arrangement between the two of you has not crossed my mind." He started to laugh, then clasped his hands together. "I simply thought the chance had run its course."

He sighed then, sinking back into his chair. "You have little to offer her, Everett. No title. No holdings. Little wealth."

I nodded once, returning to my chair. Back to where we'd started. I knew his arguments all too well, for they ran the same circles in my head.

"And yet." Mr. Lane leaned forward, his elbows resting on his knees as his eyes locked with mine. "I can think of no better man to give her to."

A rush of emotion washed over me. Gratitude so deep it ached. I swallowed hard, exerting every effort to vanquish the prickling in the corners of my eyes. "Thank you, Mr. Lane."

"Tell me, then. As a friend. What can I do to help you?" He straightened his back and looked around as though he might find the answer hidden in the shadows of my drawing room. "A loan that you could pay back over time?"

I shook my head. "To be indebted to you further—"

He furrowed his brows. "A far cry better than to the bank."

I could not argue. But again, my problems were not his to solve.

He leaned forward, serious again. "Sell Highcliffe House to fund your half of the Brighton investment. Move into my home in London with Anna. We shall find a reasonable apartment for your mother and sisters to rent nearby. I mean to ask Ms. Peale to be my wife, and I shall live with her in Bath until her mother leaves us. Having you watching over my home, protecting Anna—you would be doing *me* a favor."

Oh, how I wanted to. What he offered was better than my family could dream of. Unequivocally better than I could give them. But it wasn't, would never be, ours. "Highcliffe House belongs to my mother and sisters as much as it belongs to me. I could not sell it."

Mr. Lane harumphed. "Egad, man. Are you making this difficult on purpose?"

I blew out a breath, half laughing, half moved to tears. "Anna told me that she felt like her suitors were encouraged by your wealth and connections. I want her to know that I could take care of her without your interference. Before yesterday, we could have built something wonderful. Now, I worry if you save me from this, she will never see me as capable."

Mr. Lane leaned back. He nodded, contemplating my words. "You truly do not want my interference."

"Your advice, I will accept gratefully. But your money . . ." I shook my head. "I would respectfully decline."

Mr. Lane sat back, drew in a long, steady breath. "So this is what my father spoke of. All those years ago. What it feels like to become an old man."

I measured his words, still coming up short. "Sir?"

"You have been like a son to me, Everett. But now, you've outgrown me."

I reared back, overcome with surprise and pride to be called anything close to a son to this man. "On the contrary," I said, my voice hoarse with emotion. "I aim to be like you in every way. You are the closest thing I've ever had to a true father."

Mr. Lane met my eyes, and an understanding seemed to

pass between us. "If you *were* my son, I'd tell you you're being a stupid fool for not accepting my help."

I laughed, and nodded.

He stood, and I followed suit. "But I have seen you make responsible choices and change the course of your own life. I respect you. I respect your decision. And I am so proud of you, Everett. This loss will be but a minor bump in the road. I wish you prosperity in every form."

"Thank you, Mr. Lane," I breathed. A larger honor could not have been bestowed upon me. To be awarded Anna's love, then Mr. Lane's pride would be enough to see me through any hardship. I would spend the rest of my life aiming to become the man they saw in me.

Mr. Lane straightened his jacket and took a firm step back. "As *Anna's* father, however, I must also say, that if you cause my daughter much more pain than she is currently experiencing, we shall have to part ways for good. And that would be a devastation beyond repair. Should you change your mind and desire a loan, advice, anything at all, you know where to find me."

Another nod, and I followed him through the foyer and to the front door. He grasped my arm, and I his, in some semblance of an awkward embrace, then we offered bows in equal measure, and Roland showed him out.

Almost immediately, my mother and sisters ran out into the foyer, breathless.

"What did he say?" Ginny demanded.

"What shall we do?" Mother added.

And that, indeed, was the question.

Chapter Thirty-Four

ANNA

I awoke to the rustling of paper.

Papa was sitting in the corner chair, hidden behind a newspaper, with a cup of tea and an empty plate on a table.

I hadn't meant to fall asleep. I cleared my throat and sat up, looking around the otherwise perfectly arranged room. Sunshine beamed across the polished wood floors, and the little clock on the mantel read well into the afternoon.

Papa folded his paper and set it aside, then sat straight, eyes finding mine. "Annie, my love," he said softly. "I'm so glad you were able to rest. How are you feeling?"

"My throat is dry," I said, and he quickly poured me a glass of something and handed it to me.

I sat on the side of the bed, feet perched on the wooden frame, and took a long gulp. Wine.

"Thank you," I said. Had he seen Graham? He seemed happy, but for what purpose?

His lips twitched into a smile, then he shook his head. "I am still in disbelief that I leave you for *one* week and absolutely everything changes."

"I could say the same of you," I retorted with another long drink of wine.

Papa pursed his lips and stood, moving to sit adjacent me on the bed. "I spoke with Mr. Everett. Your feelings are indeed returned. Unfortunately, he remains adamantly opposed to my help."

I set my glass on a little table within reach. "What can I do?"

Papa shrugged, then patted my hand. "He desires to solve this problem on his own."

His pride might compel him to solve his problem on his own, but his heart? His heart was locked with mine, and we were better together. "I want to be with him. I want to be beside him. Is that not the point of loving someone? To walk through hardships together?"

"It is," Papa vehemently agreed. He smiled a quiet sort of smile; the look of someone who *knew* hardship, of a man who hadn't left the side of his loved one through the very worst sorrow imaginable.

"Then, please, Papa. What can I do?"

Papa drew in a deep breath, leaned his head back, and looked toward the ceiling. After a moment, he nodded simply. "Go to him. Stay with him."

My shoulders sagged as I weighed that option. Could I?

"It will be a burden, financially. And he did not ask me." Though I loved the idea. More than anything.

But what did Graham *need*?

Money.

I had money but not enough to compensate for his loss long-term. Not to mention the fact that he'd never accept it from me. Not even if we wed tomorrow. He was that deter-mined to pull things together himself.

No, if I went to him, I'd have to have a plan. A solid enough foundation so we could start a family. And it had to be my choice, my life to merge with his.

My investment.

I moved to the edge of the bed, feet touching the floor as I straightened with purpose. It was an impossibility. I had no idea the details nor the terms, but—

"Papa, I hate to be crude," I started, turning toward him. "But what about my dowry?"

Papa squinted in thought. "He wouldn't touch it, espe-cially after everything I offered him."

"I have fifteen thousand pounds, do I not?" I winced at the forwardness. If I didn't *need* to know, I wouldn't ask.

"Yes," Papa answered.

"And Mama left me something. I understand the sum is . . . large. But how much, exactly?"

"It is a substantial sum," Papa muttered.

"Enough, say, to buy a parcel of land?"

Chapter Thirty-Five

GRAHAM

I had a plan. It would take at least a year, likely two, of investing in the funds, the four percents, while cutting back unnecessary expenses. I had a budget, and any excess we managed to save would go toward whatever new speculation seemed profitable. It meant a long engagement, but also enough monetary stability that an engagement would even be possible.

Still, I hated it.

I could not say for certain that Mr. Lane would be agreeable. He might make me wait to offer my suit until things were more secure.

Regardless, it would mean asking my family to sacrifice for me when they'd already suffered so much at the hand of my father.

But most of all I hated the nagging feeling in the back of my mind that grew ever more present, a voice telling me that I would never measure up, listing dozens of men who would be better suited, who could give Anna an easier, more comfortable life than I could. Who was I, if I could not care for her as they could?

By the next morning, as I ushered the cow back inside after mucking out her stall, I'd half convinced myself of that truth. In my head, I started listing the reasons why Anna should move on, the foremost being the wretched smell of my current state, and the most compelling being the longevity of my current, and only, plan for a future.

How could I expect such a woman to wait potentially two years or more for me to fix my financial difficulties? How could I ask her to *stay* when staying meant settling for far less than what she was accustomed to?

I swiped the sweat from my brow, then the dirt and filth from my hands. Back in my room, I sank into a bath, though my family still slumbered. I tried to turn off my thoughts, but they pressed their way into every corner as I cleaned, shaved, dressed. I thought I heard the canter of horses down the drive as I tied my cravat, but a quick glance out the window proved the contrary.

Anna's father had sent back word that she'd recovered from her headache by nightfall. Still, I couldn't shirk the feeling that she needed me, couldn't unsee the dismal look in her eyes as she'd left yesterday. I meant to visit as soon as was appropriate to see her returned to full health. And to tell her of my plan. I could only hope she'd still want this, want *us*, after I laid it all out before her.

Was that the door?

There—a neigh—absolutely the sound of horses trotting away. I tugged on my jacket and fastened the few buttons before venturing down the hall.

"One—uh—one moment, please. If you'll just come inside." Roland's voice echoed up the staircase.

"I'll wait here."

Anna?

I bolted down the stairs, stopping only when Roland met me at the bottom.

The man looked panicked, eyes wide, face pale. "Mr. Everett, Miss Lane has come, and she's . . . Well, she's *insistent*, sir, that she see you. There are trunks and trunks, but before I have them moved—"

I patted his arm to reassure him even as I moved around him toward the open door. She stood tall, in a pale-yellow dress, one arm crossed over her middle, holding her other elbow. A coiffure of brown curls peeked out from her hat.

"Anna?" I took a step nearer, and my eyes found the trunks deposited behind her. Her many, many trunks. And her maid, Mariah, being ushered around to the side door.

"Forgive me, Graham, for coming unannounced." Anna unpinned her hat and tossed it on a trunk. "I fear I am in a bit of a tight spot. And I am hopeful for a moment of your time."

I took her hand in mine and drew her close, relaxing when she let me wrap my arms around her waist. "What has happened? Where is your father?"

She leaned back in my hold and winced. "I'm afraid I am rather homeless at the moment."

I refocused on the trunks surrounding us, then Anna's pinched look, her half smile.

"I've bought the land," she said.

Slowly, her words sank into me. *What?* I nearly let go of her and laughed. "We shouldn't jest over such things. But I am glad you came. I have a plan. One that I think will be enough to save us."

She swallowed hard, her half smile dropping into a frown

that made my stomach fill with nerves. "I made an agreement with my father," Anna said in that same serious voice. "I asked for my dowry early so that I could invest it." She raised her chin, sure and confident in herself. Or trying to seem that way, at least.

She couldn't mean what I thought. That much land would cost a fortune. Then, again, there was always talk about how Anna's dowry would be paired with whatever her mother had left her. But surely she wouldn't have—

"As it turns out," she continued as I stood there, speechless and full of assumptions, "your friend, the seller, liked me quite a lot when my father and I paid him a call yesterday. Especially when I told him how dearly I love you, and surprisingly, how dearly I've come to love Brighton."

"Anna," I managed weakly. "Are you saying you've bought my land?"

"Well, you weren't planning to buy it, were you?"

"People will talk."

She shrugged. "Let them. At any rate, I need a partner. Someone who will ensure that I succeed in my endeavor to develop it and rent out the houses for an annual income. I know nothing about anything, and I am quite overwhelmed."

I was frozen. A statue. I tried to speak, but nothing came out.

She was brilliant.

Absolutely, beautifully, brilliant.

Anna persevered. "Of course, that will mean a quick wedding. Since my father has now, lovingly, cast me to the wayside and I am indeed quite homeless at the moment." Then she pointed her finger at my chest. "But be warned: I am no fool, so I'll expect a good return on my money. I'll want my dowry back plus a ten percent increase, which shall be agreed upon in our marriage contract."

"Ten percent." I laughed, and she held her head high, raising her brows with a determined smile.

"Is that a yes, then? Oh, and I shall need a place to stay before the wedding. My father and I came to an agreement. If I am to make such a big decision, I must see it through myself. Alone."

"Alone?"

"All alone." Her smile faltered before instantly recovering. "Thus the homelessness. Indeed, as it turns out, going it alone is quite terrifying, and I am not enjoying the solitude. But I must admit, making my own decisions and planning for myself is quite freeing."

I smiled proudly. There shined the woman I loved. But I could not let her make such a sacrifice. Not on my behalf.

"As generous of a bargain as this is, I've already got things sorted. Indeed, I spent all night thinking through details, making a plan." As long-suffering as it would be. I raked a hand through my hair.

She held up a hand. A deepening crease touched her brow. "Whatever plan you've made will have to wait. *This* is the best opportunity for us, for our family, and I won't let you pass it by because of something completely outside of your control. The deal is already done. I own the land, and the man I marry will have rights to it. I would like that man to be you. Let me invest in *you*, Graham. I trust you, and I believe we can make a future here."

It all sounded too good. Too perfect. "But you hate Brighton."

As though she'd been waiting for that argument, she

turned round to where her satchel waited atop one of her trunks. "Here," she said, handing me her notebook. "Read it."

"I hardly think—"

She flung the thing at me. "I promised you could. Take it. Read the pages. There's not that much; I became distracted by the end. But I meant every word." She grabbed my wrist and tugged me toward a waiting trunk, forcing me to sit.

I looked up at her with patient frustration.

With a huff of irritation, she took the notebook from my hands and read aloud. "Day one: frustrating indeed. Mr. Everett insisted on riding inside the carriage though the weather was plenty fine to ride." She looked down at me with mock disapproval. "His home, however, is lovely. The view from my balcony window is priceless." She turned a page, reading silently down the page a bit. "Day two: Brighton's shores are rocky and unstable. The water chilly, and at times rather brown. Beautiful shells can be found, and the view all around, stunning. Easy to envision families here, laid out with a picnic blanket, perhaps with more than a handful of pillows, enjoying the sun together."

I was silent. She'd written something nice. She turned a page and handed the notebook back to me.

I reached inside my jacket and pulled out my spectacles, admiring her silky, rounded scrawl.

> *Days three and four:*
> *The Steine is pleasant, busy, with nearly every shop a person could want. More shops will likely come, though how sustainable they will be long-term and in the off-season is questionable. I particularly*

love the expansive lending library, which is a central spot for tourists. However, I found the catalog lacking in comparison to London's.

More about the sea. A whole paragraph with positive thoughts concerning the land and its location. I passed over a small paragraph about Lennox. Then read,

> *The Assembly Rooms are more than adequate for dancing the waltz with a clumsy, albeit handsome, well-intentioned gentleman.*

"Clumsy?"

Her eyes brightened, clearly remembering what she'd written, and she grinned. "You cannot have it all, Graham."

I raised a brow, but I could not help the slightest twitch of a smile.

> *Day five:*
>
> *Tourists should come here for the prawns alone. They are heaven on a plate. The Marine Pavilion is lovely, especially its gardens and stable house. I'd love a tour inside, but the opportunity did not arise. Perhaps another time.*
>
> *The most interesting part of Brighton is when the fishermen come to cast their nets just before sunset. The men appear weary and worn, yet somehow jovial and excited for the night ahead. There is room here for greater tourism, beside the already established bathhouse nearby. I cannot say I love it, but I believe in its future. I do think Brighton will continue to flourish.*

And more, I have come to find Graham the most capable of partners. He takes life's reins with a sure hand, always planning three steps ahead, and always thoughtful of my needs, sometimes before I've even considered them. He is unlike any man of my acquaintance.

I'd searched for someone like Graham in all the wrong places. And when we met, I dismissed him. Worked against him. And I regret it. But as is the case with any mistake, the best course is to move forward. I think back at all the time we wasted hating each other, but in truth, had Graham and I not argued for the last few years, I do not know that we could've understood each other as well as we do now. He is strong and capable and so smart I should feel insignificant, and yet, he'd never let me. He builds me up. He challenges me and returns my barbs tenfold in every direction. I do not know how we missed each other, but I am resolved to never lose Graham Everett again.

I turned the page, but there was nothing more. She'd stopped writing.

"I could've gone on, but you've kept me quite occupied of late. And the more time we spent together, the less I wanted to scourge you with my note-taking."

I chuckled, heart bursting, and resisted the urge to reread her every word. I removed my spectacles and studied the arms on each end.

"This investment is a huge undertaking, Anna. I love you for offering, but I am certain we can reverse this deal.

I cannot let you spend every penny you have to secure an investment that may not pay out for years."

"Well, most of it came to me from my mother. And though I did not know her, I imagine she'd approve of me following my heart. The other bit came from my dowry, which Papa was more than happy to supply early as he fully supports my scheming you into marriage." She leaned in and whispered, "Though, in truth, he is waiting in town should you lose your head and reject my offer. Which you won't. Because, as you said, you love me. And you know this is the only way forward. The only way you and I can have everything we want."

"Are you *certain* this is what you want?"

"How close did we get last time? Seventy-five percent?"

"Anna."

She laughed, stepping in between my legs. Then she wrapped her arms around my neck. "I am one hundred percent sure that you, Graham Everett, are the greatest love I shall ever find. And I am one million percent sure that this life we are creating together will be worth every penny."

"Worth risking everything?"

"If you want me as badly as I want you."

I gripped her waist. "I want you," I whispered, coaxing her down onto my leg. I reached up and brushed her jaw, thumbing her bottom lip. The weight of her on my thigh felt both rushing and grounding, with no room left to think.

She slid her fingertips up my chest, past the nape my neck, and into my hair, sending shivers all through me.

I tilted back to look up at her, at the fire burning brightly in her eyes.

She drew close, then pressed her lips to mine.

Jasmine and cherries. *Anna.*

I could not let her go. I traced my hand along the curve of her side and back down over her waist, our arms tangling together, desperate to touch, to feel, to hold on. She laughed, letting her head fall back, and I grazed every inch of her neck with my lips, feasting upon the vibrations of her laughter all the way back to her mouth. Her body in my arms made me feel, despite my unworthiness, completely and irrevocably whole.

"Say something," she said against my lips. "Tell me you're happy."

"I am very happy," I said, kissing the creases of her mouth. "Albeit a little cross."

She pulled back. "Because I surprised you?"

"Because you had to at all."

"I won't do it again, I promise," she said earnestly as I tugged on the loose curls dangling from her coiffure.

I didn't like her frown. Indeed, I never wanted to see her frown again.

"I'm so sorry, Anna. I wanted to offer you the world, but all I have is Highcliffe House and a dwindling savings."

"And a cow." She pressed her nose to mine. "And the sea."

"All the poppies you want," I offered to sweeten the deal.

"And a dead eel," she added. "Oh! And I forgot to say this earlier, about my business proposal." She straightened, looking more professional and serious again. "I'd like the balcony room for the duration of my stay. You may be permitted to join me after our nuptials."

"May be? I do not know how I feel about that phrase. Shall we draw the contract up together this afternoon?"

"As soon as possible, please. Also, in all seriousness, I am now poor, and I left the inn before breaking my fast."

I kissed my way up her jawline to whisper in her ear, "My love, are you hungry?"

She tilted her head. "Starved, dearest."

"She's back!" We heard Tabs's shriek before her little body appeared in the doorway. Her hair was braided and fuzzy from sleep, and she still wore her frilly nightdress. "Have you told her, Graham? That you love her and want to keep her forever?"

I looked at Anna, into those gorgeous, golden-brown eyes. "Can I keep you forever? Even if everything falls apart and all we have left is each other?"

She took my face in her hands and grinned, nodding. "Surely you know by now, Graham—all I want is you."

$\mathcal{E}$pilogue

ANNA

Papa's house looked exactly as I'd left it.

Marble floors so polished you could almost see your reflection as you walked down the vaulted front hall. The same paintings, the same gilded mirrors lined the walls where I'd once felt home. Now, as I walked by, I felt nostalgic for childhood.

But my home was by the sea.

I followed the servants' stairs down to the kitchen, where I found Cook in her apron and cap arranging sprigs of parsley atop the mutton she'd prepared.

"He's put you through all this trouble for me?" I teased.

She looked up, then dropped the sprigs and wiped both hands on her apron as her smile grew.

"Miss La—Mrs. *Everett*, that is!" She flushed, and it took everything in me not to embrace her, my old friend, a woman who'd imparted her fair share of wisdom over the years and saved me from more than one heartache. "Look at you. So happy." She reached out and hesitated only a second before patting my cheek.

"I miss your cooking," I said, leaning into her touch.

"Do you?" She raised a brow. "Those round cheeks say otherwise."

"Mrs. Devon!" I laughed as she cackled in return. I'd forgotten how brash she could be.

"You are in Town for your father's wedding, I presume?" she asked.

"Yes. And I'm not to bother you while Ms. Peale and her guests are here. Papa lectured me about not overstepping and letting change take its course."

"Ah." She nodded, then winked. "Then I suppose you've heard about dessert."

I tempered my humor. Apparently, Ms. Peale liked her desserts plain. A bit particular, if you asked me. "Oh, I've heard. I shall suffer through it. There is one small thing you could help me with, though."

She gave me a curious look as she rounded the table, back to her original spot in the middle of all the food. "Yes?"

I placed my hands on the table and leaned in, voice low. "If you happen to have it on hand . . . I thought perhaps my husband might appreciate a small bowl of—"

"Goat cheese?" She lifted a little plate from the side.

"You absolute saint."

Her eyes lit up with approval. "I wondered if marrying him would change your tricks. I am glad to see you are still the same girl inside."

"Anna?" Graham called from the top of the stairs. "Are you down there?"

"Coming!" I called back, then turned to Cook. "I cannot thank you enough for remembering. You always knew just what to do to make those dinners a little more exciting."

She winked again, then nodded to the stairs, and I rushed

toward Graham. I found him at the top, arms folded with a quirk to his brow and a half smile on his lips.

"We're gathering in the drawing room. Your father sent me to find you. What, pray tell, were you doing down there?"

"Not a thing, my love." I kissed his cheek as I walked past. "Hungry?"

He grasped my wrist to stop me, closing the door behind him. "Famished," he said with a wicked look in his eyes. He pulled my hand to his chest, then laced his arms around my waist. A few steps had me backed against the wall, enveloped by his strength. "You've been gone all afternoon."

I laughed and smoothed my hands up his chest to the high folds on his collar. "I've been gone only an hour to dress."

"Too long," he mumbled as he lowered his lips to mine.

Where once we'd hesitated, learning each other and savoring, now Graham kissed me hard and steady like a man making a promise. He pulled me close, and I thought of our honeymoon—of a fortnight spent a little cottage within an apple orchard not far from Brighton, of lavender pressed between sheets, and sunlight spilling through thin curtains well into the afternoon. I remembered meals around a small round table, just the two of us talking about everything and nothing at all until the candles burned low. It had been nearly a year, and yet, it felt like only yesterday that we'd made promises to never part.

How I loved him.

"Ahem."

Graham jerked back, and I wiped my mouth with a sleeve. "Papa."

His eyes were serious, lips downturned, though his voice

held a sweeter tone. "We're waiting for you in the drawing room, darling." Then, more solemn and firm. "Everett."

"Forgive me, Mr. Lane. I'd gone to fetch her and—"

"Yes. I see you've found her."

I stepped around Graham and touched my hair, ensuring every curl was in place. "I should apologize to Ms. Peale for keeping her waiting. Shall we?"

Graham followed a step behind, so I reached out my hand until he grasped it. I pulled him beside me, and we walked around the grand staircase to the drawing room.

Petite, elegant, with hints of youth still in her countenance, Ms. Peale sat with delicate, gloved hands in her lap and a growing smile as we entered.

"What a happy sight," she said, standing. "The three of you together."

"The four of us, now," Papa said, moving to her side and kissing her temple. "Tomorrow we shall make that permanent."

It still felt strange, seeing the shift in him. The love in his gaze for his intended. But it felt right, too. Like she was the missing piece. Not Mama by any means, but someone special to add to what we'd already known.

When we'd each found our places at the dining table, Papa turned his attention to Graham. "How's my house looking, Everett?"

He'd chosen first among our plots of land in Brighton, and within six months, the rest had sold. Graham and I had celebrated by taking Tabs and Ginny and Mrs. Everett out for prawns and a day spent on our favorite spot at the beach. We'd all left drenched with seawater from playing all afternoon.

"Very well. I believe they are finishing the interior this afternoon. Should be ready for the furniture next week. Right on schedule for your visit after you return from France." Where Papa and Ms. Peale would honeymoon after the wedding.

"Wonderful." Papa winked at Ms. Peale, who struggled to contain her full excitement, her happy grin.

We'd spoken enough for me to trust that grin, trust that she understood Papa and that she loved him in the same way I loved Graham. Their wedding did not feel like some looming thing I'd once imagined. It felt like something to celebrate.

I drew in a deep breath and looked around the table. At Papa, as he served Ms. Peale a generous slice of the center of the mutton, her favorite. And then at Graham, the smooth slope of his brows, the gentle curve of his lips, how they parted ever slightly as he focused on serving me.

Graham paused after spooning out a portion of peas on my plate. Tilting his head, his eyes flicked lazily to mine, lips turned up in a smirk. He gestured to the goat cheese.

"Honestly?"

I laughed as he shook his head, passing over the goat cheese to fork a slice of mutton on my plate. A playful glint in his eyes reappeared, along with the scowl he used to give me, and I wondered if I'd ever tire of teasing him.

Papa asked Ms. Peale about the wedding breakfast, and Graham leaned over to whisper to me, "I shall have to retaliate, you know. For the sake of my honor."

"Over goat cheese?" I raised a brow, bringing wine to my lips.

He sighed heavily as he sliced through his mutton. "If I

don't get you in line now, what will it be next, hmm? Jellied lobster?"

I nearly choked on my sip, and his face lit up.

"You dreadful man."

"You beautiful woman."

"What are you two blathering on about?" Papa broke in.

"Your daughter and her affinity for goat cheese, sir," Graham answered as though it was the most normal response in the world.

Ms. Peale beamed as though she wanted to laugh but didn't quite feel allowed. Papa, however, looked between us, half amused and half stern. "If you two cannot have proper conversation or proper manners during a dinner with your family, how the devil do you function in Society? People will start to talk."

I met Graham's eyes, enraptured by the light—the love— glowing behind them. Nothing else in the world mattered than those eyes gleaming into mine.

"Let them talk," I said softly, gently, and he took my hand in his.

He smiled, then said, "Let them talk."

$\mathcal{A}$cknowledgments

A huge thank you to Heidi Gordon for believing in me and talking me through ideas to craft this story into something stronger and more meaningful than I'd first imagined; to Lisa Mangum for sitting with me during times of vulnerability, for listening and guiding and giving me freedom to find my own voice, and for being the most excellent and thoughtful editor; to my fabulous marketing team: Amy Parker, Haley Haskins, and Ashley Olson for everything they do to promote my book and set up events. Thank you to my unrivaled cover designer, Heather G. Ward, for creating the most stunning images for every book.

To everyone at Shadow Mountain Publishing: I could not do this without you. Thank you sincerely for your support and hard work to make this book and my dreams possible.

Highcliffe House has seen many a friend. To my beta readers, I'm sorry for the bad jokes and poor descriptions, but thank you so much for all your honest feedback and for helping me shape this story into something I'm so very proud of.

To my beloved Critique Partners and dearest friends,

Heidi "Believe in yourself" Kimball—A girl couldn't ask for a better champion. Every time I feel doubts creeping in, you're there to lift me up. One day, we'll write a rom-com together that will take this world by storm.

Joanna "Let's do dual POV's!" Barker—You know story so well, and you make me work, and I just love you for it. Thank you for pushing me and making my writing stronger and for being so kind and loving through it all. Your kindness inspires me.

Arlem—"Take his shirt off"—Hawks—Don't kill me; I love you. Darling friend, I wouldn't have survived without you. Thank you for reading this story, for not missing a single detail, for letting me whine, and for always having my back.

I love you three so much. Thank you, most of all, for being my friends.

I'm so grateful for my family—my parents and sisters, nieces and nephews, who constantly ask after my writing, and who love and encourage me despite knowing zero about the Regency Era. I love you all so much. Thank you.

To my three precious children, especially Owen who has whined and complained that there is no book of mine dedicated to him, *but now there is.* I love and adore you more than you will ever know. Thanks for putting up with my deadlines and those times when the words are flowing and I just have to write. You are my joy. I would be nothing without you.

To Ted, for standing beside me, for picking up my slack, for loving me despite my wandering and dreaming, and for being a dang good man, husband, and the best friend of my life. Words will never be enough. I love you.

For all of my growing talents, my life, and my blessings, I thank my Father in Heaven, Whose hand is in everything I do.

Discussion Questions

1. Anna and Graham both make assumptions based on perceptions they each have of the other. What do you think was the turning point in their relationship?
2. Anna's relationship with her father changes after she meets Graham. What contributed to these changes, and ultimately, what keeps their relationship solid by the end?
3. Do you think Mr. Lane was right to keep his relationship a secret from Anna in the beginning? Why or why not?
4. Graham has worked hard throughout his life to appear more well-off in Society's eyes than he actually is. How do we do this in our modern day? How can we overcome feelings of inadequacy among our friends?
5. Do you relate more to the Lane family or the Everett family? Why?
6. A main theme of the story is taking risks in life. Is there a time where you wish you would've taken a risk but didn't? Or one where a risk paid off well for you?
7. Anna ultimately learns to love Brighton. What do you think changed her mind?

About the Author

MEGAN WALKER was raised on a berry farm in Poplar Bluff, Missouri, where her imagination took her to times past and worlds away. While earning her degree in Early Childhood Education, she married her one true love and started a family. But her imaginings of Regency England wouldn't leave her alone, so she picked up a pen. And the rest is history. She lives in St. Louis, Missouri, with her husband and three children.